Praise for Frédéric Beigbeder

"Beigbeder is smart and amusing, and issues a busy, entertaining broadcast of high-low cultural references."
The Guardian

"If anyone has breathed new life into literary stardom, it is Frédéric Beigbeder, the most glamorous writer in France."
De Volkskrant

Praise for A Life Without End

"It's funny, profound, brilliantly researched, and fiendishly artful."
Le Figaro

"A touching and contemplative literary curve ball."
Femina

"Beigbeder has produced one of the most human, touching, relevant, and funny stories about passing time, the acceptance of aging, and the need to love. If you're looking for something quite unlike anything else to read, then choose this."
Le Parisien

"A call to arms against transience from a Beigbeder who is back in top form, with all his trademark wit."
Lire

"This mad philosophical and biological quest is a life-affirming and intelligent reflection on the meaning of life. Decidedly ambitious, Monsieur Beigbeder!"
Psychologies Magazine

"An audacious romance, between obsessions and hope."
Marie Claire

"Only a rogue like Beigbeder could pack so much serious-ness, cheerful simplicity, and self-irony into such a complex current topic."
Basler Zeitung

"This novel, which spills over in all directions, is also rich with the striking and beautiful observations of a man who is only now learning how to look."
NDR Kultur

"It's a dark topic, but not a dark novel. Beigbeder narrates with wonderfully black humor and a desire for abysmal considerations."
ORF

"Although this book may not be able to extend your life, it could certainly change it."
Sächsische Zeitung

Praise for Windows on the World

"Beigbeder invests his narrators with such profound humanity that the book is far more than a litany of catastrophe: it is, on all levels, a stunning read."
Publishers Weekly

"Powerful—the combination of banality and panic is quietly devastating. Affecting and disconcerting."
Financial Times

Praise for A French Novel

"When a book is as honest as this, it can lead, almost unintentionally, to genuine revelations about what it means to be human."
MICHEL HOUELLEBECQ

"Despite its title, *A French Novel* seems to betray literary and hereditary Anglo-Saxon roots; Beigbeder's Gallic cynicism keeps getting undermined by a romantic sensibility that ultimately reminds me more of Fitzgerald than of Houellebecq. A wry, funny, and compelling novel from an important French novelist."
JAY MCINERNEY

"Cool, self-mocking, but heartfelt as well as ingenious."
BOYD TONKIN, *Independent*: Books of the Year 2013

"In its mixture of wildness and rigor, exhaustion and rapture, impudence and earnestness, *A French Novel* reminded this reader of—to adopt for a moment Beigbeder's name-splattering style—Michel Houellebecq with a human face, Nabokov in both his huffy and dewy modes, Marcel Proust at his most Paul Morley-ish ('Nutella has not yet arrived from Italy'). Beigbeder's gifts are remarkable, but for a book so steeped in its native land and language to retain its exhilarating sharpness and the jazziness of its juxtapositions requires the work of a translator no less rare. Frank Wynne has shared prizes with Beigbeder in the past and again he finds the right pitch of measured mania."
New Statesman

Frédéric Beigbeder

A LIFE WITHOUT END

Translated from the French
by Frank Wynne

WORLD EDITIONS
New York, London, Amsterdam

Published in the USA in 2020 by World Editions LLC, New York
Published in the UK in 2020 by World Editions Ltd., London

World Editions
New York/London/Amsterdam

Printed by Lake Book, USA

Library of Congress Cataloging in Publication Data is available

ISBN 978-1-64286-067-2

First published as *Une vie sans fin* in France in 2018 by Grasset & Fasquelle

Twitter: @WorldEdBooks
Facebook: @WorldEditionsInternationalPublishing
Instagram: @WorldEdBooks
www.worldeditions.org

Book Club Discussion Guides are available on our website.

for Chloe, Lara and Oona

"May almighty God have mercy on us, forgive us our sins, and bring us to everlasting life. Amen."
The Roman Catholic Ordinary of the Mass

"We love death as you love life."
OSAMA BIN LADEN

"Even if there were nine hundred and ninety-five million of them and I were all alone, they'd still be wrong, Lola, and I'd be right. Because I'm the only one who knows what I want: I don't want to die anymore."
LOUIS-FERDINAND CÉLINE
Journey to the End of the Night

A NINE-STAGE JOURNEY TOWARDS IMMORTALITY

A MINOR (BUT IMPORTANT) DETAIL.

"The only difference between reality and fiction is that fiction needs to be credible," according to Mark Twain. But what happens when reality is no longer credible? These days, fiction is less harebrained than science. This is a work of "science non-fiction"; a novel in which all of the scientific developments have been published in *Science* or *Nature*. The interviews with actual doctors, researchers, biologists, and geneticists are transcribed as they were recorded between 2015 and 2017. All of the people, companies, addresses, discoveries, start-ups, machines, medication, and clinical institutions mentioned actually exist. I have changed only the names of friends and family to spare them embarrassment.

When I embarked on this investigation into human immortality, I never imagined where it might lead.

The author accepts no responsibility for the effects of this book on the human species (in general), or on the lifespan of the reader (in particular).

F.B.

1

DYING IS NOT AN OPTION

"Death is stupid."
FRANCIS BACON to FRANCIS GIACOBETTI
(September 1991)

IF THE SKIES are cloudless, you can see death every night. You need only look up. The light of dead stars has traversed the galaxy. Distant stars that burned out thousands of years ago continue to project a memory onto the firmament. Now and then I will call someone who has just been buried and hear their voice, intact, on their voicemail. Such situations provoke a paradoxical feeling. How long does it take the light to wane when the star no longer exists? How long does it take a telephone company to delete a corpse's voicemail greeting? There is a gap between death and extinction: stars are proof that it is possible to shine on after death. Once this *light gap* has passed, comes the moment when the radiance of a bygone star flickers like the flame of a candle about to gutter out. The glow falters, the star grows weary, the voicemail falls silent, the fire trembles. If you study death attentively, you will see that a dead star shimmers a little less than a sun that is still alive. The halo grows fainter, the glimmering dims. The dead star begins to blink as though sending out a distress signal. It clings on.

MY RESURRECTION BEGAN in Paris, in the district of the recent terrorist attacks, on a day when there was a spike in fine particulate air pollution. I had taken my daughter to a neo-bistro called Jouvence. She was eating a plate of *salchichón de bellota* and I was drinking a Hendrick's and tonic with cucumber. Since the invention of the smartphone, we had grown out of the habit of talking to each other. She was checking her WhatsApp messages while I stalked supermodels on Instagram. I asked her what she wanted as a birthday present. She said, "A selfie with Robert Pattinson." My first reaction was alarm. But thinking about it, in my job as a television presenter, I also demand selfies. A guy who spends his life interviewing actors, singers, sportspeople, and politicians in front of the cameras is simply shooting long takes next to people more interesting than he is. And, in fact, when I'm out in the street, passersby ask if they can take pictures with me on their mobile phones and if I gladly accept, it is because I have just done the very same thing on set surrounded by television cameras. We all live the same non-life; we want to shine in the reflected glow of others. Modern man is a collection of 75 trillion cells all striving to become pixels.

A selfie posted on social media is the defining ideology of our times: what the Italian writer Andrea Inglese calls "the only legitimate obsession, that of constant self-promotion." There exists a noble hierarchy dictated by the selfie. The solitary selfie, where one appears next to a famous monument or a landscape, means: I've been here and you haven't. This category of selfie is a *curriculum visuale*, a virtual visiting card, a social springboard. The selfie taken with a celebrity has a more loaded meaning. The Selfist is seeking to prove to his followers that he has met someone more famous than they have. One does not ask to take a selfie with an ordinary individual, unless that person has some physical peculiarity: achondroplasia, hydrocephalus, elephantiasis, or third-degree burns. This form of selfie is a declaration of love, but more than that, it is proof of identity (when he predicted that "the medium is the message," Marshall McLuhan never imagined that the whole world would become the medium). If I post a selfie of me standing next to Marion Cotillard, what I am expressing is something very different than if I were to post a selfie with Amélie Nothomb. The selfie is a means of introduction: see how handsome I look next to this monument, with this celebrity, in this landscape, on this beach—and I hope you feel green with envy! You have a better understanding of me now—see me lying in the sun, resting my finger on the top of the Eiffel Tower, stopping the Tower of Pisa from falling—I'm a traveller, I don't take myself too seriously, I exist because I bumped into a star. The selfie is an attempt to usurp some greater notoriety, to prick the bubble of aristocracy. The selfie is a form of communism: it is the weapon of the foot soldier in the glitzkrieg. The Selfist does not pose next to just anyone, he wants the personality of the other person to rub off on him. A selfie with a "GOAT" (Greatest of All Time, for the digilliterate among you) is a form of cannibalism: it absorbs the aura of the star. It launches him into a new orbit. The selfie is the new language of the narcissistic era: it replaces Descartes's *cogito ergo sum*.

"I think therefore I am" becomes *fingo ergo sum*: "I pose therefore I am." If I take a photo with Leonardo DiCaprio, it eclipses your selfie with your mother on a skiing trip. Face it, even your mother would rather be standing next to Leo DiCaprio. And DiCaprio next to the pope. And the pope next to a child with Down syndrome. Does this mean that the most important person in the world is a child who suffers from Down syndrome? No, I'm straying from the point: the pope is the exception that proves the Instagram rule of celebrity overkill. The pope has shattered the self-obsessed snobbery instigated by Dürer in 1506 with "The Feast of the Rosary," where the artist painted himself photobombing Holy Mary, Mother of God.

The logic of the selfie might be encapsulated thus: Britney would like a selfie with Bono, but Bono does not want a selfie with Britney. As a result, a new class war is taking place every day, on streets all over the world, whose sole aim is media domination, the vaunting of greater popularity, the ascent along the greasy pole of fame. The war involves comparing the number of UMAs (Units of Media Approval) amassed by each individual: appearances on radio or television, photographs in the press, likes on Facebook, views on WhatsApp, retweets, etc. It is a battle against anonymity in which points are easily tallied; one in which the winners snub the losers. I propose naming this war *Selfism*. It is a world war fought without armed forces, one that is waged permanently, 24/7, with no hope of a ceasefire: *bellum omnium contra omnes*—"a perpetuall warre of every one against every one," as expressed by Thomas Hobbes—now fought technologically and scored instantaneously. At the first press conference following his investiture as President of the United States in January 2017, Donald Trump made no attempt to expound on his vision for America, or the geopolitics of the world: he was content simply to compare the size of the crowd at his inauguration with that of his predecessor. Nor do I exclude myself from this existential struggle: I have been only too happy to flaunt selfies with Jacques Dutronc or David Bowie on my fan page which, as I write, has amassed 135,000 likes. And yet, for more than fifty years, I have considered myself terribly alone. With the exception of selfies and television studios, I spend little time with human beings. By vacillating between solitude and chaos, I avoid any awkward questions about the meaning of my life.

There are times when the only way to confirm that I am still alive is to check Facebook to see how many people have liked my most recent post. More than 100,000 likes and I sometimes get a hard-on.

What I found troubling that evening with my daughter was that she did not dream of kissing Robert Pattinson, or talking to him or getting to know him. She simply wanted to post his face next to hers on social media to prove to her friends that she had actually met him. Like her, we are all caught up in this headlong rush. Short or tall, young or old, rich or poor, celebrity or nobody, uploading a photo has become more important than our signature on a cheque or a marriage certificate. We are desperate for recognition. The majority of earthlings are screaming into the void about their need to be looked at, or at least noticed. We yearn to be contemplated. Our faces are hungry for clicks. And if I've received more likes than you, that proves that I'm happier, just as on television a presenter with higher viewing figures believes himself to be more loved than his colleagues. This is the tactic of the Selfist: to humiliate others by maximizing his share of public love. Something happened during the digital revolution: egocentricity mutated to become a planetary ideology. Having lost all sway over the world, we are left with only an individual worldview. Time was, dominance was reserved for courtiers and the aristocracy, later it was conferred onto film stars. Now that every individual is a medium, everyone wants to dominate their fellow man. Everywhere.

When Robert Pattinson came to Cannes to promote his movie *Map of the Stars*, though unable to arrange for my daughter Romy to take a selfie with him, I was at least able to get her a signed photograph. In the green room of my television show, he wrote the following message in red marker on a photo ripped out of a copy of *Vogue*: *To Romy with love xoxoxo Bob*. In lieu of thanks, she simply asked me a question: "You swear to me you didn't sign this yourself?"

We have given birth to a mistrustful generation. But what I found most hurtful was that my daughter never, ever asked for a selfie with her father.

THAT YEAR, MY mother had a heart attack and my father had a fall in a hotel lobby. I began to become a habitué of hospitals in Paris. This was how I came to understand the working of vascular stents and discovered the existence of titanium knee replacements. I began to loathe old age: the antechamber of death. I had an overpaid job, a pretty ten-year-old daughter, a triplex apartment in the centre of Paris, and a BMW hybrid. I was in no hurry to lose all these benefits. When I got back from the hospital, Romy came into the kitchen with one eyebrow raised.

"Papa, the way I understand it, everyone dies. First Grandpa and Grandma, and after that Maman, you, me, the animals, the trees, the flowers ..."

Romy stared at me fixedly as though I were God, when in fact I was simply the father of a mononuclear family experiencing an accelerated acquaintanceship with cardiovascular surgery and orthopaedic wards. I had to stop dissolving Lexomil tablets in my morning can of Coke if I was to propose a solution to her anxiety. I'm a little ashamed to admit it, but I never imagined that my mother and father would one day be octogenarians, and that afterwards it would be my turn, and then Romy's. I was hopeless at maths and at old age. Beneath the flaxen hair of a living doll, two blue spheres began to fill with tears as she stood between the purring fridge and the microwave. I remember Romy's tantrum the day her mother told her that Santa Claus didn't exist: Romy hates lies. Then she said something kind: "I don't want you to die, Papa."

How delectable it is to shuck off one's armour ... Now it was my turn to tear up as I buried my nose in the sweet smell of her mandarin and lime shampoo. I still could not understand how a man as ugly as I am could produce such a beautiful little girl.

"Don't you worry, darling," I said, "From now on, no one is going to die."

We were a beautiful sight, as unhappy people so often are. Sadness makes the face more beautiful. Happy families are all alike, Tolstoy writes at the beginning of *Anna Karenina*, but he adds that every misfortune is unique. I don't agree: death is a banal misfortune. I cleared my throat the way my army-issue grandfather used to when he sensed he needed to restore order in his house.

"Listen, darling, it's true that for millennia people and animals and trees have died, but starting with us, that's all over."

All I had to do now was make good on my promise.

ROMY WAS VERY excited at the prospect of going to Switzerland to visit the Institute of Genetics and Genomics.

"Can we eat fondue?"

This is her favourite food. This whole adventure began in Geneva with our meeting with Stylianos Antonarakis. On the pretext of making a documentary about immortality, I had arranged an interview with the Greek geneticist so that he could explain how modifications to deoxyribonucleic acid could prolong our lives. I was looking after my daughter that week, so I took her with me. The recent publication of a number of essays on transhumanism had given me the idea of organizing a televised discussion on "The Death of Death," with Laurent Alexandre, Stylianos Antonarakis, Luc Ferry, Dmitry Itskov, Mathieu Terence, and Sergey Brin from Google.

Romy was asleep, sprawled in the back of the taxi that was driving along the banks of Lake Geneva. The sun glistened on the snowy peaks of the Jura, clouds tumbling down the slopes like an avalanche of translucent mist. This was the bone-white landscape that inspired Mary Shelley to write *Frankenstein*. Is it a coincidence that Geneva is the city where Professor Antonarakis is working on the genetic manipulation of human DNA? In Switzerland, home to the most fastidious clockmakers, nothing comes down to chance. In 1816, while staying in the Villa Diodati, Mary Shelley sensed the gothic soul of the city. Here, tranquillity is based on a facade of rationalism. I have always been unconvinced by the cliché of Switzerland as a peaceable country, especially after a few champagne-fuelled brawls at the Baroque Club.

Geneva is Rousseau's noble savage as domesticated by Calvin: every Helvetian knows that he is at risk of falling into a ravine, of winding up frozen in a crevasse or drowned in a tarn. In my childhood memories, Switzerland was a country of wild New Year celebrations on the *grande place* in Verbier, of curious cuckoos, of fairy-tale chalets glittering in the night, of deserted palaces and valleys haunted by eerie mists, where protection against the cold was a glass of Williamine. Geneva, the Protestant Rome, a city of banks in mourning for their banking secrets, seems to me the perfect illustration of the maxim of the Prince of Ligne: "Reason is often a thwarted passion." What I like about Switzerland is the fire that smoulders beneath the snow, the secret folly, the focused hysteria. In a world as heavily policed as this, life can change dramatically in an instant. After all, the name Geneva contains the word "gene": welcome to the country that has always longed to control humanity. All along the shores of the lake, posters advertised an exhibition on "Frankenstein, Creation of Darkness" at the Martin Bodmer Foundation in Cologny. I was convinced that the Bentleys silently gliding past Geneva's famous fountain, the *Jet d'Eau*, were filled with artful monsters.

"Can we go and see the exhibition, Papa?"

"We have other priorities."

The fondue at the Café du Soleil—half Gruyère, half vacherin—was almost light. Nothing like the thick yellow gloop wolfed down in Paris. My daughter dipped her bread in the molten cheese and whimpered with pleasure.

"*Oh là là!* Ish b'n sooooo long! Nom nom!"

"You shouldn't talk with your mouth full."

"I'm not talking, I'm *onomatopaying*"

Romy has excellent genes: on my side, she is descended from a long line of doctors; from her mother, she has inherited a richly inventive vocabulary. Before she left me, Caroline would regularly transform nouns into verbs. She coined new words every day: I'm off "yoga-ing," or I'm "cinema-ing" tonight. Someday, her neologisms will be included in dictionaries: "snacktivate," maybe, or "instagrammatize." When she dumped me, Caroline didn't say, "I'm leaving you," she said, "It's time to slow-fade." Although Swiss fondue is not a dish recommended by the World Health Organisation (20 Avenue Appia, 1211 Geneva) —especially for breakfast—Romy's happiness was more important than our immortality. We dropped our suitcases off at La Réserve, a palace on the shores of Lake Geneva, and while I was leafing through the brochure for the hotel's Spa & Wellness Centre, which offered an "anti-aging programme" including a genetic appraisal of my "bio-individuality™," my little girl dozed off on the velvet sofa personally chosen by on-trend design mogul Jacques Garcia.

The lobby of the Geneva University Hospital was filled with antique radiotherapy machines, strange outmoded contraptions, early precursors of scanners. The nuclear medicine of the 1960s has given way to infinitesimal manipulations that are much less cumbersome. Outside the hospital, groups of medical students were sitting on the grass, while, inside, young interns wearing white coats were bustling around bubbling beakers, test tubes, and petri dishes of cells. Here, people were accustomed to domesticating the human animal, trying to correct the flaws of *Homo sapiens*, perhaps even enhance the aging vertebrate. Switzerland was not afraid of post-humanism, since it recognized man as imperfect from birth. Here, happiness looked like a cool campus, the future was a teen movie set in a medical facility. Romy was spellbound: in the middle of the gardens was a gantry hung with swings, a trapeze, competition rings, there was even a merry-go-round.

The Genetics Department was located on the ninth floor. In his bottle-green polo shirt, Stylianos Antonarakis looked less like Doctor Faustus than a cross between Paulo Coelho and Anthony Hopkins, with all the benevolence of the former and all the magnetism of the latter. The president of the Human Genome Organisation (HUGO) stroked his white beard and polished his wire-framed glasses like an absent-minded Professor Calculus while, in a joyous and relaxed manner, he explained how humanity was going to mutate. Romy was immediately struck by his new-age approach: the benignant gaze, the friendly smile, the idyllic future. His office was an indescribable mess. A huge plastic model of a double helix lay on its side on a wooden trestle. I glanced at the spines of the books: *History of Genetics Vol. 1, Vol. 2, Vol. 3, Vol. 4, Vol. 5* ... Even recent genomic discoveries were ancient history to this international specialist in the field. A disembowelled computer had been transformed into a jardinière in which some post-atomic designer had planted steel stems blossoming with Nespresso capsules to create a bouquet that would never wither.

"Thank you for setting aside a little of your precious time to meet with us, Professor."

"We have all eternity ahead of us ..."

His glacier-blue eyes perfectly matched the sky outside.

"Could you explain DNA to my daughter?"

"We are each born with an individual genome: a vast text that runs to three billion characters multiplied by two (half from your mother and half from your father). We are all unique individuals because our genomes are unique—except in the case of monozygotic twins. Once we are born, we are subject to somatic mutations caused by the sun, by air pollution, by the food we eat, the medicines we take, and our general lifestyle. This is what we call epigenetics. Aging is also dependent on the individual phenotype. Some people age more quickly than others."

The professor spoke French with a pleasant Greek accent. One would feel at ease in a posthuman world if it was populated by clones of Doctor Antonarakis.

"A cell is immortal. Human beings first appeared in Morocco 300,000 years ago. What existed before that was a different species, and before that a different species again. And the most common ancestor was a cell. That cell is present in me and in both of you. I pass on the cell to the next generation through my sperm, and you, young lady, will pass it on through your oocyte."

Romy was perhaps a little young for a lesson on human reproduction. I quickly changed the subject.

"So there is something immortal in every one of us?"

"Precisely. It is impossible to create a new cell. Cells can be reprogrammed, new genes can be introduced into cells, others can be erased to alter the fate of a cell, but it is not possible to create a new, living cell. Nor is it possible to create a new bacteria today, although it seems likely that we will be able to do so two or three years from now."

"Talk to me about genome sequencing."

"These days, it is an easy process. We take two millilitres of saliva and isolate the DNA. When I first started this work thirty years ago such things were done by hand, but these days we can work out the three billion letters in your genome in about a week. Using powerful software, we can compare the differences in your genome with the reference sequence completed in 2003. This was the result of an international project launched in 1990—one I was fortunate enough to work on—the Human Genome Project. The dataset is open to anyone."

"The reference sequence is of an American called Craig Venter, isn't it?"

"He did his own sequencing in parallel to ours. In the United States, the first sequencings were of him and a number of others, including Hamilton O. Smith, who won the Nobel Prize in Physiology or Medicine in 1978. It is simply a benchmark, it does not mean that Craig's DNA is normal, it was simply the first to be decoded and, since then, we've studied differences in relation to that reference."

"Can I go and play outside, Papa?"

I looked at the professor and he looked at me. It was obvious that our discussion on advances in genetics was less appealing to Romy than the prospect of playing on the swings.

"Alright, but don't go far from the playground, that way I can see you from the window. And keep your phone turned on. And don't stand up on the swing. And don't ..."

"Papa, I'm programmed to live for a thousand years, so I think I can go down a slide. Don't sweat it."

Doctor Antonarakis burst out laughing. "Your genome hasn't been sequenced yet, mademoiselle, that's something we would need to verify."

He turned to me.

"If you like, my assistant can keep her company while we're talking."

He pressed a button and a young lab assistant appeared. Her brown hair stood out against her white coat, and she seemed delighted to be suddenly promoted to babysitter, which would allow her to get some fresh air. Giggling, the two beautiful children left the office.

"Now, where were we?" Antonarakis asked.

"Craig Venter. I've seen his work online. He's a real Victor Frankenstein: he created a synthetic mycoplasma genome. I heard he shouted 'It's alive!' like the mad scientist in Mary Shelley's novel, remember? Doctor Frankenstein shouts 'It's alive!' when the hand-stitched creature he created here in Switzerland starts to breathe, to stir, after a few jolts of electricity, before it gets off the table and starts strangling everyone."

"I've never read *Frankenstein*, but I can see where you're heading. Craig Venter replaced a natural chromosome with a synthetic one created in his laboratory. And he succeeded in reimplanting it into a microscopic living organism. He even included his initials in the genome: 'JCVI-syn3.0.' It's an artificial organism that lives and thrives."

"Personally, I see it as a playful experiment by researchers. It must be thrilling to design synthetic bacteria on a computer, but I can't see how it helps humanity."

"One day, it will allow for the creation of new materials, hybrid fuels, new alloys ..."

Here I did something that TV professionals often do when they're completely lost: I looked down and read the next question on my piece of paper. I'd thought I was coming here to research a talk show, but in that precise moment I realized I was here for something else.

"Do you think that sequencing my DNA could prolong my life?"

"If you were ill, it could help determine the cause of

your illness. There are around 8,000 genetic diseases and, with access to your DNA, we can diagnose 3,432. We can also conduct a prenatal diagnosis to determine whether to terminate a high-risk pregnancy. Sequencing also makes it possible to treat certain genetic conditions, it provides information about cancers. It allows us to categorize different cancers and develop individual treatment regimes. Lastly, using statistical models, sequencing allows us to study the predisposition towards certain diseases. These are tests I recommend only for Alzheimer's and breast cancer."

"Here at the 'Genome Clinic,' you make these kinds of predictions. Would it be fair to say that DNA has replaced the stethoscope?"

"The Swiss government doesn't like me calling it the Genome Clinic, they prefer us to talk about 'genomic consultations.' But you're wrong: we detect illnesses, not predispositions."

"Which predictions are scientifically reliable?"

"If a woman carries mutations of the BRCA1 or BRCA2 genes, like Angelina Jolie, there is a 70% probability that she will develop breast cancer, whereas the probability in the population at large is 9%. In such cases, the patient needs to get herself screened every six months, or have a double mastectomy."

He talked about catastrophic operations casually. Incomprehensible chemical equations scrawled on the wall in felt tip might hold the secret to the Fountain of Youth. Good doctors have always questioned their patients about their parents and grandparents; predicting the future is part of job, whether they like it or not. Cancer is like a terrorist: it needs to be neutralized *before* it can carry out an attack. This is what is so new: with genetics, doctors don't have to wait for you to fall ill in order to treat you. The genome is the *Minority Report* within your body.

"Do you carry out genetic manipulation here, yes or no?"

"Of course. I'm particularly interested in Down syndrome. I try to identify the important genes in chromosome 21. Here, we create transgenic mice to study human diseases. I have a laboratory in which we create induced pluripotent stem cells—iPS cells. We test different medications for treating intellectual disability. There's hope. We conduct clinical experiments. I dream of one day seeing an intelligent person with Down syndrome."

I don't know whether he was aware of the shocking aspect of this sentence. Whether we like it or not, the rate of Down syndrome has been declining since the development of amniocentesis. We are all eugenicists, even if we avoid using the word.

"What do you think about the Californian transhumanists who want to correct, or improve, or 'enhance' humanity?"

"People dreamed of such things even before the Second World War: the experiments of the Cold Spring Harbor Laboratory. It was the same beautiful, utopian ideal of developing a humanity without disease.

"A humanity without disease: this is the goal of the foundations established by Bill Gates (ex-Microsoft), Mark Zuckerberg (Facebook), and Sergey Brin (Google), three of the richest men on the planet. Zuckerberg has promised to invest three billion dollars to cure all diseases by the year 2100.

"Back in the 1930s, researchers at Cold Spring Harbor wanted to eradicate diseases by way of eugenics. By sterilizing certain people and forcing others to breed. This charming little dream was adopted by the Nazis and has since been discredited. But every family dreams their children will be healthier than others."

"Are you implying that transhumanists are Nazis?"

"I'm simply saying that if we change something in the human genome, we have no idea of the consequences. For example, ten years ago in India I encountered a large family of forty members, all of whom had six fingers and six toes. Every individual in the family had twenty-four phalanges. I thought, 'These people have an evolutionary advantage if they ever decide to become pianists!'"

I was watching as Romy hoisted herself onto a trapeze, thinking that Mary Shelley would have liked this affable Greek doctor. Behind the roguish charm lurked an audacious scientist. I was beginning to feel a dull ache in my stomach, but maybe I was simply having trouble digesting the fondue.

"Did their six fingers all work properly?"

"They had no trouble using them. It was simply an extra, perfectly articulated little finger. Imagine playing the harp!"

"Yes, twenty-percent better technique. Pretty useful for cleaning your ear, too …"

"At the time, I genuinely thought it would be a brilliant idea to introduce this genomic variation into humanity at large. So I took blood tests, thinking that I'd be improving the human condition. And I eventually tracked down the mutation to a specific gene. Like you and me, these people had two copies of the gene: one from their mother, one from their father, either of which might contain the mutation that produced twenty-four phalanges rather than twenty. But if a member of the family had two mutated copies of the gene—which occurred quite often—the foetus died at eight weeks' gestation. One copy of the mutation was advantageous, but two was deleterious."

"Damn—so much for the harp concertos."

"The reason I'm telling you this story is to highlight the fact that if we meddle with our evolutionary genome, we have no idea what price we might pay as a species. Every time we introduce something into the genome, we have to watch to see what damage it causes. If we want to improve our species, that has to be a decision made by society as a whole."

"But it's inarguable that human beings are imperfect ..."

"Exactly. The fruit fly has more powerful eyes than we do, bats have better hearing than we do. Our ribcage doesn't protect our liver or our spleen, which means that, if we're in an accident, we can die from a haemorrhage. We walk on two feet, something our ancestors didn't do, and that causes lumbago. The internal plumbing of the human animal is too complicated, menopause could occur much later."

"And despite all these defects, we shouldn't touch anything?"

Doctor Antonarakis got up and went to the window to look out at the trees. Down in the gardens, the dark-haired research assistant was spinning Romy on a merry-go-round similar to the centrifuges used to separate liquids from solids we had seen in the lab. We could hear her laugh, at once liquid and solid, rising in the air and crashing against the picture windows like a reckless robin.

"We've been talking now for about half an hour. During that half hour, thousands upon thousands of our cells have been replaced. A million in my bloodstream. Half a million in my intestines. Replacing cells requires copying the genome. Six billion letters of genetic code have been copied approximately two million times between us in the past thirty minutes. For cells to be renewed, the human body requires an extraordinary and remarkably precise copying system. In fact, the system is not always accurate. It makes mistakes. Every time cells are renewed there is an error rate of 1 in 10^8, meaning forty or fifty errors over every three billion nucleotides. It is those errors that make it possible for us all to be different from one another. We need them, because we need to carry on living if the environment changes. In the face of a virus, or of global warming, we need diversity in order to evolve. Certain mutations cause illnesses, but that's the price we pay for our adaptability. A flagrant example of the evolution of our species is diabetes. It has become more and more common because food and especially sugars are more plentiful. A hundred years ago there was virtually no diabetes. Three hundred years ago, the same genes that these days cause Type II diabetes offered us protection when food was more scarce."

I scratched my head. Seeing that he had disappointed me, Doctor Antonarakis tried to console me.

"You know, the people who produce clean water do more in terms of prolonging our life expectancy than all the scientists and geneticists put together."

"How can we go about postponing death, Professor?"

"Our concern is the brain: the liver, the intestines, the blood, even the heart can be regenerated. We can inject cells into endocrine glands. But I don't think we could create an artificial brain. That's something we just have to accept. I encounter a lot of patients in their eighties or nineties, and they all say the same thing: it's okay to end life. There comes a moment when you're weary of it. You'll see. There is a species, the mayfly, that lives for only one day. The whole lifecycle: birth, adulthood, old age, and death in a single day. And it's possible that that species is happy."

I ran my fingers through my hair: it's a tic of mine when I don't know what to say. I had no particular admiration for the Buddhism of ephemeropteran insects. The sun was fast sinking behind the trees, and I didn't want to abandon Romy for much longer. I thanked the kindly geneticist who did not save my life, and hurried to catch the lift. Romy was in the lobby with the pretty medical student. A twisted thought occurred to me: if Romy got along well with this young woman ... maybe ... we might ... eventually ... envisage ...

"Papa, this is Léonore, she wants a selfie with you. She's a fan of your TV programmes."

"I owe you that at least, mademoiselle. I don't know how to thank you."

Léonore had already taken out her mobile phone.

She had a dainty little chin

And looked like Charlotte Le Bon's twin.

Click. In the fraction of a second I stood posing next to her, I inhaled everything. The brunette with the rounded forehead had just brushed her teeth, her skin had been soaped with cherry-scented shower gel, her hair smelled of orange blossom, she had a wholesome smile, she was the kind of person who has no sense of irony. The way she looked me straight in the eye, her lips parted, said: *I know what I want in life, and you could be part of my schedule.* I held her gaze, a challenge, until she turned away to look at the Alps. There was enough space behind her ear, between her hair and her neck, to reveal three square centimetres of bare, downy skin on which planting a kiss would probably be the best decision of the year. To cut a long story short, I instantly wanted to have a child with this beautiful intern. For a man, creating a life is much easier than postponing death. I swear it's true: I didn't just want to make love to her, I wanted to see her belly swell with my fecund seed. I felt like an alien in heat: I wanted to bury a tentacle inside this person. I had just fallen into a trap hatched by my daughter in collusion with the Greek professor. After so much talk about DNA, it was my penis that now took itself for Victor Frankenstein.

"Your daughter is a sweetheart," Léonore said as she looked at the selfie on her mobile, "and a talented sportswoman—a real expert on the swings and the seesaw."

"Can we invite her to dinner with us at La Réserve, Papa? Please ..."

"But I've booked a Better-Aging Signature body massage at the Nescens Spa ..."

"I already asked her and she said yes! Promise I won't ask for anything else ever ..."

"That'll be the day," I said in the voice of John Wayne, as dubbed in French by Raymond Loyer, in *The Searchers*.

I felt an immediate revulsion at my old man's drawl. No one says "That'll be the day" anymore, but I couldn't help it, it just came out. There are some encounters in which you find yourself on autopilot. The conspiracy of women to make me happy was fomenting a new attack.

So we went and bought meringues, double cream, and some raspberries. The three of us sat on a jetty overlooking Lake Geneva. We listened to the water lapping against the boats as we dipped the meringues into the tub of thick cream. Léonore explained the principle of eternal snows to Romy.

"You see the mountain peaks over there, it's so cold that the snows never melt."

"Like the cream in Papa's moustache?"

"Exactly."

I wiped my face on my shirtsleeve. On the glistening water, a duck quacked. The lake shimmered in the twilight, then grew dark: God had just turned out the light. Clouds had gathered and a summer storm burst directly over our heads. Léonore was even more ravishing with her hair wet, sensual as a photo by Jean-François Jonvelle (a dead friend).

"What's your blood group, Léonore?"

"O+, why?"

"Mine too. Have you had your DNA sequenced? Your eggs frozen? Do you have plans to have your stem cells preserved in a cryogenic biobank? Do you have ethical problems with brain uploading? What about self-regenerating blood shots? Will you marry me?"

At this point, she assumed I was a lunatic, which says much about her perspicacity. Romy invited Léonore up to our suite so that she could dry her hair. We finished the meringues and watched *Black Mirror* until Romy fell asleep. Then CNN informed us that George Michael had just died at the age of fifty-three. They played the video of "Don't Let the Sun Go Down on Me" where he sang with Elton John. When the singer—of Greek extraction, like Doctor Antonarakis (George Michael's real name was Georgios Kyriacos Panayiotou)—sang the line "All my pictures seem to fade to black and white ..." a tear fell from my right eye and Léonore watched as it trickled into my beard. I was crying selfishly about my own mortality, but she assumed I was altruistic. Embarrassed, she said, "Right, well, it was lovely to meet you, I've had a lovely time, but it's getting late, I think I'll let you get some rest."

... I didn't let her let me get some rest.

Sometimes my shyness turns into firmness. With my forefinger, I tucked a lock of her hair behind her right ear. My other hand had grasped her wrist. I pressed my cheek against hers in slow motion, turned my eyes to her, tilted my head toward her lips. Holding my breath, I smiled, then gently slipped my tongue into her mouth. It is at this point that the mission might have ended. All it would have taken was a sign of reluctance on her part. If she had hesitated, I wouldn't have insisted: she could destroy my life with a single tweet. But she whetted her tongue, and nibbled at my lower lip as though it were her own. We both gave a sigh, perhaps of relief. I think we were both relieved that our porn-star kiss had not been ridiculous. I slid a hand over her breast and, lower down, a few fingers beneath the thin cotton. I was able to confirm that my attraction was reciprocated. Our epidermises longed to make contact. I was inheriting a new woman. It is rare to encounter such straightforward foreplay. As I peeled off her T-shirt, I took out my hard penis. This type of manoeuvre is generally complicated, even embarrassing (cock-blocked by boxer shorts, T-shirt stuck over the head, prick scratched by the zip: such minor incidents can spoil the fairy tale). No such problems here: our movements were as fluid and logical as in a wet dream. I think Léonore was surprised by my impatience; she didn't know that I had spent centuries wanting to get her pregnant. Nothing now separated us, not even a condom. I loved Léonore as one might inhale the pure air of French-speaking Switzerland in the middle of a summer storm. I rapturously sullied her pristine clothes, and her two spheres, their nipples erect like my penis between them. We fucked standing to attention, our mingled sweat sweetening each other.

She whispered in my ear, "It's obvious you do this regularly."

I didn't dare tell her she was the first woman I had touched in two years. She mistook my enthusiasm for wantonness and there was no question of me shattering her illusions. Her pleasure heightened mine, I spurted when she came. Every time she squealed in my ear, I put a hand over her mouth so that she didn't wake Romy, and being gagged simply excited her more. The best sex occurs when two egotists stop being egotists.

THE FOLLOWING MORNING, Romy insisted we go and visit the Frankenstein exhibition at Colony. It was still raining, but not the fine summer drizzle I love: big, fat raindrops from this Swiss monsoon trickled down our necks like icy love bites. We dropped Léonore off at the hospital, having said little in the car; but it was not an awkward silence, quite the reverse, it was the silence of three people who aren't afraid to say nothing and simply listen to the song of the windscreen wipers. When she had gone, Romy said, "She's cool."

"You don't mind that she stayed the night?"

"No, I'm sad that she had to go now."

(*joyful silence*)

"Right, shall we go see the monster exhibition?"

The same taxi dropped us off at the Bodmer Foundation, outside an imposing building perched on a lush hill overlooking Lake Geneva. The private library has one of the most important collections of manuscripts in the world. The exhibition "Frankenstein, Creation of Darkness" paid homage to a source of national pride: it was in a neighbouring village that Mary Shelley wrote her great novel about artificial life. The city had even erected a statue of Frankenstein's creature in its Plainpalais district. At the entrance to the exhibition, in gold letters, was a line from the novel: *I am by birth a Genevese, and my family is one of the most distinguished of that republic.*

"You see, darling, it was here that Mary Shelley wrote

Frankenstein, exactly two hundred years ago."

"Duh! I know that," Romy said pointing to the wall, "I'm not stupid. It's written right there!"

Romy lingered for a long time in front of every painting, every manuscript, and read all of the explanatory notices in their entirety. I couldn't understand how I, a shallow TV presenter, had managed to sire someone so meticulous. We were able to study a number of manuscript pages, and a first edition of *Frankenstein* (1818) signed by Mary Shelley: *To Lord Byron, from the author.* The engravings of the monster wandering the streets of Geneva did not frighten Romy, a fan of *The Walking Dead.* The illustrations in the grimoires on display showed dancing skeletons, rotting corpses, and the circles of hell—in short, the commonplace tragedy of the human condition. I pored over Mary Shelley's private diary. The young novelist had lost her mother as a little girl. She had written *Frankenstein* at the age of twenty. Later, three of her children died (typhus, malaria, miscarriage), then her husband drowned when his sailing boat sank in the Ligurian Sea, all this before Mary turned twenty-five. This is what happens when you conjure up someone who triumphs over Death: you attract its attention.

In the preface to the 1831 edition, on the subject of *Frankenstein*, she writes: "... it proved a wet, ungenial summer, and incessant rain often confined us for days to the house." I looked up and saw the rain hammering on the windows and on the paved courtyard, a black torrential rain. "Frightful must it be," she writes about her novel, "for supremely frightful would be the effect of any human endeavour to mock the stupendous mechanism of the Creator of the world."

"What'cha doing?"

"Argh!"

Romy made me jump out of my skin. I was beginning to understand how the Swiss weather had scared the shit out of the young Mary Shelley, and, through her, the whole world.

"There's nothing but old books, it's boring," Romy said. "Can we go?"

"Hang on, there's just one more old book I want to show you."

In the room containing the permanent collection, we passed a first edition of Goethe's *Faust*. It was open at an original illustration by Delacroix.

"Who's Faust?"

"He's a guy who wants to live forever. So he makes a deal with the devil."

"And it works?"

"At first, yes: he gets his youth in exchange for his soul. But later, things get complicated."

"So it ends badly?"

"Inevitably: he falls in love."

"Is this what you wanted to show me?"

"No."

A few metres further on, the Egyptian *Book of the Dead* impressed with the solemnity of its mysterious hieroglyphs from beyond the sarcophagus. Five thousand years ago, a scribe had put stylus to papyrus to write this user's manual to the afterlife. To broadly summarize, after death, the heart was weighed in a balance before the gods. The soul underwent a certain number of ordeals (notably, being forced to face snakes, crocodiles, and revolting beetles) before "emerging forth into the light," or, in other words, sailing across the sky aboard the solar barque of the god Ra to Sekhet-Aaru, the heavenly city. Later, the three great monotheistic religions of the world simply plagiarized the concept.

"Is this what you wanted to show me?"

"Nope."

I felt a wave of tenderness. Romy had an unruly tuft of hair that reminded me of photographs of myself at her age: do we love our children simply out of narcissism? Is a child a living selfie? In another room, we finally came to the Gutenberg Bible. The holy book glittered like a precious stone behind the thick bulletproof glass. The gilt and multicoloured illuminations and the letters printed on vellum 562 years earlier seemed to hover above the page like subtitles in some 3D blockbuster.

"There: this is the first book ever printed. It's important for you to see this book, to remember this moment. Soon, books won't exist anymore."

"That way I can say I saw the beginning and the end of books."

She looked me up and down with those blue eyes that will never again know innocence. I never felt prouder than when Romy calmly said those words. It was one of the first times I had spent two days alone with her, without Clémentine (her nanny). It was high time I got to know my daughter.

LIFE IS A hecatomb. A mass murder that slaughters 59 million people a year. 1.9 deaths per second. 158,857 deaths a day. Twenty people have died around the world since the beginning of this paragraph—more if you're a slow reader. I don't understand why terrorists wear themselves out adding to the statistics: they will never manage to kill as many people as Mother Nature. Humanity is decimated into general indifference. We tolerate this daily genocide as though it were a normal process. Personally, I find death shocking. I used to think about it once a day. Since turning fifty, I think about it every minute.

Let's be clear: I do not hate death; I hate *my* death. If the vast majority of humankind accept that it is inexorable, that's their problem. Personally, I can see no advantage to dying. In fact, I'd go so far as to say, Death stops with me. This tale is an account of my efforts to stop foolishly dying like everyone else. It was unthinkable that I should die without fighting back. Death is lazy, only fatalists truly believe it is inevitable. I loathe those resigned to their fate, who sigh and mutter "*Oh là là*, we all go that way one day or another." Fuck off and die somewhere else, puny mortals.

Every corpse is first and foremost a has-been.

There is nothing extraordinary about my life, but even so, I would rather that it carry on as long as possible.

Vainly, I got married twice. As a reaction, ten years ago

I had a child without marrying her mother. And then, in Geneva, I met Léonore, curvaceous brunette, doctor in molecular virology. I asked her to marry me straightaway. I'm not very skilled at picking up women; that's why I marry in haste (except for Caroline, which is probably why she left me). Romy and I sent Léonore a text message: "If you come to visit us in Paris, don't forget to bring double cream from Gruyères, we'll supply the meringues." I don't think the metaphor was deliberately erotic. I can't come up with a definition for love: personally, I feel it as a gnawing ache analogous to drug withdrawal. In marrying me Léonore was not simply marrying a father, she was agreeing to be stepmother to a pale-eyed preteen girl. After our wedding in a pink church in the Bahamas, Léonore divided her time between Paris and Geneva. We would take it in turns to catch the TGV Lyria. Sometimes we'd take it together so we could fuck on board. We talked a lot while making love between two carriages, between two countries.

"I should warn you, I'm not on the pill."

"So much the better, I want to impregnate you."

"Stop it, you're making me horny!"

"My gametes want to ravage your oocytes."

"Keep going ... I love it ..."

"I'm going to shoot three hundred million flagella at your fallopian tubes ..."

"Oh, yessss ..."

"Do I look like a guy who fucks just for the fun of it?"

"Oooh, gonad me!"

Nine months later ... Lou arrived so quickly that we didn't even have time to move in together. I've speeded up the story to get to my point: the subject of this book is not life, but non-death. Fathering a child at fifty is like trying to correct a film script that's already been written.

Usually, a man is born, marries, reproduces, divorces, and when he turns fifty, he rests. In choosing reproduction over retirement, I contravened the rules.

On the same evening that our baby was born, David Pujadas announced on the TV news that life expectancy in France had stagnated at seventy-eight. I had only twenty-six years left to live. But this was how old Léonore was, and we both knew how quickly twenty-six years flash past: in five minutes.

Twenty-six years, or 9,490 days left to live. Every day, from waking to sleeping, had to be slowly savoured as though I had just been released from prison. I had to live as though I was reborn every morning. To see the world through the eyes of a baby when actually I was a beat-up second-hand car. I needed an advent calendar with 9,490 windows to open. Every day that passes is one day less: 9,490 days are all that separate me from the Answer. I taught my youngest daughter a trick that my mother had taught me: turning over the shell of the boiled egg you've just eaten. Lou pretends she has barely started on her egg and I pretend to be annoyed. She cracks the shell with her spoon and I pretend to be surprised that the shell is empty. We're both laughing at a prank that relies on everyone playacting: Lou forces herself to believe that she has genuinely tricked me and every day I act like I'm surprised by the same prank. Could this little Sisyphean game be a metaphor for the human condition? Your shell is empty, so turn it over and pretend it's funny. Growing old is laughing at a joke you know by heart.

My fear of death is ridiculous, I know that. It's time to admit it: my nihilism is a failure. I have spent my whole life making fun of life; I have made irony my stock-in-trade. I don't believe in God: that's why I want to keep body and soul together. (Actually, I'd be happy just to keep body together.) I'm a nihilist who ended up with two children. And here I am forced to publicly confess, sheepish yet proud, that procreating is the most important thing that ever happened to me, to me, moderator of TV squabbles and director of satirical films.

There are two kinds of nihilist: those who take their lives and those who create new ones. The former are dangerous, the latter are pathetic. Violent nihilists have succeeded in discrediting my armchair pessimism. Cioran is the sort of pessimist jihadists assassinate. I bitterly resent Islamists for making derision derisory. But that's the way it is, it has to be admitted: every life, however worthless, is superior to nothingness, however heroic. If you don't believe in an eternal life-after-death, you inevitably want to prolong your own life. And this is how, from being a melancholy cynic, one becomes a posthuman scientist.

The life story you are reading guarantees my immortalization; it is preserved in Human Longevity, Inc., file number X76097AA804. But we'll come back to that later.

Until the age of fifty, you run with the crowd. After that, you're a little less eager to hurry. Around you, you see fewer people, and in front of you, a yawning abyss. My life has dwindled. I can clearly feel that my brain is younger than my body. I get beaten 6–2 at tennis by my twelve-year-old nephew. Romy knows how to change the cartridges in my printer; I'm completely incapable. It takes me three days to recover from a night drinking tequila. I've reached the age where you're afraid to take drugs: you snort "bumps" rather than the "fat rails" of yesteryear. You constantly look like a prude because you're afraid of having a stroke. You drink apple juice on the rocks so people think it's whisky. When you pass a girl in the street, you don't turn around for fear of getting a crick in your neck. The minute you decide to go surfing, you end up with an ear infection. Every night, you wake up once or twice because you need to pee. These are the joys of being a fiftysomething: if someone had told me that one day I'd fasten my seat belt in the back of a taxi ...!

Old people constantly have an ache somewhere or other. The body is worn out; few are the days without a pain in the foot, a cramp in the leg, a shooting pain in the chest. To say nothing of the neurological and psychological problems. The worst of which is constant kvetching. Old age broadly consists of pissing off those around you. Old men moan and grumble, and put young people to flight.

The one thing all fiftysomethings have in common is that we're scared shitless. You can see it in certain gestures: we're terribly careful about what we eat. We give up smoking and drinking. We stay out of the sun. We avoid oxidation of every kind. We're permanently freaked out. Former party animals turn into chickenshit wimps desperate to save their skin. Even the word "wimp" is an indication of the author's advanced age. We safeguard our last moments. We take out personal pension plans, life insurance policies, real estate investments. In the blink of an eye, my generation has gone from heedlessness to paranoia. I feel as though it happened overnight: suddenly all my wild and wasted friends from the '80s are obsessed with organic food, quinoa, veganism, and biking tours. As though we're all tripping on GHB (Generational Hangover Bug). The more time my friends spent holed up in the toilets of Le Baron twenty years ago, the more they now spend lecturing me on superfoods and healthy living. It's all the more surreal since I never saw it coming. Maybe I'd been sucked into the black hole of my divorces and my TV shows, I thought it was still cool to do drugs with call girls, I never saw the world around me changing. Guys whose idea of a night out was ending up in a gutter at 8:00 a.m. are now ayatollahs of the paleo diet and my former drug dealers are now devotees of mountain trekking in North Face clodhoppers. Now, you spark up a cigarette and you're a suicide bomber; order a caipirovska and you're the scum of the earth. You haven't read Sylvain Tesson? Poor bastard. It's their own past they're railing against. Even Sylvain Tesson once nearly snuffed it while drunkenly climbing across rooftops. Stop making Tesson out to be some eco-friendly monk! He's just like me: an alcoholic Russophile who's scared to die.

I started watching every single cookery programme: *Masterchef, Top Chef, Les Escapades de Petitrenaud*. I'm an ou olubbor who'o movcd into Lo Ɔal ɔuisinc. And somothing that was bound to happen has happened: I signed up for a gym. Even in my worst nightmares, I'd never predicted such a cataclysm: me on a Cross-Trainer, me vibrating on a Power Plate, me propped on my elbows doing Core Strength Exercises, me squatting against the wall imitating an Air Chair, me pulling on Bungee Cords, me pumping iron to turn my moobs into pecs. Down the centuries, man has fought in many heroic wars; in the twenty-first century, the struggle against death has taken on a new form: a guy in shorts with a skipping rope.

I'm afraid, because Romy and Lou don't deserve to be orphaned. I'm trying to postpone my end. Life is ending, and I refuse to accept that. Death doesn't fit with my Reverse Schedule. This morning, I walked barefoot over strawberries my baby girl had thrown on the floor.

Could this great joy, won at such great cost,
In the next five minutes somehow all be lost?

I'm going deaf: I'm forever asking people to repeat

things. But maybe there's no problem with my hearing, maybe I'm simply not interested in other people. I'm at the age where men start to drink Coke Zero because they're getting a paunch and they're afraid they'll never see their prick again. Every night, in the bath, I count the hairs I've shed floating on the surface of the water. If there are more than ten, I get depressed. With a pair of tweezers, I hunt down the grey hairs sprouting from my nose, my ears, and I trim my eyebrows, which look like they've been borrowed from Groucho Marx. I keep a close eye on moles and beauty spots as though waiting for milk to boil. I wear "razor-thin" suits by Hedi Slimane in the hope that if Death encounters a bearded guy squeezed into a slim fitting jacket, it'll assume it's got the wrong man. The knuckles on my hand are numb, my back aches after fifteen minutes' physical exercise. At fifty, there's no time left for lounging around. Life works on a tight schedule. My smartwatch constantly displays my heart-beat and the number of calories I burn when I walk. My Hexoskin Smart Shirt transmits my sweat rate to my iPhone 7. I find knowing these futile statistics reassuring. At any moment, I can tell you the number of steps I've taken since this morning. The World Health Organization recommends taking 10,000 steps a day; I'm only at 6,136 and already I'm shattered.

I've lost something along the way, and that something is called my youth. In our unshockable era, death alone is shocking. Since the beginning of this chapter, 10,000 people have died across the world. I prefer not to enumerate those who will die between here and the end of the book; the carnage would be too terrible to contemplate.

THERE'S SOMETHING I don't understand: you need a licence to drive a car, but to father a child, nothing. They'll let any asshole be a father. All he has to do is plant his seed and, nine months later, he is lumbered with the most colossal, the most crushing responsibility. What man is prepared for such an undertaking? I recommend a "paternity permit," requiring something like a driving test, that would assess a man's generosity, capacity for love, exemplary nature, human warmth, tenderness, politeness, education and, obviously, absence of incestuous or paedophiliac tendencies. Only perfect men should be authorized to procreate. The problem with such a "paternity permit" is that no one I know would qualify, certainly not your humble servant. The generation that introduces the "paternity permit" will probably be the last. Thereafter, no man will be authorized to father children. Humanity would die out as men were disqualified from fathering children.

Fatherhood, even when planned, is a profession that involves thinking on your feet. Unsurprisingly, nature has programmed for a surge of paternal affection, a joy that overwhelms you from the moment of birth. The father takes the squalling infant in his arms: he instantly falls in love with this sticky, wriggling, bluish creature. Nature sets great store by this moment when the witless youth becomes a senile old man. This is the paternal tripswitch: suddenly, the man forgets all thoughts of his car, his apartment, his job, or even cheating on the mother of his child. The man is no longer a man, he is a father, what Péguy calls the "great adventurer of modern times": in fact, a happy fool. Does he know what awaits him? No: here, too, nature has been cunning. If men knew what awaited them, they would think twice before embarking on such an insane venture. They would choose easier adventures: swimming across the Pacific, climbing the Himalayas barefoot. A piece of cake by comparison. Fatherhood alights on the incompetent without warning. It is a catastrophe known as happiness.

I have two daughters: child number one is ten years old, the younger child has just learned to say her name. You'll note I say "the younger child" rather than "child number two": this is superstition. I'm hoping to disprove the old maxim "never two without three," but the very fact that I've written the words means I'm already prepared for the worst. Have I been a good father? How can I know? Sometimes I was absent or thoughtless, clumsy or simply stupid; I did my best. I gave hugs and kisses, I worked so that my daughters had a nice house and healthy food, so they could holiday in the sun; the things they take for granted have required considerable effort on my part. For me, fatherhood means two things: 1) it has given my life meaning; 2) it has prevented me from dying. We need to stop thinking that a father is someone who looks after others. That's not true. I am being completely sincere in writing this. Mine is a generation in which children look after their parents. When I became a father, I thought I was Kurt Cobain; he also had a daughter. But, unlike him, I didn't commit suicide. I often think about Frances Bean Cobain, who is twenty-five now. When I think about her, I like Nirvana a little less. Fatherhood is a job you have no right to chuck in.

This doesn't stop me from feeling guilty all the time. I'm not proud that I wasn't able to stay with the mother of my elder daughter. How can you bring up a child when you've done everything in your power to be infantile? I think I've tried to be equal to the task. To be worthy of my children, even if my father had less to do with looking after me than my mother. It wasn't his fault; it's long since been forgiven. I know so many fathers who think they take good care of their children, but never spend a moment with them, they spend their days at the office and their nights in front of a laptop, they never ask questions and never listen to the answers, they allow TV news, urgent phone calls, and irrational fears about illegal immigration to come between them and their children. It's so easy to avoid the little excrescences who live with you. You make sure you don't step on them, when in fact you should use them as the missing rung on your ladder. Our society is one of absent fathers and deadbeat dads, apparently: though that's not how I've experienced it. When I separated from Caroline, I made sure I looked after Romy every other weekend and later every other week. I probably did more to raise her than I would have if I'd lived with her full-time … And now, with Lou, I've experienced custody that isn't shared. It's not so terrible to watch someone grow every day. I've experimented at being various kinds of father: absent, part-time, full-time. Someday, I should ask my daughters which father they would have preferred: the one who leaves, the one who stays, or the one who comes and goes. Show business isn't the only profession where you can have a walk-on part.

I was lucky to have daughters. I don't know whether I could have loved a son as much: for me, fatherhood is marvelling at a fringe of blond hair, gap teeth, little pink ears, dimples, peach-like skin, an impish profile, a snub nose, braces on teeth, a pointed chin above a swan's neck. Fatherhood is also lazily allowing your child to play their video game or watch *Harry Potter* so you don't have to deal with them between meals. Divorce forced me to play endless cheesy games, like UNO (a sort of modern variant of Mille Bornes, a card game I played as a child). These days, my elder daughter is better than I am at many things. She can trounce me 21–08 at ping pong. She speaks Spanish fluently. She wants to make films like Sofia Coppola (which would make me Francis Ford!).

People sometimes say a director's films are his children. I've rarely heard such utter bullshit. I have produced only two masterpieces, and no pixels were involved.

I WAS LIKE everyone else: I wanted a mansion with a swimming pool in Los Angeles, and if the basement was fitted with a private cinema, a bar, and a strip club, so much the better. It was the first time in history that all of humanity wanted to live in the same place.

I didn't introduce myself because most of you already know me. It's pointless to recount a life that no longer belongs to me since it appears in the pages of *Voici* every Friday. I'd rather talk to you about something that does belong to me: my death.

I'm allergic to autumn, because it is followed by winter and I have no need of winter: I'm already cold enough inside. I am the first man who will be immortal. This is my story: I hope it will last longer than my notoriety. I wear midnight-blue shirts, midnight-blue jeans, and midnight-blue moccasins. Midnight blue is the colour that allows me to wear mourning without looking like Thierry Ardisson. I present the first chemistry show in the world. I'm sure you've seen my *Chemistry Show* on YouTube, where French law doesn't apply and television has the right to do anything and everything without censorship. It is a talk show where I organize arguments on topical issues. The USP is that all the guests have to pop a pill an hour before we go live: Ritalin, Methadone, Captagon, Xanax, Synapsyl, Rohypnol, LSD, MDMA, Modafinil, Cialis, Solupred, Ketamine, or Stolnox, at random. They pick the gel capsule from a jar wrapped in black silk, not knowing what they will be taking. Amphetamines, opiates, steroids, tranquillizers, anxiolytics, aphrodisiacs, or hallucinogens: they have no idea what state they will be in as they engage in the most mediatized debate of their lives. The shows get millions of views on every conceivable platform. In terms of presentation style, I pitch myself somewhere between Yann Moix and Monsieur Poulpe—highbrow but wacky (the press release describes me as "pertinent and impertinent"). I have a veneer of culture, but don't flaunt it so as not to scare off the uncouth: the sort of smartarse capable of easily navigating between theology and scatology. Last week, a priest fell asleep on my shoulder sucking his thumb while trying to defend a parliamentary bill, a comedian slipped her tongue into my mouth and flashed her breasts (I had to call security to stop her fingering herself in front of Camera 3), and a singer burst into tears and then pissed his pants while talking about his mother. As for me, it depends: on one show it took me ten minutes to say, "Good evening, ladies and gentlemen," while on another, I interviewed the sofa for half an hour (I provided the questions and the answers); last month I threw up over my "blue suede shoes." The most famous episode was the one where I whipped the guests with my Gucci belt before spraying champagne all over the studio and announcing that my mother had had a heart attack. I have absolutely no memory of the long, paranoid monologue that racked up four million views on YouTube: I refuse to watch it. Apparently, I was drooling. If the argument isn't heated enough, I look down at my prompt cards—my researcher always prepares a list of embarrassing questions designed to unsettle my guests. They all leave furious. Some ask me to "sort things out" in the edit. It is at this point that I tell them the programme is livestreamed. (It's called a "live hangout" but it's like a good old-fashioned episode of *Right to Reply*.) Personally, I don't understand why artists come and make fools of themselves in my studio, given that I'm the only one who gets paid (not much, €10,000 a week, it's not the 1990s anymore). Recently, the audience figures have stagnated; that's why I've got into directing movies. On the set of my first feature, when the technicians found me too impatient, I'd say, "Why are we only shooting two minutes a day? On YouTube, it takes an hour and a half to film ninety minutes!" Films should be shot live; it would take much less time—a single take and it's in the can, like the movies of Iñárritu or Chazelle. The current fashion for extended takes comes from their films: the public don't want cinema anymore, they want to observe life on the screen, and that's not the same thing. Movie actors would be a lot less like divas if they felt the same fear as stage actors. I released a rom-com called *Do You Love Me or Are You Faking It?*—financed by an old pay-per-view channel—that had audience figures of 800,000: the channel covered its costs, despite "mixed" reviews. My second film, *All the Supermodels in the World*, didn't fare so well, there was no TV funding and the audience figures fell by 75%. I don't know whether I'll direct a third film, now that I've found another way to become immortal.

ADVANTAGES AND DISADVANTAGES OF DEATH

PROS

CONS

Putting an end to the suffering of the elderly	Depriving your children of your wisdom and experience
Finally getting the hell out of this sordid life	The most sordid thing about life is that it ends
Not having to suffer fools and fuglies	Missing the next few thousand seasons of *Black Mirror*
Refusing to become a vegetable	So many books to read and films to watch
Not being a burden to society	You paid social security and pension contributions, why feel guilty?
Why live if you can't fuck anymore?	Viagra exists for men and women
Things were better in the past	Things will be better in the future
Free up space on an overpopulated planet	All we need to do is colonize Mars
I don't understand the world anymore	It would be a pity not to be around to criticize the next few centuries
Suicide is beautiful	You can always kill yourself later
Living to be 300 would be a bore	No one has ever tried
Old age is a disaster	Woody Allen was 80 when he directed *Café Society*

PROS	CONS
Not having to endure modern art	So many old masters still to see
It's the end of the world anyway	It would be a pity to miss the show
Screwing the 72 virgins in paradise	What if there are only 71?
Not having to watch your kids get old	It would be a pity to miss the show
I'd have a beautiful funeral	I wouldn't be there to see it
People would miss me …	… for about three days
You can die with dignity in Lausanne	But it's a lot less fun than a donation to a sperm bank
After a certain age everyone is pretty much unfuckable	Four words: Clint, Eastwood, Sharon, Stone
Life is exhausting	Which means death is for slackers
No more bills and taxes to pay	Your kids pay death duties
No more lying about your age	No more birthday presents
When you're old you're not allowed to drink and take drugs	Four words: Keith, Richards, Michel, Houellebecq
Avoiding family get-togethers (Christmas, New Year)	You'll still see them on All Saints' Day
People say nice things about you when you're dead	You won't get to read the obituaries
You can finally get some rest	A detox would be rest enough
In death, everyone is equal	Just vote communist
I wouldn't have to put up with reality TV anymore	You can switch off the TV without switching off reality
No one should be obliged to live forever	Just because you don't like life, don't put others off

PROS	CONS
Death offers closure	Life is an opening
Without death, what would be the purpose of literature?	The only function of art is to celebrate beauty
It is death that makes every moment in life so precious	Who's to say it wouldn't be more precious if it was longer?
Millais's painting of "Ophelia"	Mexican death heads
Père-Lachaise Cemetery	… it's already full
"Death helps us to live" (Lacan)	"Death is a final solution" (Hitler)
It would make those who hate us happy	It would make those who love us sad
Without death, Goethe would not have written *Faust* and Oscar Wilde wouldn't have written *The Picture of Dorian Gray*	Without immortality, the Sumerians wouldn't have written *Gilgamesh* and Bram Stoker wouldn't have written *Dracula*
Without death, what would be the point of the Panthéon?	Without life, what's the point of the Académie Française?
It's cool when shit people die	It's shit when cool people die
Not ending up looking like Jeanne Calment	Not beating Jeanne Calment's record (122 years, 5 months, 14 days)
It's the ultimate detox, the apotheosis of rehab	… with a huge side order of FOMO

SINCE THE DAWN of humanity, there have been approximately a hundred billion deaths. I'm not claiming that attaining immortality would be easy. I envy my daughters their age. They'll see the twenty-second century. André Choulika, CEO of Cellectis (the leading French biopharmaceutical and genome engineering company) claims that babies born post-2009 will live to be a hundred and forty. I envy Lou. I am a selfish bastard refusing to give up my place. The work I do is ephemeral; I know all too well that what I do on television will be forgotten when I die. The only chance for me to carry on is to cling to life and to the screens, whether big or small. For as long as my image survives, people will remember. My death will sound the death knell of my work. I won't simply be forgotten—worse, I'll be replaced. It's funny to see former TV presenters, feeling their fame threatened, rushing to perform in provincial theatres, hoping for a few last crumbs of glory, recounting their memoirs to half-asleep old biddies with purple rinses. They spend their lives interviewing artists and writers, then, when the merry-go-round stops, they want to be the ones getting standing ovations, but nobody wants to interview them, it's too late, so they find themselves performing in a village hall in Romorantin, like tribute acts to Johnny Hallyday or Patrick Modiano. They want to shrug off the ephemeral for the permanent, to replace fleeting fame with something for posterity. The most upsetting case is

Thierry Ardisson, the man who gave me a start in the industry. Thierry dreamed of being a writer, but nothing that he says is written by him: his comments, his jokes, and his questions are all written by hacks. All Thierry Ardisson has done for the past thirty years is read words written by other people. It's hardly surprising that he's now obsessed with producing box sets of clips from his old shows—the frustrated novelist desperate for a place on your bookshelf. If I want to escape this dismal fate, I have to be immortalized for real. Physically, by which I mean, medically.

In a world where all men are mortal, an optimist is a charlatan.

The few real friends I had are dead now. Christophe Lambert, the CEO of EuropaCorp, killed by cancer at fifty-one. Jean-Luc Delarue, President of Reservoir Prod and my neighbour on the Rue Bonaparte, dead at forty-eight. Philippe Vecchi, his roommate, at fifty-three. Maurice G. Dantec, cyberpunk writer, dead at fifty-seven. Richard Descoings, Director of the Paris Institute of Political Studies, died from a heart attack at fifty-three. Frédéric Badré, founder of the literary magazine *Ligne de Risque*, dead from a neurodegenerative illness at fifty. Mix & Remix—real name Philip Becquelin—who illustrated my column in *Lire*, dead from pancreatic cancer at fifty-eight. They were all guests on my TV shows: they were great television, always ready to put themselves out there, never waffling. I remember Dantec lighting a firework with a page torn from the Bible and intoning: "Forgive them, for they know not what they do"; Jean-Luc tearing his shirt off and throwing himself on the floor for a breakdancing lesson; Christophe miming a bullfight with Luc Besson, fingers pressed to his temples as horns, playing the bull; Philippe pogoing to "Should I

Stay or Should I Go"; Richard winning an air-guitar competition; Frédéric imitating animal noises; the other Philippe drawing *vagina dentata*. They felt as though they had nothing to lose. A few months later, they lost everything. After fifty, death is no longer an abstract concept. I hate the insidious way it creeps closer with every medical check-up. It reminds me of the rain of arrows in *The Revenant*: you have to run, to zigzag like Leonardo DiCaprio to avoid the hissing downpour, burning and poisonous. I am zigzagging faster and faster. I long to stop, to rest for a while, but in order to rest, I need a new life, like in *Call of Duty*, where it only takes two clicks to come back to life after a shootout. Give me another few decades and I promise I'll make better use of them. I'm still hungry. I want seconds, okay? Just a handful of seconds. A second life.

I'm in no hurry to become an orphan. I didn't like the spectacle of my parents, the people who gave me life, lying in hospital beds, it felt somehow vulgar, predictable, like a bad reality-TV scene. Something told me I had to save them. I didn't want to lose them; they were my human shields. Giving me life is not a crime that warrants the death penalty.

My father on crutches in a physiotherapy clinic at the Buttes-Chaumont, my mother lying in Cochin hospital, shattered after a fall: neither suspecting that they might end up alone. My parents' brutal ends were twin advertisements for divorce and cardiovascular disease. They had lived apart for years, yet I foolishly imagined they would die together. For months, on the set of my TV shows, I pasted on a hideous smile—the grinning rictus of a bad actor off his face on coke—whenever the camera light turned red. It was around then that I started presenting charity phone-ins: Téléthon, Sidaction, the Concert against Cancer ... I was offended to find myself grieving over an event as banal as my parents' illnesses, to discover I had a heart capable of such a statistically conventional emotion. Over lunch at the Ritz, the cartoonist comic artist Sfar had warned me, "If you lose your parents when you're ten, everyone comforts you, you're suddenly an interesting person; if you lose them at fifty, no one pities you, that's when you're truly the loneliest orphan in the world."

If I lost my parents, I knew that no one would ever take as much interest in me as they did. So my grief was just more narcissism. Grieving for one's parents is grieving for one's own fragility. I pleaded with the woman in make-up to hide my grief with concealer as I roared at the floor manager to drown out the applause for the warm-up man: "Good evening and welcome, mortal friends: this is not a programme, it's a prescription!"

A threat looms over the populace of Europe; our peace of mind is transitory; we have learned to behave as though the chaos that exists between the Big Bang and the Apocalypse can be organized on our smartphones between two suicide attacks livestreamed on Periscope and a Snapchat of the *plat du jour*. Since birth, we've been repeatedly told we'll come to a bad end. Before I started this investigation, I knew that a human being was a physical body, but not an agglomeration of a billion reprogrammable cells. I'd heard of stem cells, of genetic engineering, of regenerative medicine, but if science could not save my parents, what was the point of it? To save us, my wife, my daughters and me—the next names on the death list.

The epiphany came while I was doing a New Year show. As always, the show was pre-recorded, so that I could spend the holidays on Harbour Island. Surrounded by the Pink Paradise dancers and professional comedians, I pretended it was December 31, that I was waiting for midnight and the countdown—"Five! Four! Three! Two! One! HAAPPY NEW YEAAAARRRR FRANCE!"—when in fact we were celebrating at 7:00 p.m. on November 15 in an icy studio in Boulogne-Billancourt. We had to restart the countdown three times because the fucking balloons didn't fall. As it turned out, that year, two of my guests died between recording and transmission. A singer with a drug problem and a gay comedian didn't make it to New Year. Because of them, four hours of fake-live video had to be ditched: my producer lost two million euros (less my commission); viewing the rushes, it was clear the show couldn't be broadcast, even if it was reedited— the dead comedian was camping it up in all the wide shots. All my guests were pissed off; the poor bastards had had to spend a bleak winter afternoon pretending to celebrate New Year's Eve, in black tie and evening dresses, in return for zero Media Impact Score. This was the straw that broke the camel's back: I was sick and tired of death ruining my life. This was the moment that I started to look more closely at advances in genetics.

The world of today feels to me like a speeded-up traffic jam. As if we were stuck in a tailback but, rather than drive slowly, bumper to bumper, we're hurtling into the abyss at 200 kph, like the scene in *Fast & Furious 7* when Vin Diesel's Lykan Hypersport crashes through the window of a skyscraper in Abu Dhabi and completely destroys the 74th floor of a second Abu Dhabi skyscraper, before landing in a third Abu Dhabi skyscraper. It's a spectacular stunt, but how many of us want to live like stuntmen? We age faster these days: by thirty, we find the younger generation incomprehensible, their slang unintelligible, their way of life impenetrable, and they are only too eager to push us out. In the Middle Ages, we were all dead by fifty. Today, we sign up for the Club Med Gym and wave our arms on a yoga mat while watching Bloomberg TV, with share prices scrolling every which way. I'm pretty sure that if I opened a gym called "Death Row," people would be fighting to sign up for it.

If you think I'm crazy, close this book. But I know you won't. Because you're like me, an "autonomous individual," to use the term coined by the sociologist Alain Touraine, meaning free, modern individuals with no ties to the land or to religion. According to a market-research study conducted by my own production company, my show only appeals to urban singles, rootless people, mavericks, AB consumers, high-earning atheists; nobody else watches my shows. In his report, the market researcher who questioned the panel about my image, quoted the German philosopher Peter Sloterdijk, who talks about modern man as a "self-generated citizen," a "bastard with no ancestry." I very nearly took this badly; as I left the presentation, I looked at my reflection in the mirror in the lift and realized I looked like a "creature of dis-continuum." I am part of the first human generation raised with no sense of patriotism, no family pride, no deep roots, no sense of belonging, no particular beliefs, beyond catechism lessons at the Catholic school when I was very young. This is a fact about which I have no reactionary lament: I only see a historical reality. I am the product of the obsolete utopia of the seventies, of an era when citizens of the Western world tried to shrug off the chains of previous centuries. I'm the first man with no ball and chain. Or I'm the last ball and chain of the next generation.

No one, except depressives and suicide bombers, actually *wants* to die. If there is even one chance in eight billion that I might succeed in prolonging my life for two or three centuries, you'll want to do likewise. Bear in mind this one fact: you're going to die because you'll let yourself. You're dying and I'm not. Humankind has mastered everything: the deepest oceans, the most inaccessible mountains, the moon, even Mars. It's time for medicine to put an end to death. Once that's done, we'll work out how to find space to deal with the overcrowding. In twenty years' time, there'll be no Social Security. Faced with a rapidly aging population and a massive deficit in tax revenues, it will be every man for himself: the rich will stop paying to subsidize the poor. Short of postponing the retirement age to 280 ... As for health insurance and life insurance companies, DNA sequencing will let them know the precise level of our health risk, and an algorithm will rapidly calculate the corresponding premiums. Extending life span will have a positive financial impact: everyone (except those with faulty genomes) will be able to buy eye-wateringly expensive houses on mortgages repayable over several centuries. Example: a €10,000,000 mortgage repayable over three hundred years with monthly payments of €2,700. You've always wanted a yacht? No problem if you've got centuries ahead of you.

I'll spare you the religious spiel about life after death. I've never been a fan of casinos or horse racing: don't count on me to endorse Pascal's wager. I don't give a shit about life after death, what I want is to indefinitely extend my life *before* I meet the Grim Reaper. Catholics pray for eternal life; me, I want eternal life without all the praying. The problem with God is that if you don't believe in Him, you come across as a complete loser. Especially at fifty, when your body starts to malfunction; something that we know—despite all our anti-aging creams, Botox injections, hair transplants, and Ayurvedic massage—

will only get worse until the final humiliation. This is why the congregation at mass are all over fifty. The Church as health spa for the soul.

Have I lost the taste for danger?

2

GONZO CHECK-UP
(Georges Pompidou European Hospital, Paris)

"But exactly how were they to live? How?"
MIKHAIL BULGAKOV, *The White Guard* (1926)

ROMY AND LOU had much more of a future than I did: I respected their longevity. They were posthuman from birth. Children are wonderful multicellular organisms that run around the living room and reward our attention.

The birth of Lou somewhat complicated the writing of this book. When your baby is chanting "papa, papa, papa," writing becomes a superhuman effort in resisting a smile waiting to be seen. I typed this paragraph on my computer while Lou was hiding behind the curtains waiting for me to find her, before erupting into peals of laughter beneath her flaxen hair when I tickled her. How can anyone be expected to write *War and Peace* in such conditions? Dickens apparently managed to write *Oliver Twist* while surrounded by his brood, but it was the story of children being abused: he was getting his revenge. My revenge is to nibble Lou's ears and toes until she begs for mercy: "Stop Papa! Stop Papa!" She has the softest skin of anyone in the world. And the gap-toothed grin of Vanessa Paradis, only forty-five years younger. The face of a goddess, a domed forehead, plump cheeks, an impish nose, and a generous mouth stuffed with apricots. It's impossible to imagine anything more joyful than her dimples. How can anyone be creative when their most glorious creation is prancing around them? Sorry, I've got a nappy that needs changing. I'll get back to work tomorrow. Literature will have to wait: the tiny hand in my big hand is stopping me from writing.

I don't want Lou to grow up, and I'm dreading the day when Romy leaves. When I see Lou playing with the shower, discovering that a car horn goes *beep-beep*, biting into a cherry, or playfully knocking over all my obsessively catalogued DVDs despite my protestations, allowing me to finally find the copy of Cukor's *Adam's Rib* I thought I'd lost, I remember Romy performing those same miracles at that age, and then I see myself, knocking over tables in Neuilly, and I relive my childhood for a third time, again and again, getting younger each time. With each new birth, I am reborn.

I ALLOW ROMY to do all the things her mother forbids—to eat peanut butter and *Mi-cho-ko* before dinner, to watch TV until midnight, to make phone calls in bed, to FaceTime her classmates ... As for Lou, no one can say no to her, especially not me. My TV shows come second to finger painting. My daughters have taught me how not to waste time. My priorities have significantly changed over the course of the 2000s: making a plasticine seahorse has become more important than a threesome with a couple of Slovak girls. A good day is Lou watching *Peter Rabbit* and me watching Lou and drinking beer (I've realized that alcohol puts me on her level; a drunk is just like a baby, but flabbier).

Yesterday, I dreamed that my parents were cremated. Lou was in the living room playing with their urns. She was spilling my mother's ashes onto the carpet. A heap of grey dust on the floor. Then I realized she had also tipped out my father's ashes. It was impossible to separate the piles: my parents were a single heap of dust in the middle of the living room. As my Dyson 360 Eye Robot Vacuum started to hoover up my mother and father, I woke up.

There are numerous ways to overcome death, but they are the preserve of a handful of Chinese or Californian billionaires. Better to be a living posthuman than a human reduced to ashes. I realized I didn't care for my humanity as much as I'd thought, otherwise I'd have chosen to be something other than a TV presenter. I'm not a traditionalist when it comes to the physical body. If, to carry on living, I have to become a machine, I'll give up my already approximate humanity without a second thought. I don't owe murderous Mother Nature anything. Besides, I've fucked up everything in this life. I need a second chance: I'm not asking for much, just another century. A life to spend playing catch-up.

Lou looks me straight in the eye and demands butterfly kisses. I blink rapidly, fluttering my eyelashes against her cheeks. Then she demands I play Incy Wincy Spider. So I do. "Again!" She giggles as my fingers tickle her neck. "Again!" I love this glorious time of the morning when Lou still prefers me to SpongeBob.

I make the most of these beginnings that enliven my death pangs.

THE FIRST STEP in my quest for eternal life was to get a check-up from the doctor favoured by A-list celebs at the Department for Functional Testing and Predictive Medicine at the Georges Pompidou European Hospital in the 15th arrondissement of Paris, near the former head office of Canal+, designed by Richard Meier, the studios where my TV show and Yann Barthes's *Quotidien* are filmed.

Frédéric Saldmann is a famous cardiologist and nutritionist whose first book, *You Are Your Own Best Medicine*, has sold 550,000 copies. In theory, there's a two-year waiting list to get a consultation, but I'm a celebrity and the system we live in isn't totally democratic. I was predisposed to trust Saldmann. A doctor who is so well known in the media has to be more careful than his colleagues: he knows that if I die, it will ruin his reputation.

The imposing glass and steel building resembled a gigantic spacecraft bristling with tubular structures that looked like Terminal 2E at Charles de Gaulle Airport. In the centre, two soaring palm trees provided a touch of environmental exoticism. It would be the perfect setting to shoot a U2 video or house a contemporary art institute. The architecture was part of the utopian atmosphere, it had to offer a dazzling spectacle, otherwise no one would believe: medicine has changed very little since the plays of Molière. It was at the Pompidou Hospital that "Carmat," the world's first artificial heart, was implanted. Although the patient who received the transplant died three months later, it was a noble attempt. The newspaper *Les Échos* even namechecked the futuristic establishment in their October 2016 issue: "The wildest hopes for tissue regeneration were revived earlier this year when Professor Philippe Menasche of the Georges Pompidou European Hospital announced that a patient who had suffered a heart attack had been successfully treated using cardiac cells derived from human embryonic stem cells." I know where to bring Maman if her dicky heart starts to act up again.

On the second floor of Building C, I passed the Department of Pharmacology/Toxicology. I took the name as a personal warning. As I walked through the reception area, I met several stooped, doddery old men; they didn't seem to realize that they didn't need to check in at reception anymore. Around me, interns were scurrying towards electron microscopes, but the star of the department was standing motionless in front of me. At sixty-four, Doctor Saldmann looked ten years younger. Svelte and cheerful, the doctor who had treated Alain Delon, Sophie Marceau, Bernard-Henri Lévy, Isabelle Adjani, Jean-Paul Belmondo, and Roman Polanski shook my hand and ushered me into his consulting room. This was not a place where they washed the grubby sheets of bed-ridden patients; this was a place dedicated to extending humanity by means other than TENA incontinence pants. Saldmann was wearing a white coat, and glasses with chrome steel frames. He reminded me of Michael York in *Logan's Run*. Eternal life favours the crisp sci-fi look. I prefer "crisp" to "clean," which sounds more like "clinical." He took my blood pressure: high. My electrocardiogram: predictable.

Then he took a cold, sticky transducer and performed an ultrasound of my abdomen. Saldmann's only problem is that he's balding: his scalp was visible through his hair. On the other hand, his smile looked devilish, probably because of the gaps between his incisors. For a doctor promising longevity, having gap teeth—which, in France, we call "lucky teeth"—is a guarantee of integrity. He peered at the monitor, studying my stomach, my gall bladder, my pancreas, and my prostate (black and white scudding clouds, like a painting by Soulages). All my organs were functioning correctly, he told me, except one, which was giving off a strange gurgling sound.

"You have fatty liver."

"I eat foie gras all the time."

"Fat in a duck's liver is a lot better than fat in your own. The liver is what filters waste from your system. Yours looks like a clogged sieve."

He showed me an image of a greenish yellow piece of rotting meat. It reminded me of the diseased organs they put on packs of cigarettes to terrify those following in the footsteps of Humphrey Bogart (an allusion for the oldsters).

"That's what your liver looks like. You look pretty weird on the outside, but you look even weirder inside."

At this point, I started to sulk. One of the most frustrating consequences of working as a boorish TV presenter is that even casual acquaintances think they can be boorish with me.

"Don't play the martyr," he said. "It takes five hundred days for your liver to regenerate. You just have to change your eating habits. If you do what I tell you, you'll soon have the liver of a twenty-year-old who's only ever drunk Evian from crystal bottles. Come on, let's do a stress test."

He made me get on a cross-trainer. After pedalling for one minute, my heart was racing at 180 bpm. He pleaded with me to get off the machine.

"Help, he's about to do a René Goscinny impersonation!"

"But that's not surprising, I don't do any running."

"Well don't go having a heart attack in my office."

René Goscinny is every cardiologist's nightmare, ever since the author of the *Asterix* comics died of a heart attack during a routine stress test in 1977. He was fifty-one: precisely my age.

"Come on, we'll do a full check-up. Including a cardiac MRI. I'd like to take a close look at your coronary arteries."

I left the consultation depressed. I fasted overnight, and the following morning I went to a medical clinic to provide blood, urine, and a stool sample. After a few days I began to find something sensual about the young lab assistant to whom, every day, I had to hand the little pot labelled with my name that contained my faeces. The humiliation commonly known as "old age" was like some particularly twisted sexual fetish—I never imagined that I'd ever come to find shitting in a plastic tub every morning to see how long I was going to live sexy. Although we never broached the subject, I felt a sort of scatological complicity developing between her and me.

I also went for a CT coronary angiogram at the Labrouste Institute. An iodine-based dye was injected into my bloodstream to make it possible to see my ribcage in 3D. As I lay holding my breath in a tunnel filled with radioactive rays, I noticed a sign warning against looking directly at the laser. Predictably, I looked around for Darth Vader's lightsaber. Fifteen minutes later, I was looking at my heart, my aorta, and my arteries on a series of LCD screens. It looked like a knuckle of veal.

I said to the radiographer studying the images, "I've often wondered what death looks like. I'm guessing he looks like you."

"Disappointed?"

My life depended on this cross-section that looked like a three-dimensional turnip from a horror movie. It would be a great idea for a talk show: "Show Me Your Guts!" Shot at the Labrouste Institute, viewers would be able to watch the beating hearts and clogged arteries of the guests. There would be live ultrasounds. The tear-jerking section would be when the guests are told their prognosis in front of the cameras. Something to think about for next year.

The following week, the glass surfaces of the Pompidou Hospital reminded me not of a spaceship, but of the pyramid at the Louvre. I began to understand where I was: in a steel and glass mausoleum similar to the sarcophagus built by François Mitterrand. My mood had changed; I wasn't swaggering anymore. Check-ups take a toll on your self-esteem. Doctor Saldmann had called me in to give me the results. He reviewed my test results with the sadistic slowness of a judge waiting for silence in court before delivering his verdict. This is my heart, for you to contemplate.

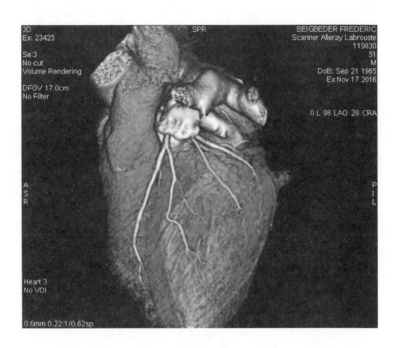

HOW MANY NOVELISTS do you know who are prepared to reveal the inner workings of their body? Louis-Ferdinand Céline said that a writer had to "put his skin on the table." My CT coronary angiograph is a decisive step in the history of literature.

(Note from an author prepared to do anything.)

"YOU'RE SUFFERING FROM hepatic steatosis and hypertension. It's just about within normal limits, given everything you've been putting into your body. But your heart is sound and your arteries are clear. It's amazing! You have zero risk of a myocardial infarction. Did you make a pilgrimage to Lourdes or something? Your coronary calcium level is zero; it's like you've just been born! Your stomach, your lungs, your balls, are all functioning normally. You don't even have an enlarged prostate. Much more of this and I'm going to start taking Class A drugs!"

I thanked God for giving me a second chance. Saldmann seemed as relieved as I was. He had been expecting to find a ruined body.

"The thing I find surprising," I said, after the long sigh of a death row inmate who has just been pardoned, "is that it's taken fifty years for my liver to protest. Is there any way you can prolong it indefinitely?"

"What?"

"I'd like to postpone my death to such an extent that death will die before I do. My goal is to live for four hundred years, with my fatty liver."

"Let's be realistic and talk about the next four months. (*grim laughter*) The average life expectancy for a man in France is seventy-eight, my friend; it's eighty-four for women because they're more intelligent. This means you should have thirty good years ahead of you as long as you follow my low-fat diet. Your sugar level is 133 mg/dL, uric acid is 9.1 mg/dL, and triglycerides 236 mg/dL. Too much fat, too much booze, too much sugar. You have to find some other way to get your kicks beyond eating and drinking: travel the world, fuck whoever you like as long as you use a condom, read books, go to the cinema, to the theatre—think old school! Most importantly, forty minutes daily exercise will lower your risk of cancer by 40% by releasing 1004 protective molecules. But don't work yourself to death. Are your audience ratings still good?"

"Three to five million a week."

"That's not bad."

"We get more when I throw up on set."

"Do you have to take the same pills as your guests? All this substance abuse isn't exactly recommended by the medical establishment."

"Don't worry about the pills, I only take them when we broadcast live. Then I spend the following week drinking mineral water and preparing the next programme. I'm not trying to kill myself, you get that, Doctor? Either through work or through play. These days, I'm as keenly aware of death as a stag at a fox hunt."

"You're the only hypochondriac I know who pops pills without knowing what's in them."

"Look, I'm pretty careful. I track every possible symptom, any suspicious pains. I bought myself a BP monitor so I can take my blood pressure morning, noon, and night. I look stuff up online. I know the best specialists for every part of my body. These days I spend more time hanging out in pharmacies than in swanky bars. Every day, the chemist on rue de Seine greets me the way Alan, the bartender, used to do when I was propping up the bar at Castel! The cash I used to fritter away on vodka and Coke is now invested in vegetables and vitamins."

The doctor to the stars clearly thought I was a halfwit, something he signalled by nodding slowly and gazing into the middle distance muttering *"Oh là là."* And the Academy Award for Best Feigned Emotion goes to ... Doctor Frédéric Saldmann. He listened to my lungs with his icy stethoscope. He peered into my ears and my throat with his penlight.

"Look. I'll be blunt with you. I consider any death before the age of a hundred and twenty as premature, but I need you to work with me. When you get to fifty, life is a shooting gallery. We can't carry on like you're thirty. You're slowly killing yourself. Even if I freeze and store your stem cells so I can transplant them later, it won't be enough. You have to cancel your *Chemistry Show*. If you've got a problem with that, then there's nothing I can do for you. If you have to, let your guests pop pills, and you can just pretend. You've got no choice. Pop a Tic-Tac or an M&M, screw your face up and people will fall for it."

"I've already tried that, but everyone can tell something's wrong if I'm not off my face. The show has no spark. People who don't work on TV assume being a presenter is easy. Then again, maybe you have a point, I could finish this season and then take a year out."

"Maybe you could use the time to see a shrink, too, so you can work on your death wish. I really enjoyed the show you did about death. I particularly enjoyed the moment when the founder of Google swallowed his earphone."

"Generally, death doesn't get a spike in ratings. But that one time, we hit the jackpot."

"Maybe because it still affects most people. As for you, the situation is very simple: you either quit drugs or you quit living. The choice is yours."

"I feel like popping something now just so I don't have to hear what you're saying."

"In that case, I'd like to buy your house."

"Really?"

"Yeah—for a life annuity."

Being a "doctor to the stars" has its privileges: you're entitled to more gallows humour than the national average. It was June: the TV season had just ended and I had more than enough money in my bank account to quit working for a year without it impacting my lifestyle. My only worry was whether the production company would pick up the show again the following year, or whether I'd have to produce it myself. A sabbatical year was a good idea. I could travel the world with Romy; Léonore and Lou could come and join us at the more relaxed destinations. I was going to save all our lives. I could take on Doctor Saldmann as my agent. He gave better advice than my producer, whose plan was to have me work myself to death until the final triple bypass.

"Can I be honest with you?" he went on. "You need antioxidants. Eat radishes, raisins, quinoa, clementines, and grapefruit. Give up the pills, the hard liquor, the barbecue, saucisson ..."

"Oh no, not saucisson ... So, all you are saying is give peas a chance?"

I apologize for the terrible pun. At least on my chat show, the warm-up act forces the audience to laugh to drown out clangers like that. It's nice to have a cushion of applause when you flop. Unperturbed, my bestselling author-cum-doctor carried on, à la Michel Cymes. (Michel was a great guest on my show, he ate the bunch of flowers on set, gave backstroke lessons in an inflatable pool, and said positive things about sodomy.)

"Eat garlic, almonds, lemon, melon ..."

"With serrano ham?"

"No sir, and no ham. Ease up on the meat, butter, cream,

cheese, fries. No foie gras, no grilled meat ..."

"Aaargh!"

"... carrots, tomatoes, broccoli, fennel, leeks, courgettes, aubergines ..."

"Listen, if you're going to tell me that I have to be vegan in order not to die, I didn't need to see you, I could just have read the latest issue of *Men's Health*. You don't need to worry, I've already tried this grim diet. For example, I only eat the green crocodiles in Haribo Starmix."

"Look, you ask me a question, I give you an answer. It's not me talking, it's science. And you don't need to go vegan, you can eat fish. Sardines are animals, aren't they? But for god's sake, give up the Haribo Starmix, they're full of pork gelatine. And not a drop of Coke. That stuff's poison! Drink tap water instead. Drink lots of water, it suppresses the appetite and no one has ever found anything healthier for the stomach."

"Shit ... So, no sweets and snacks?"

"Pistachios, dark chocolate, and honey are okay. And not too much salt either."

"Jesus ... And no booze?"

"Make your mind up. You want to be immortal or a wino? Drink wheatgrass juice!"

"I'd rather die."

"Just as well, since you probably will."

"It's just a turn of phrase. Don't worry, I regularly eat acai bowls, I drink matcha latte. I'm guessing I shouldn't spend too much time in the sun?"

"Only if you've smeared your body with Factor 50. But a little vitamin D is very good for your health."

"So you're saying, in order to live longer, you can't be Basque or American. Pity: they're my two favourite nationalities."

"Oh. One last thing—how did you get here."

"On a scooter."

"Well, stop that right now, you idiot! It's by far the most dangerous thing you're doing. It's suicide on two wheels. You get distracted for a split second and *ciao*."

"That's funny, I've just realized why the model name of my old moped was Ciao. Fine, I'll walk home."

"You don't seem to realize: this is the dawn of a period of amazing medical progress; you just have to hang on for thirty or forty years. I'm studying a rodent from East Africa (Somalia, Ethiopia, Kenya) called the naked mole-rat—an animal that's immune to everything and lives for thirty years, in comparison to the common mouse, which lives for two to three years. It's the equivalent of humans living for six hundred years in perfect health. The naked mole-rat never contracts cancer or Alzheimer's or heart disease. Its skin and arteries don't wear out, it remains fertile and sexually active to the end. Researchers have tried implanting it with aggressive cancerous tumours, its body rejects them. The same thing happens if it's exposed to chemical carcinogens. We're talking about an animal that holds the secret to eternal life. All you need to do is hang in there until help arrives."

(*After Googling "naked mole-rat" to see photos*) "What a hideous animal!"

"Immortality isn't like choosing Miss World."

"But we're talking about an animal that's unfuckable!"

"You're right, I forgot one essential point. Sex is crucial to longevity. It's estimated that having sex twelve times increases life expectancy by ten percent. If you can get your leg over twenty times a month, you *reduce* your risk of prostate cancer by a third. Essentially, you need to replace the blow-outs and the booze with a lot more fucking: doesn't sound like such a bad deal."

"So an orgasm a day keeps the Grim Reaper away?"

"Right. I've got to go, I wish you a happy resurrection. Do you mind taking a selfie with me so I can impress my wife? She's a huge fan. She loved the episode where Depardieu and Poelvoorde decided to neck all the pills at the same time."

"Yeah, that worked out well, it was a brilliant idea to stay on air until they had their stomachs pumped at 4:00 a.m. live from the Hôtel-Dieu. How much do I owe you for the check-up?"

"Send me some of your foie gras at Christmas!" (*derisive laughter*)

Outside, the summer was obscene. Being in mourning for your life is a great excuse for a public meltdown. I disparage death but I tolerate disintegration. I often cried for no reason; perhaps it was the particulates floating in the Paris air. As Salinger said, "Poets are always taking the weather so personally." I sniffled as I passed a blonde mother pushing a pram. Looking at the green plane trees against the grey backdrop. Gazing up at a sky the colour of fatty liver. My celebrity doctor had just brought illness into my life. I was feeling sorry for myself and my own decline. Whatever you do, don't pity me. I'm capable of blubbing to order. Sometimes, when one of my guests says something poignant, I shed a tear just for the feels.

I'm jealous of the clock on the Place Vauban that is never out of order. As I wandered the bleak streets of the 7th arrondissement, I bought a bunch of violets. A storm was brewing in the air. The shops were closing, a bell tolled. I didn't even notice night drawing in. I went into a lighted church, St. Pierre du Gros Caillou, which looks like the Acropolis but in better repair. The smell of incense made me light-headed; I was afraid I might faint. I set down the violets on a purple altar; they clashed, which is embarrassing in a place of worship. I lit a candle for my father and my mother. I didn't want to suddenly be the next to face the final curtain. The candle flame set a shadow dancing on the stone wall. It gave me courage. Churches save hundreds of atheists every day. I emerged into the Paris night. I called my producer to tell him that I was cancelling the show: the advantage of voice mail is that no one can try and convince you (once again) to stay. I felt a surge of relief, like a man who had almost, but not quite been, crushed by a Boeing 747. I should cancel things more often.

In the dark sky above the treetops, planes flickered. I felt as though they were sending me a signal in Morse code, but I didn't know what it said. "Get the fuck out," maybe?

That evening, I took Léonore, Romy, and Lou to eat French fries at L'Entrecôte—a nutritionally incorrect restaurant. The children were overjoyed, and because they were, so was I. Despite my ailing liver, I felt we were much more alive than usual.

3

MY DEATH DEPROGRAMMED

"Old age ain't no place for sissies."
BETTE DAVIS

THERE IS A memory that haunts me. It was after Gérard Lauzier's funeral at the church of Saint-Germain-des-Prés in 2008, I was having a beer at the Café de Flore with Tonino Benacquista, Georges Wolinski, and Philippe Bertrand. Just for the hell of it, I posed the question: "So, which of us is next?"

We all looked at each other and laughed. Two years later, I saw Benacquista and Wolinski at the funeral of Philippe Bertrand, dead from cancer at sixty-one. I had just delivered a eulogy at Montparnasse Cemetery. I tried to be light-hearted: "So, who's next this time?"

We didn't laugh as loudly.

On January 7, 2015, Georges Wolinski was slaughtered during an editorial meeting at the offices of *Charlie Hebdo*. He was eighty years old. Back in Montparnasse cemetery for his funeral, Tonino and I did not laugh at all.

We eyed each other, like Charles Bronson and Henry Fonda in *Once Upon a Time in the West*.

INCREASINGLY FREQUENTLY, WHEN out in the street, I run into people I know, but when I go to kiss them I remember they're dead and realize to my horror that I'm about to kiss a doppelganger. It's pretty unsettling, having to stop yourself saying hello to the dead.

"Hi Régine!"

"Excuse me?"

"You're ... you're not Régine Desforges?"

"No."

"Oh fuck, I've just remembered, she died three years ago ..."

"It's obviously not me."

"Are you often mistaken for her?"

"Sometimes—it's my red hair. People also mistake me for Sonia Rykiel ..."

"She's dead too! Does it bother you, being the spitting image of all these dead redheads?"

"Does it bother you that you're not as funny in real life as you are on TV?"

You have to hurry if you want to talk to the living. A worm lives for eighteen days, a mouse three years, a Frenchman seventy-eight. If I consume nothing but vegetables and water, I'll add ten years to my life, but I'll be so bored it will feel like a hundred. Maybe that's the secret of eternal life: an ocean of tedium so vast it slows time itself. The statistics are unarguable: in France, in 2010, there were 15,000 people over the age of a hundred. By 2060, there are expected to be 200,000. I'd prefer to be a transhumanist superman to a vegan old-age pensioner: at least a transhumanist superman can gorge on saucisson and booze, provided he has his organs regularly replaced. All I want in life is for someone to repair me like a machine. I dream that in the future doctors will be called "human mechanics."

I made an urgent appointment with Madame Enkidu, my psychoanalyst. I hadn't seen her for ten years; she helped me deal with my cocaine addiction and get over my first two divorces. Her consulting room near the Place de l'Étoile was still painted magnolia, a box of Kleenex still lay in ambush on her desk. The box of tissues in a shrink's consulting room is the modern-day equivalent of the sword of Damocles. There is no sofa in Doctor Enkidu's office: she and her patients talk face to face. Then, face buried in Kleenex. Her bookshelves are full of psychoanalytic monographs with convoluted titles: theses on suffering, dissections of grief, cures for melancholy. Ring binders full of scientific articles dealing with the struggle against depression and suicide.

"When all's said and done, psychoanalysis is just badly written Proust," I said.

My psychiatrist nodded politely.

"It's weird," I added, "I'm paid to talk to millions of viewers, but you're the only person who listens to me."

"Because you pay me."

"Anyway, the reason I'm here is that I've decided not to die."

Her pitying look had not changed either. She had a few more crow's feet, the bags under her eyes were darker, her hair probably dyed. Spending all day listening to a torrent of human misery is clearly not the secret to eternal youth. When she saw me, she looked startled. I probably looked a lot older too. She never watched television; if she had, she wouldn't have been surprised at the grey in my beard.

"Not dying is a wise decision." Her eyes twinkled sardonically behind her half-moon glasses. "It makes a change, I have to say. Last time I saw you, you seemed intent on pursuing a very different goal."

"I've never been more serious. I am not going to die, full stop."

"And when did it occur to you, this resolution?"

"Oh ... My daughter asked me if I was going to die. I didn't have the courage to say yes. So I told her that, from now on, no one in our family is going to die. Does that make me a bad father?"

"A good father is one who worries that he's a bad father."

"That's clever. Is it a quote from Freud?"

"No, it's a quote from you. You said those words in 2007, probably to reassure yourself when you were cheating on her mother. At our very first session, you were already talking about your fear of getting old. It's the Peter Pan Syndrome, very common among Western men in their forties. Fear of old age is a fear of death dressed up as latent hedonism."

"I wasn't aware hedonism was an illness. Pretty soon, our society is going to be locking Epicureans up in asylums. These days, pleasure in every conceivable form is punishable by law, while being promoted by advertising. It's a paradox that produces millions of schizophrenics. You have capitalism to thank for that—without it, you might have to shut up shop."

"Please, you're not going to give me that middle-class libertarian spiel, are you? We're not on TV. You can check: there's no hidden cameras."

I suddenly remembered why I stopped coming to see

this dour therapist: I hated her clear-sightedness. I've always been frightened by intelligent women, ever since my mother. But it was my fault: I'd just had a cardiac CT, and now it felt like I was having a brain scan. I felt like an archaic libertine in a world where hedonism was dismissed as the perversion of dirty old men. To think that, when I was young, people felt they had to at least *pretend* to be swingers if they wanted to be cool. We used to make up stories about things we'd done at Les Chandelles, the swanky Paris sex club. These days, Dominique Strauss-Khan has made orgies seem sordid, and the word *libertine* conjures up images of doddery old men in stained kimonos, like Hugh Hefner (also dead). We're living in a time of extraordinary sexual regression. You might even call it the sexual counter-revolution.

"Doctor, cemeteries are full of corpses rotting in coffins while people dressed in black stand around, trying to focus on the grieving orphans and look sympathetic. A bunch of bastards who knit their brows to make it look like they're concerned—I feel like punching them. I have no time for empathy, or for sympathy."

"Death makes people vicious," she said without smiling, just to justify her salary (€120 for a thirty-minute session). "When animals sense it, they sometimes become dangerous."

"There must be some way to solve the problem."

"Which problem?"

"Death. Mankind has always come up with a solution. We invented electricity, the internal combustion engine, radio, television, spaceships, vacuum cleaners that don't lose suction … By the way, I had a dream that a vacuum cleaner hoovered up my parents' ashes which had been tipped out onto the carpet. What would Lacan have made of that?"

"A typical case of morbid delirium, aggravated by paranoid narcissistic megalomania, exacerbated by celebrity and multiple-drug dependence. What I find interesting is you attempt to remarry your parents by mingling their ashes. Was it nice, seeing them reunited in your dream?"

"Listen, science is on the point of eradicating death, and I don't want the discovery to come *after* they kick the bucket. You have to admit, it would be pretty shit to die just before science discovers immortality. We need to hold out until 2050 but, based on the average life expectancy of French men, I'm scheduled to die in 2043. I'm not asking for much, just to narrow this seven-year gap. Everyone in the world wants what I want. In my dream, it felt comforting, hoovering up death. It made death disappear. I woke up feeling great. You don't want to die, do you?"

"I'm reconciled to accepting human mortality. I can't say I find the prospect thrilling, but I've learned not to rail against things I can't change."

"In a minute you'll be paraphrasing Montaigne: 'To psychoanalyze is to learn to die.' I don't give a shit about philosophy, or about psychoanalysis. I don't want to learn to die, I want deal with the problem. My time is limited: I've got twenty-six years to defer the final deadline. Oh, and I want my family to be immortal too. Personally, I think this should be the aim of every normal human being."

"No, to be normal is to be mortal. The countdown started the day you were born. Accept it. You can control everything but that."

"You don't understand where I'm coming from. You think I'm Don Quixote while actually I'm James Bond. My death is a bomb set to explode, and I have to defuse it. To music by John Barry if necessary. I don't care if you think I'm a control freak."

Madame Enkidu looked at me sadly, the way you might look at a homeless person holding a hand out when you've got no small change. Outside her window, cars honked their horns, revved their engines, spewed exhaust fumes into the street. Down in those gridlocked cars, newly minted fiftysomethings were breathing in particulate matter while listening to air-pollution warnings on France Info every five minutes. You could hear them thinking, "Shit, it's going to be at least another hour before I get to Porte Maillot, and I'll die in two decades. On my deathbed, I'm going to regret spending this hour in a traffic jam breathing in poison." That's the real mystery of modern society: why do mortal individuals accept traffic jams on ring roads?

"What I'm saying is pretty simple," I went on, "I belong to the last mortal generation, but I want to be part of the first immortal generation. My death is just a matter of timing."

My therapist smiled as though I had just scored 100 on the Levenson Self-Report Psychopathy Scale. She was probably considering having me sectioned and transferred to the nearest psychiatric unit. She's used to listening to bullshit, but I'd gone too far; I was irritated to see her condescending sneer as she took notes for an upcoming book to be published by Odile Jacob. Eventually, she scribbled an address on her pad with her Montblanc, peeled off the page, and handed me the prescription.

"Okay, maybe I know someone who can help—but he's in Jerusalem. He's a researcher working on cell renewal. It's worth a punt. If worst comes to worst, a vitamin cure wouldn't hurt. Can I take a selfie with you? It's for my niece. The stupid girl is a real fan of your show. She loved the episode where lockjaw stopped you being able to speak."

A cloud shaped like an unknown country scudded across the sky. "Cell Renewal." As I stepped out of the grey building it occurred to me that the crazy old bat might have put me on the right path. Having accepted her own impending death, she'd offered me a way to postpone mine. This didn't stop me sobbing in front of a luxury travel-goods store that shall remain nameless, since I don't want to give free advertising to Goyard. A passerby clapped me on the back and said, "Hey, you had me in stitches that time you threw up on TV! Can I get a selfie with you?" I dried my tears and posed, making the V-for-victory sign. The public always expect me to be hilarious and outrageous. They're disappointed when they discover I'm shy and boring. Fans want to have a drink with me so they can tell their mates we got rat-arsed together. There was a point in my career when I did everything I could to live up to my reputation. I handed out drugs to strangers so they could tweet about it. I posed for shirtless selfies with a bottle in one hand and a baggie of white powder in the other. This was the night when I stopped burnishing my character as a trash-punk TV presenter, all I wanted was to be left in peace for the three centuries I had left to live.

I summoned an Uber that took fifteen minutes to find me. Do you know how I finally realized I was old? When I asked the driver to turn on the radio, the guy looked at me for a long time in the rear-view mirror and then tuned to Radio Nostalgie. I was utterly devastated: I clearly looked like a fan of Gérard Lenormand's greatest hits. Then he dictated my address to his GPS system, which took us in the wrong direction, dropping me at the rue de Sèvres instead of the rue de Seine. The driver trusted the machine, and the machine was deaf. Or maybe robots take pleasure in humiliating us? I found it surprising that a major company such as Uber should adopt such a blatantly Nazi name. All too often, our faith in software is disappointed. Okay, there's always some trial and error, a few failures. But we have to believe that scientific progress will one day lead humanity to ultimate freedom.

In *Manhattan* (1979), Woody Allen lists ten reasons to live:

– Groucho Marx
– Willie Mays
– the second movement of Mozart's *Jupiter Symphony*
– Louis Armstrong's recording of "Potato Head Blues"
– Swedish movies
– Flaubert's *Sentimental Education*
– Marlon Brando
– Frank Sinatra
– those incredible apples and pears by Cézanne
– the crabs at Sam Wo's
– Tracy's face (as played by Mariel Hemingway)

On the next page, I intend to complete this list of things that make the idea of death unbearable.

SUPPLEMENT TO WOODY ALLEN'S LIST OF REASONS TO LIVE

– all Woody Allen movies, except *The Curse of the Jade Scorpion*
– Edita Vilkevičiūtė's breasts
– September twilight over the bay of San Sebastian, seen from Monte Igueldo
– Paul-Jean Toulet's *Les Contrerimes*, especially number LXII:

Will you return to me, rivage Basque,
With vanished fortune fair
And your dances in salt air,
two eyes, ablaze behind the mask.

– Roger Federer's backhand passing shot, especially during the fifth set of the Australian Open final in Melbourne, January 29, 2017
– the back room of Café La Palette, on the rue de Seine (listed building)
– "Perfect Day" by Lou Reed
– the (pierced) breasts of Lara Stone. Her words on the day she got married at Claridge's in London: "I know every room in this hotel."
– I still have three bottles of Château de Sales 1999 in my cellar
– the songs of Cat Stevens
– Kellogg's Frosties
– every film starring John Goodman
– "Salvator" caramels from Maison Fouquet

– lightning during a summer storm
– the beds on the first floor of Shakespeare and Co. bookshop in Paris
– "Only You" by Yazoo
– the sun's first rays filtering through closed curtains
– let's not forget that at some point an Italian invented tiramisu
– making love and then falling asleep listening to your lover taking a shower
– Kate Upton's breasts as she dances to The Rej3ctz's "Cat Daddy" in a video by Terry Richardson (2012)
– this quote from *Full Metal Jacket*: "The dead know only one thing: it is better to be alive."
– the grounds of the Villa Navarre in Pau in autumn, when the Pyrenees veer from mauve to blue, with a warm breeze and an ice cube tinkling in a glass of Lagavulin
– "The Offshore Pirate" by F. Scott Fitzgerald
– "La rua Madureira" by Nino Ferrer
– the purring of a cat lying by a crackling fire
– the purring of a fire lying by a crackling cat (rarer)
– listening to rain drumming on the roof when you're indoors
– when, after lovemaking, you start to get hard again
– the version of "People Have the Power" by Eagles of Death Metal with U2, live in Paris, three weeks after the Bataclan massacre
– Ricky Gervais's monologues at the Golden Globes
– Marisa Papen's Instagram account
– Jean-Pierre Léaud's monologue in *The Mother and the Whore*
– discovering a dusty old Colette paperback with a cracked yellow spine, and reading it from cover to cover while standing in the living room

– parties that end up in my kitchen at 5:00 a.m.
– turning your laptop off
– Ashley Benson's breasts in *Spring Breakers*. The scene
where she spends a night in a holding cell in just a
bikini. The scene in the pool where she kisses Vanessa
Hudgens. Of course life is worth living.
– Paul Léautaud's literary journals (published in three
volumes by Mercure de France). Worth leafing through
whenever you doubt the power of literature.
– the former French penal colony of Poulo Condor, on
Con Dao Island in Vietnam, now a Six Senses five-star
chain
– lying in a hammock on a hot night beneath a starlit
sky and thinking about nothing
– the Musée Gustave Moreau on the rue de La Rochefou-
cauld, especially when you're the only visitor
– coming in a mouth full of ice-cold Perrier
– the blue and pink hydrangeas of Arcangues when
you're waiting for a juicy mushroom omelette, surrounded by drunken friends
– the voice of Anna Mouglalis
– the places I have not visited: Patagonia, the Amazon,
Lake Victoria, Honolulu, the Great Pyramids, Popocate-
petl, Mount Kilimanjaro. There can be no question of me
dying before I've sailed the Emerald River and the Black
Dragon River.
– a Nestlé Milkybar
– *The Big Lebowski* obviously, especially the scene where
John Turturro says, "Nobody fucks with the Jesus."
– baked tagliolini with ham at Harry Cipriani on Fifth
Avenue
– "Hearing the song of a little girl as she walks away
having asked you for directions" (Li Bai)
– Monty Python's "Ministry of Silly Walks" sketch

– Léonore's breasts
– Romy's laugh
– Lou's flaxen hair: like downy feathers on a baby chick

I had a child at a time when I didn't give a fuck about the future. No, correct that.

I had two daughters. Now I long for a future.

THE PRESS RELEASE on the Morandini website announcing that I had resigned and been replaced by Augustin Trapenard sparked a wave of reactions on social networks: a third of them were polite regrets, a third said "good riddance," and a third were brownnosing plaudits for my replacement. The headline in *Le Parisien* read: "Chemistry Show Overdose." In *Voici*: "Can the has-been make a comeback?" *Le Figaro*: "Garbage In Garbage Out." I was forced to do an interview for Jeanmarcmorandini.com to defuse the negative press.

Jean-Marc Morandini: Are you washed up, TV-wise? (*laughter*)

Me: I don't know and I don't care. Unlike some people, I have a life outside of TV. I also think TV is dying, which is why I'm planning to do a weekly radio piece on France Inter, starting in September.

JMM: This has to be a first—a presenter giving up a one-hour TV show for a three-minute slot on radio. And you're trying to tell us it's a promotion? (*laughter*)

M: Yeah, I genuinely think it is. Because I'll be able to speak freely. And anyway, radio shows have been filmed for years now. People will be able to stream the videos online. Radio isn't radio anymore.

JMM: Were you tired of having to swallow that shit? (*laughter*)

M: The reason I'm giving up is so I can look after my daughters. Here's a riddle for you: name the one thing that doesn't appear on primetime?

JMM: Losers? (*laughter*)

M: No: life. Most TV presenters are terrified of the idea of stepping down. They're willing to present some dumb cheesy game show rather than not be on TV: look at Dechavanne, Sabatier, Nagui ... I had to get out before I ended up spinning the wheel of fortune for the long-term unemployed.

JMM: Is this your midlife crisis? (*laughter*)

M: I'm fifty, so it isn't midlife, it's two thirds of the way through. And it's not a crisis, it's a lesson. The lesson of two thirds.

JMM: What's the lesson of two thirds?

M: You wouldn't understand.

JMM: How are you planning to go around the world if you've got a regular radio show? (*laughter*)

M: Pay attention, Jean-Marc, I'm about to use two highly technical terms: dual-location and RTB—that stands for "ready to broadcast." Apologies for using industry jargon.

JMM: But you're seriously planning to return to TV after a year? You do realize it's not up to you, it's up to the production companies? (*laughter*)

M: The largest audience for the *Chemistry Show* is YouTube Live. Anyone can broadcast on YouTube. We don't need permission from Vincent Bolloré or Martin Bouygues to make television these days—or didn't you know? Augustin is a friend, I hope he has an amazing time conducting live chemistry experiments. I'm sure he'll enjoy it and the viewers will too. As for production companies, I'm a producer, as I know you are. I'm looking at all the options.

JMM: You haven't answered my question. Aren't you pissed off that the company replaced you so quickly? (*laughter*)

M: We'll see how it goes. The viewers will decide. But trust is important. It's like when a teenager auditions for a porn flick with you. An underage guy has to be pretty trusting when you ask him to jerk off in your office. (*mocking smile*)

JMM: You're such a fucking dickhead. Cut! Back to the studio. You little shit! (*He gets up to punch me, my bodyguards intervene*)

That last joke was a cheap shot, I'm not proud. It was retweeted four million times: celebrity deathmatch of the year.

BACK AT HOME, I pleaded with Romy to put down her mobile phone and listen to me for five minutes. She sighed but did as I asked. I like her manners. They're as bad as mine.

"Hang on a second," she said. "Name an insect that stings, four letters beginning with T."

"Tick. T, I, C, K."

"Are you sure that's a real thing? Oh, cool, it's right!"

In recent weeks, Romy has been playing 94%, a word game on her iPhone. I am much happier at the thought of her improving her vocabulary rather than playing *Candy Crush* or playing truant and hanging out in clothes shops.

"So, I've been thinking: how about we go on a trip together?"

"But it's not school holidays."

"They're not far off. You'd only miss one month, then it's summer. Maman has said it's okay. I'll write a note to your school. A real one—you won't need to fake our signatures."

"Ha ha, very funny. What about my friends?"

"You can email them and call them on Skype."

"What about Lou and Léonore?"

"They'll come and meet up with us as soon as possible. We're going to see the ocean, the mountains, far-off lands ..."

"Hang on, name a tree, six letters beginning with P?"

"Poplar? Privet?"

"It accepts both! Sixteen points!"

"We need a change of scene, it would do us good."

Since her mother and I separated, Romy has been suppressing her emotions. It's not fair, having to grow up so soon. I can't bring myself to raise the subject, it's too depressing. From time to time, I try: "You okay? You sure?"

She says nothing. Then I give her a chocolate croissant, a pack of bubble gum, or a Netflix subscription. She's a huge fan of *How to Get Away with Murder*.

"To be honest, honey, I preferred it when you watched *Hannah Montana*."

"Yeah, yeah, things change: these days Miley Cyrus is a skank."

I remember a weekend we spent in Corsica when Romy asked me to put sunscreen on her back and I suddenly realized she was becoming a woman; it was the first time I felt embarrassed to touch her: my daughter was not a little girl. For the last time, I massaged the back of the little girl to whom I had given life, under the disapproving gaze of the Murtoli tourists I could hear whispering behind my back: "When is that filthy pig going to stop pawing his daughter." There was no way I could escape this child; she was the only person who really knew me. She knew how stupid I was and she forgave me. Romy didn't resent me for replacing her mother with a Swiss girl. This is what children are for: making adjustments. Sometimes, when she smiled, I saw her mother's face, sometimes her grandmother's. I restrained myself from hugging her too often so as not to smother her. Maybe I was wrong.

"You're not happy?" I say to Romy.

"Sure I am. The trip is to die for."

"No, no, it's not to die for. It's exactly the opposite."

At this point, in one of my films, there would be a three-second close-up of my enigmatic expression, to underscore the double meaning of this piece of banter.

"You remember when I told you that we're not going to die?"

"Yeah."

"Did you believe me?"

"Um … You come out with a lot of stupid stuff."

"Don't I know it, it's how I make my living! Well, the thing is, if we're planning to not die, we have to visit a bunch of doctors who can take care of us. You see what I'm saying? That's why we're going on this trip. But don't tell anyone."

"Why not?"

"Because we're going to be the first. It has to be our secret, otherwise everyone will want to do it. And remember how much you hate queuing for the rides at Disneyland?"

"I can't even post on Instagram? #100% Jesus!"

"Nope."

"Where are we going first?"

"Jerusalem."

"LOL. You mean the place where Jesus came back from the dead?"

"Rose."

"What?"

"You say 'Jesus *rose* from the dead.' But, no, it's nothing to do with him. It's just a coincidence. Or … at least I *think* so."

Another close-up of my face, this time with an inscrutable expression, think Bruce Lee in *Way of the Dragon*. Maybe with an aside to camera and tracking shot (and a surge of synths on the soundtrack).

"I just need you to promise me one thing, Romy. Look me in the eyes."

"What?"

"Promise you won't go disappearing on me again."

"That wasn't my fault!"

"Whose fault was it, then?"

"itwuzmamansfault ..."

"Sorry? I didn't hear that. Enunciate your words."

"I said it was Maman's fault."

"Skipping gym class and hiding in a fitting room at a branch of Brandy Melville didn't bring your mother back. Maybe you can tell me how hiding in a changing room or in a sweet shop helps anyone."

"sbecuzklementinesedmamahadanuboyfrend."

"Please, try to speak a bit more clearly, you can be a real pain, sometimes!"

"I said it's because Clémentine told me Maman had a new boyfriend."

"Clémentine?"

"Yeah, that's why I skipped class. I couldn't breathe, so I ran to Le Luco. I wasn't thinking. And the lady in the sweet shop was really nice. When I told her my parents were divorced, she said I could have all the marshmallows I could fit in both hands. But after that, I wasn't hiding, I was just sitting in the park, in the bandstand, everyone could see me. I knew you'd find me. You should be happy, it's not like I ran away to Syria!"

It suddenly occurred to me that I was about to go around the world with a gifted, ungrateful, cheeky little madame who I could have hired to present a talk show for paedophile fans of *Kick-Ass*. Now there's a concept: talk shows hosted by kids—I need to file a copyright notice with the Society of Dramatic Authors and Composers! I made a note on my laptop.

"So?" I said, "It's normal that your mother is moving on with her life."

"So what?"

"So, do you promise not to disappear on me?"

"I have a shell and I begin with an *S*."

"What?"

"Hurry up ... I have a shell and I begin with an *S*—what am I?"

"Shrimp? Scallop?"

"No, it's only five letters. Come on, Papa, ten seconds left!"

"Snail?"

"Wow, you're good!"

"So, do you promise?"

'Okay ... You're better than Maman at this game."

I got up from my daughter's bed and shouted down the hallway: "Clémentine? Could you help Romy pack her suitcase? We're going on a trip. Oh, and another thing— we won't be requiring your services any longer. To quote the TV presenter who's now President of the United States: You're fired!"

4

NOBODY FUCKS WITH THE JESUS

(The Hebrew University of Jerusalem)

"That is not dead which can eternal lie,
And with strange aeons even death may die."
H.P. LOVECRAFT

WHAT DO WE chiefly die from? In 2014, the British medical journal *The Lancet* published a study funded by the Bill Gates Foundation: 800 international researchers reviewed 240 causes of death spanning 188 countries around the world. The top four are not particularly surprising: the heart gives out (coronary heart disease accounted for eight million deaths in 2013), our brain fries (stroke accounted for six million deaths), our lungs collapse (three million deaths), and the fourth cause is Alzheimer's disease (1.6 million deaths). Traffic accidents (1.3 million deaths) are tied with AIDS for seventh position.

I wrote to the Israeli professor specializing in cell renewal whose email address my shrink had given me:

> Doctor Buganim, I am contacting you at the suggestion of a psychoanalyst you know, Doctor Enkidu in Paris—I hope you don't find her recommendation unsettling. Would you be prepared to meet me in order to defer my death? I have a sizeable budget at my disposal. On that subject, could you tell me: how much is eternal life? I would be grateful if you could send me a detailed costing for immortality by return. All the best.

When you send this kind of email to a bigshot in the biotech industry, either he marks it as JUNK MAIL, or he calls you back within the hour because chatting to fruit loops is always entertaining. Doctor Yossi Buganim got back to me within fifteen minutes. Worriedly, he enquired in what context Madame Enkidu had mentioned his name to me, and whether I could send him a confirmation email from the Head of External Relations at the Hebrew University of Jerusalem. I suddenly had the strange impression that I was in a spy novel. The world of biological research is very paranoid these days: the quest for immortality is a race between the Chinese, the Swiss, the Americans, and the Israelis (the French are lagging behind: not enough money and too many ethics). In this scientific war, there is fraud, there are phoney press releases (such as the discovery of NgAgo—an enzyme that can be used as "genetic scissors" to modify genomes—by Han Chunyu of the University of Science and Technology, Shijiazhuang), risky publicity stunts, and a lot of disinformation and espionage. Genetics is worse for competition than the Oscars. In 2016, Doctor Yossi Buganim received the Boyalife Prize from *Science*: He is one of the world's leading researchers in the field of iPS cells (induced pluripotent stem cells). So I sent an email to the comms director of his laboratory.

Could you please inform the doctor that I'm not ill. I do not need him to cure me, but to prolong me. We're working on a major documentary about immortality and I just want to know whether injecting stem cells would make it possible for me to slow the aging process. My daughter will be with me at the consultation: her cells are a lot fresher than mine. I would be grateful if you could suggest some convenient dates. We are available immediately.

A little information about stem cells. Don't worry: I'm not going to copy/paste the Wikipedia page, which is incomprehensible. In 1953, an American biologist in Maine named Leroy Stevens researching the effects of smoking on mice, notices that one of the subjects has an enlarged scrotum. He kills and dissects it. In fact there is a tumour on the mouse's testicles. Well, first off, this confirms that smoking is bad for your health. But Stevens notices that the tumour itself is bizarre. Inside, it contains hair, and fragments of bone and tooth. What the actual fuck?! He forces more mice to inhale cigarette smoke, and dissects more tumours, which look more like embryos. It's *Alien* in miniature. He decides to graft these tumours onto younger mice to see what happens—and also because there is no Universal Declaration of Rodent Rights. He discovers that the tumours adapt to their new environment and develop into repulsive non-viable embryos, all hair and teeth. People really knew how to have fun in Bar Harbor (Maine) back in the day! Leroy Stevens had discovered stem cells. Put simply, humans are multicellular animals: huge mice comprising 75 trillion cells. At embryo stage, our cells replicate endlessly and are able to become anything: bone, liver, heart, eyes, skin, teeth, wavy hair, your pussy. (Apologies for that little ruse, just getting my readers' attention.) If someone could control these stem cells, it could either save our lives (e.g., by recreating a malfunctioning organ), or turn us into giant slimy tumours. Warning: this is where things get complicated. Embryos contain an abundance of stem cells, but we're not going to terminate thousands of foetuses to steal their stems cells: even if the idea sounds logical—as we'll see later, there is something vampiric in the fight against aging—it would be deeply amoral and, besides, it was banned in France under the

2004 Bioethics Law. A decade ago, a theory was proposed that human cloning might be used to cultivate stem cells, but in 2006 two Japanese scientists found another solution. Kazutoshi Takahashi and Shinya Yamanaka of Kyoto University managed to rejuvenate adult skin cells by "reprogramming" them such that they become iPS cells. Put simply, the Japanese scientists succeeded in genetically manipulating human dermal cells by introducing four factors (Oct3/4, Sox2, c-Myc, and Klf4), making it possible to reprogramme mature cells into "all-terrain" embryonic cells capable of adapting anywhere inside the body and of self-renewing. In 2012 Yamanaka was awarded the Nobel Prize in Physiology or Medicine for his achievement. And this is why, for the past five years, thousands of biologists around the world have been torturing millions of mice hoping to find the philosopher's stone. Got it? End of information dump. Now I'm expecting the Nobel for scientific simplification.

THE BUSINESS CLASS cabin on our flight to Tel Aviv was full of businessmen reading *The Discreet Charm of the Intestine*. Many of them were wearing yarmulkes. I was surrounded by mortal creatures who were not afraid of death. Jews brush with death on every street corner; they seem to have grown accustomed to the Grim Reaper hanging around. They don't seem to care about it one way or another. Unlike Romy, I don't find the phrase "to die for" to be synonymous with "amazing." In the same way, I hate it when she loses at some video game because she invariably says, "I'm done with my life." To which I reply with pride, "I've got first dibs!"

Romy stifles a yawn as I explain the prodigious scientific discoveries that have led us to this city; though she keeps her mouth shut, her flaring nostrils betray her. I have never before set foot in Jerusalem; I don't have much interest in holy sites. For example, I never succumbed to the fashion for walking to Santiago de Compostela. Romy is watching *Hunger Games*—another survival story—on her computer. Katniss Everdeen, played by Jennifer Lawrence, is forced to win a series of increasingly Sadean "games" as the plot progresses. If I'd seen the movie when I was her age, I'd have been traumatized, but Romy dozes off without a care in the world. Young people have become inured since every-man-for-himself became the dominant storytelling approach for our children.

I sent this message to Léonore, who was back in Paris with our baby:

Love of my life,
 Though I do my best to seem blasé, it is no mundane thing to land in the Promised Land. You fly over the Mediterranean and, all of a sudden, through the window, you see a straight line, white and shimmering: this is Israel, a country that, for three millennia, has been a utopia. The elderly couple in the seats next to us held hands as the plane touched down. I envied them, because your hand was not here for me to hold. I know you think my quest for immortality is futile. You're probably right, but even before my appointment with your boss's colleague, it has already been a success, since every kilometre that separates me from you and Lou spans an eternity. I'll phone you when I've been filled with stem cells. Bite one of Lou's toes for me: it'll grow back. I'm not going to write a long email, because I'm afraid I might cry in front of Romy. I cannot bear to do anything but hold you in my arms.
 Your legally wed lover whose feelings are imperishable.
 PS: I'm not kidding—holding you in my arms is my definition of paradise.

I should probably buy a yarmulke. I wore one to my producer's wedding and it suited me, it gave me the gravitas I lack. After all, with my aquiline nose and pale eyes, I have the face of a good Ashkenazi. Even though I also possess a deeply Catholic foreskin, I appear on the list of "Jews who control the media" published on some neo-fascist website. I let them think what they like because I'm flattered. As long as someone, somewhere is talking about me.

Romy woke up when we landed. I asked our taxi driver

to drop us directly at the Centre for Genomic Technologies at the Hebrew University of Jerusalem. It is a one-hour drive from Tel Aviv, via a highly secure motorway flanked by barbed wire. Since I don't believe in God, in Yahweh, or in Allah, I tried looking out the window, as though this was just another country, but this was not just another country. Groups of police officers surrounded bearded men dressed in black who wore black hats and long braided sideburns. Israel is like the Marais in Paris but bigger, with a wider sky. Even the light here is metaphysical. I realized I did not know a single word of Hebrew other than *shalom*. I didn't even know how to say "yes" or "thank you"! Luckily Romy had 4G roaming: she told me the words I needed were *ken* and *toda*. The cab driver was driving like a lunatic, foot to the floor, with the air conditioning turned up to max: I was afraid Romy would catch a cold.

"Put your seatbelt on and wear my scarf."

Fatherhood often requires the use of the imperative.

Tall, dark, slender beauties strolled along the pavements, they had silken hair, green eyes, white teeth, and triumphant breasts, but I tried not to allow myself to be distracted from my scientific undertaking. What is the word for the hollow at the back of the knee, that soft, golden curve? If anyone knows, please email me. After all, I could hardly ask my daughter to Google it.

"See those Israeli women, Romy? They adopt that sullen expression because they think it makes them look beautiful. Don't ever do that, are you listening to me?"

It looked as though young Israelis wanted to be Californians, to spend their lives wearing t-shirts and sandals: all Jews looked like Jesus in shorts. Like Paris, Rome, London, or New York, it was difficult to tell the Jews from the hipsters. Who was copying whom? Was the hipster just a hyper-cool Jew in disguise? Was the Jew just a hipster with a spiritual dimension? It looked to me as though a war was looming, and the Israelis had opted to side with the hipsters. By the time the cab dropped us off at the hospital cafeteria, Romy had the beginnings of a tummy ache.

I felt relieved; nobody recognized me when we got out of the taxi; my face was on holiday. To live is wonderful; to live in voluntary rather than imposed anonymity is bliss. Especially when you know that anyone trying to phone you is getting the same posh robotic message: "The voicemail of the person you are trying to reach is full." Which is a polite way of saying, "I'm more popular than you, so fuck off!" After the press release announcing my resignation, I had received not one single phone call from the hundreds of guests I'd invited onto my show. Though their ingratitude was unsurprising, it was no less upsetting: after twenty years in television, the number of celebs who had become friends was zero. I'd simply been an intermediary between the artists and their audience. Do I look like a go-between?

Romy and I drank Coke and had a burping competition. Romy's nose was sunburned where the taxi window had been open. After too many burps, she started throwing up her French toast. Thankfully, by that point, we had pulled up outside the hospital.

The Hadassah Ein Kerem Medical Center is a modern citadel perched atop a mountain. It comprises thirty buildings, including a shopping centre, a synagogue, several restaurants, and a university. I think it's the largest hospital I have ever set foot in. Though not as modern as the Pompidou Hospital spaceship in Paris, it inspires more respect, as do all strictly monitored zones. This vast hive is guarded by armed soldiers. To gain admittance, you have to pass through security gates more fearsome than those at an airport, and those who do not have an appointment with an eminent doctor are escorted back to the perimeter.

Doctor Yossi Buganim is a young research prodigy at the Faculty of Medicine of the Hebrew University of Jerusalem. The shaven-headed Israeli researcher looks as though he should have a part in a Jason Statham action movie. He has long, nervous, elegant hands; the hands of a pianist playing the four notes that make up DNA: A, T, G, C (adenine, thymine, guanine, and cytosine). Hands that would look perfect holding a cigarette, though, needless to say, given his profession, Doctor Yossi Buganim did not smoke. His laboratory is minimalist high-tech: highly sophisticated microscopes, 3D videos of multicoloured cells, biologists in lab goggles wielding pipettes ... He showed us around his office and I found myself dreaming of a posthuman world in the very place where monotheistic religions were born.

"Shalom, Professor, thank you for agreeing to see us. I'll get straight to the point. Can stem-cell transplants cure people who are ill?"

"Yes: we dream of treating Alzheimer's, Parkinson's, diabetes, leukaemia ... Here, we create iPS cells to regenerate the placenta in some pregnant women."

"So, if you inject me with stem cells induced from me, could I live to be five hundred?"

"You're not ill: I might just as easily give you cancer at the site of the injection. That's the problem: iPS cells are unstable, sometimes aberrant. Given what they do to mice, imagine what they would do to you: a guaranteed tumour."

"So when will people be able to live to be three hundred?"

"I thought you were aiming for five hundred."

"I'm happy to lower my expectations to two-fifty or even two hundred."

Romy, who had her whole life ahead of her, was profoundly bored by this conversation. To a ten-year-old girl, the idea of living to be two hundred is as tedious as having to watch a 52-minute documentary on the glories of the Chateaux of the Loire Valley with Lully's *Marche Royale* on the soundtrack. Doctor Buganim addressed himself specifically to her, forcing himself to use words that would be intelligible to a little girl. You could tell he was a veteran of medical conferences. One of the most time-consuming aspects of techno-medicine is persuading the rich to provide funding at medical conferences; researchers have to hard-sell their discoveries to pay for their test tubes. He had been prepared to meet with me because I had led the hospital's PR department to believe that I was a major French TV journalist. He was hoping that my fame would provide him with some crumbs he might use to save the rest of humanity.

"Miss Romy," he said, "let me explain how you came to be here. First a sperm fertilizes an oocyte, and this produces and egg called a zygote. This single cell begins to divide: two, four, eight, sixteen. When it reaches sixty-four cells, it becomes a precursor to the embryo, called a blastocyst, and looks like a hollow ball. When scientists cultured these cells, they discovered that they replicated themselves indefinitely and continued to remain identical."

Romy was spellbound. I prompted him, just as my mentor Yves Mourousi prompted me.

"A colleague of yours told me that some cells are immortal."

"Yez. Ze embryonic ztem zellz are immorrrtal."

I forgot to mention that we were speaking English. Romy was having a hard time following Doctor Buganim, and I was having a hard time taking him seriously, since his Israeli accent reminded me of Adam Sandler in *You Don't Mess with the Zohan*, the best comedy about Israel I've seen. To avoid bursting out laughing in such a situation, it was essential for me to ignore his accent and focus on the fact that, in twenty years working in television, I had never been awarded a prize by *Science*.

"Embryonic stem cells are immortal," he had just calmly announced.

"So, the cells are like chameleons?" Romy said, astounding her co-interviewer.

"Exactly. They can become anything you want them to be. Well … almost anything. Hence their name: *pluripotent*."

On a whiteboard, he drew a round cell that looked like *Les Shadoks* (another outmoded reference).

"Tell me about the Japanese scientists who first discovered how to create stem cells. What is the iPS system?"

"Careful. They're not just stem cells, they're embryonic stem cells. That is to say, cells capable of generating any kind of cell within the human body. As adults, we all have stem cells in our organs. Romy does too. But they only know how to regenerate the cells of that specific organ. The Japanese scientists wondered whether it would be possible to take adult cells and reprogramme them to become embryonic—meaning pluripotent—stem cells. This would address two issues: 1) the ethical problem: the idea of destroying human embryos is not pleasant, even though I'm not sure that I would consider the blastocyst—a microscopic ball—as being alive; 2) transplant rejection: if I inject you with embryonic cells from someone else, they will almost certainly be rejected.

On the other hand, cells taken from your own body, collected from a skin biopsy, will not be rejected."

He was scratching under his arm. Romy turned to me, worried.

"He's not going to give us an injection, is he?"

"No, no one is going to do anything to you, chérie."

"But even if I did," the researcher said, "it's just a little scratch on your arm, it doesn't hurt."

"If I understand what you're saying, the Japanese scientists collected adult cells and managed to … rejuvenate them?"

"Exactly. That's precisely it. I collect your skin cells, I introduce a few transcription factors, wait two or three weeks, and suddenly we see "induced" embryonic cells—that's the 'i' in 'iPS.'"

"That's insane!"

"Completely insane! No one believed it could be done. Certainly, no one imagined that it would take only four genes. There are 20,000 in the human body. And it takes only four to travel back through time. The British scientist John Gurdon deserves some credit for the discovery—he was the first person to reprogramme cells. He shared the Nobel Prize with Shinya Yamanaka in 2012. He was the man who first devised the technique that was later used to clone Dolly the sheep. Gurdon took a frog zygote, collected DNA from a tadpole's intestinal cell and, by introducing the DNA into the enucleated egg, produced an embryo. If you take the nucleus of an adult cell and introduce it into an enucleated zygote, it produces a clone. The egg begins to divide: two cells, four, eight, etc. Using his system, anything can be cloned."

"Anything? You mean I can be cloned?" Romy shrieked.

I was amazed that my daughter could understand his English despite the heavy Israeli accent.

"Not like in *Star Wars*, but we can create a genetically identical Romy. I take a skin cell from you, extract the DNA, and insert it into an enucleated human egg, let it grow for a few days, implant the embryo into a surrogate mother, and nine months later, we'll have a clone, a baby genetically identical to you."

Romy was really starting to panic now; I decided to intervene to avoid any further trauma.

"Nobody's going to clone you, darling—it's exhausting enough having to cope with one Romy. It's strange, Doctor. Fifteen years ago, everyone was obsessed with human cloning but no one really talks about it anymore. Has it gone out of fashion?"

"It's not about fashion, as you put it. Human cloning is prohibited for ethical reasons. But I'm sure someone, somewhere in China, is working on it."

"You really think so?"

"I don't think so, I'm certain of it. They've already cloned pigs, dogs, horses ... The first successful human cloning was done in 2013, by Shoukhrat Mitalipov, a Kazakh-born American professor at the Oregon Health & Science University in Portland."

"But there was no mention of that anywhere!"

"Yamanaka's discovery made his approach obsolete ... for now."

"So, in your lab, do you use cloned mice or genetically reprogrammed mice?"

"Both. In 2009, the first mouse entirely made of reprogrammed cells was born. It was born alive, viable, and capable of reproduction. In 2011, scientists generated a functional larynx, in 2012, a thyroid gland. Eighteen months ago, a mouse liver was artificially recreated using induced pluripotent stem cells. IPS cells are amazing, the only problem with them is that only thirty percent are capable of generating a viable mouse. The vast majority of ips cells produce embryos that are malformed or miscarried during pregnancy; not all ips cells are viable. Whereas, if you take the actual embryonic stem cells of a blastocyst, almost all of them can successfully produce a cloned mouse."

"I don't understand. I'm talking about extending my life expectancy, and here you are singing the praises of cloning ..."

"No. I'm just trying to explain that we haven't yet discovered the ideal conditions for cell regeneration. The concept is a solid one, but we do not yet have the means. The goal of cloning, and of genetic reprogramming, is to go back to square one. We call it a 'reset.'"

"I want a reset, Doctor! It's time to reboot me! Beigbeder 2.0!"

By now, Doctor Buganim was completely convinced that I was deranged. Romy, meanwhile, was playing *Brick Breaker* on her mobile phone. In a way, I found this reassuring: knocking down the red brick wall on her iPhone was more important to her that finding out how to reset our lives.

"So, if I understand you correctly, Professor, neither human cloning nor genetic reprogramming can grant immortality."

"You're right. A clone will be an exact copy of you, but first it has to be brought to life: nine months of pregnancy, birth, rearing, food, everything starts from scratch. The clone will *look* like you, but it will never *be* you. In any case, we don't use the term 'cloning' anymore, it's too controversial. We prefer to say 'somatic cell nuclear transfer,' although in practice the two are exactly the same.

"Dolly the sheep was cloned back in 1996. Since then, science has moved on; now we're trying to generate a maximum number of high-quality rejuvenated cells that can be safely reimplanted."

"But you just told me that if you injected me with iPS cells, I'd end up with a tumour. So, I'll pass, thanks!"

(*He laughs*) "Imagine you have Parkinson's disease, you're constantly suffering from tremors, and I inject you with genetically modified neurons that lessen the symptoms. You'll be thrilled, even if it means that, ten years later, you might develop a tumour. Here we have discovered four genes (Sall4, Nanog, Lin28, and Esrrb) capable of producing better-quality iPS cells. At the moment, they work on cloned mice."

"And that's why you were awarded a prize by *Science*."

"Exactly. We're testing different factors to those used by Yamanaka."

"So why does it take three weeks, when an egg only takes three days?"

"Reprogramming is slower than programming! Besides, during that time there may be aberrant genetic mutations; we have to be able to control the process."

"So, immortality is a long, arduous process."

"I'm not looking to achieve immortality. I'm looking to collect a dermal cell from a patient with Parkinson's or Alzheimer's, and to reprogramme it to create a neural iPS cell so that I can study how neurons are affected by these conditions. By studying these genetically rejuvenated neurons, I might be able to treat such conditions. Develop new drugs that can eliminate these diseases. And there's another possibility: regenerative medicine. We can try to repair the defective neuron and reimplant it into the patient's brain."

"Aha. Now we're getting somewhere. This has something to do with the discovery made by two researchers in 2012? CRISPR-Cas.9?"

At this point, I'm worried I may have lost even my most determined readers. Let's do a brief summary of the current state of genetics: in 2012 (an important year, since it was also the year that Yamanaka won the Nobel) two biologists, Jennifer Doudna (from California) and Emmanuelle Charpentier (from France), developed a technique that allowed them to splice DNA and reintroduce the modified PD1 gene. Having noticed palindromic repeats (that is to say, inverted repeats of the letters A, C, T, and G) when sequencing bacterial DNA, they gave it the acronym CRISPR (clustered regularly interspaced short palindromic repeats). Don't ask me to explain how they did it, it would take me ten years of study to even begin to understand. The two researchers used CRISPR to insert a gene into the DNA. "Cas.9" is the name given to the protein used in the operation. This new technology has significantly simplified human genetic modification. Yossi Buganim was amazed that I was aware of these scientific developments, when actually, I'd simply asked my assistant to prepare a crib sheet before my trip. He now talked without any attempt at simplification, as though he was chatting to a colleague at the Annual J.P. Morgan Healthcare Conference in San Francisco.

"Imagine the mutant DNA of a patient with Parkinson's," he says, "In theory, we can treat the patient using the CRISPR method and introduce new DNA. Using the Cas.9 protein, guided by RNA, we cut DNA and perform the modification. We use this technique every day now."

"Aren't you terrified at the thought of creating a GMH (genetically modified human)? The Americans, the Chinese, and the British have recommended a moratorium on human genetic engineering."

(*He smiles*) "In China, Doctor Lu You, at Chengdu University, is using CRISPR to modify T-cell lymphocytes in patients suffering from metastatic lung cancer unresponsive to chemotherapy. They take a blood sample, collect the patient's T cells, and alter the DNA of the PD1 gene that "protects" the cancer. By reinjecting these genetically modified cells, they believe that the PD1 gene can no longer instruct the T cells not to attack the tumour."

"So, these experiments are actually taking place right now?"

"Yes. They've started human testing. In theory it might work, but at the same time, since the cells are no longer sending out signals saying 'do not attack,' there's a risk that the genetically modified cells will attack healthy cells ... creating the risk of autoimmune disorders."

"Why aren't you doing experiments like this here in Jerusalem?"

"It'll take us years to get permission. In the US, a similar immunotherapy trial on patients with leukaemia (called the "ROCKET trial") was discontinued after five patients died. And then there are the tragedies caused by quack doctors. A Russian family living here in Israel, whose son had a neurodegenerative disease, paid a fortune to have him injected with stem cells in Kazakhstan. When the boy came back, he had to be admitted to the emergency unit at Sheba Hospital: they found two brain tumours. He died shortly afterwards."

"So, you're saying that only Western scientists are respecting the moratorium?"

"Yes. But if someone from India, Russia, Mexico, or China offers you a miracle cure, be very careful: there are no medical controls."

"In Switzerland, I found an online clinic that injects stem cells taken from sheep foetuses!"

"I hope what they're injecting are placebos, otherwise they could kill you. In China, fifty years from now, people will be demanding blond, blue-eyed children, and people will be able to supply the demand."

"With the legacy of the one-child policy, they haven't got enough women: now they'll be able to create Barbie dolls to order!"

"Or clone vicious animals, or engineer super-soldiers. Or uncontainable bloodthirsty monsters."

"We're getting close to the Nazi dream—the creation of a super-race."

"Exactly. The researchers here work to make pluripotent stem cells. We were the first lab to create iPS cells from placenta. And also single cells, called *totipotent cells*, which can differentiate into nearly all cells—though that study hasn't yet been published. Embryonic stem cells are injected into a blastomere and produce new cells capable of becoming placental cells. These cells occur much earlier in embryonic development than those used by Doctor Yamanaka. We've managed to go farther back in the process of gestation. We're not looking to clone human beings, or to create a superman. We're simply looking to treat people who are ill, but this will take time."

Doctor Buganim glanced at his watch. I suddenly remembered that I wasn't on the set of my TV show but in the consulting room of one of the world's most prestigious biochemists. I felt it was time to leave the researcher to his research. As he walked us to the lifts, Doctor Buganim tried to reassure me—though the way he went about it was strange.

"Maybe in two or three hundred years, we'll be able to slow the aging process. But I think the Earth will have died before then. Given the way we treat the environment, within a hundred years the problem will have been solved: the whole planet will die, and humanity will die along with it. So, there's no need to worry about immortality. Now, if you'll excuse me, I have mice to exterminate."

"Ah, Jewish humour!"

Thankfully, Romy hadn't heard a word: she was involved in a game of *Angry Birds*.

ATHEISM IS A religion like any other. Its one original concept is that heaven and hell are the same place: here. There is no afterlife; not even in celestial Jerusalem. The point-blank objections of the Israeli researcher had not discouraged me. Was I possessed by some kind of supernatural geographical contagion? Anyone who has not set foot here cannot understand why so many people fought for thousands of years to conquer this city. Another taxi ferried us back downtown, to a wall of pink stones hidden behind a bus queue.

"Are we going to visit the three gods?"

Romy had insisted on seeing the old city; like all children, she was hungry for magic. I was hungry for a good shawarma with hummus, fresh pita bread, minced lamb, and chopped parsley. I thought, let's go visit King David's city: four thousand years of bullshit metaphysics and the Crusades is like catnip to spiritual tourists. Jerusalem is the least secular city on the planet. A religious hypermarket: there's something for everyone here. As we passed through the Old City walls, built by Suleiman the Magnificent, walking along cobblestones worn smooth by rapturous hordes of sandals, we quickly became lost in this labyrinth of the three monotheistic religions. I booked a table at a Palestinian restaurant.

"The Coke here tastes funny," Romy said.

"Maybe it's kosher?"

The passageways were covered, I had never imagined

Jerusalem as a maze of vaulted passageways, stone walls with no windows, narrow alleys as crooked and crowded as the metro station at Châtelet–Les Halles at rush hour, and a lot dustier. Romy insisted that I buy her a "SUPER JEW" T-shirt that I told her she can't wear back in France (too risky). As we left the restaurant, we realized that we were near the Wailing Wall. As good a place as any to start our tour. But we were refused entry to the site because: 1) I had to wear a yarmulke; and 2) Romy is female. We turned our backs on the wall to take a selfie together. Then I found a disposable cardboard yarmulke that kept being blown away by the wind, forcing me to run and pick it up from the sand. I think many true believers would have happily had me crucified. I told Romy to wait for me on the other side of the barrier, to the right of this section of wall, while I went down and formulated a wish.

The light at the foot of the Mount of Olives had the dull white sheen of sacred stones and mausoleums. The steps leading down to the plaza made me feel dizzy. I wasn't sure whether I had vertigo or whether I had suddenly become an Israelite. I slowly approached the Wall, savouring the moment, waiting for a miracle, and I slipped my little supplication (scribbled on a paper napkin folded in four and, unfortunately, written in French) into a gap between two stones: *Dear Yahweh, if You exist, please grant eternal life to Romy, Léonore, Lou, to my mother, my father, and my brother. And to me. Many thanks, toda, shalom, and mazeltov.* I felt as foolish as the mugs who attach padlocks to the Pont des Arts. Romy was overwhelmed by the solemnity of the visitors; she was terrified of disturbing them. To me, it was the antiquity of this place that I found overwhelming. To me the ancient stones seemed to be more respectable than the sobs of a few elderly rabbis in Roman sandals. One thing did surprise me: the Al-Aqsa Mosque partially rests on the Wailing Wall. Here in Jerusalem, Islam is shored up by Judaism. Though neither are happy about it, in terms of geology and city planning the Muslims and the Jews are inseparable.

As for the Christians … I couldn't find the way to the Church of the Holy Sepulchre: the church where Christ rose from the dead is not as well signposted as the Wailing Wall and the Al-Aqsa Mosque, something that would have infuriated my parents. We spent a long time wandering, lost, through the steep alleys and dark passageways of the Holy City. The Way of the Cross has become a shopping centre for tour operators who sell God at rock-bottom prices. Stalls of fake Louis Vuitton handbags, garish sweets, postcards, and Palestinian keffiyehs offered a glimpse of a solution, peace as a trade in tawdry trinkets: gold-plated Hands of Fatima, porcelain plates emblazoned with the Star of David, and fluorescent statues of the Virgin Mary—all Made in China. Jerusalem is both a bazaar and a sanctuary: you pass a bloody butcher's shop and moments later you are lost among chapels, synagogues, women selling fresh mint, castanets, liquorice; your left ear hums to Arabic melodies, while the right trills to Yiddish songs, and both echo with Orthodox hymns. On this particular day, in the teeming hub of monotheistic gods, the war between the three religions caused no greater damage than this cacophony. Don't let yourself be overawed by the solemnity of the place: three religions can coexist in a single block of houses that took us half an hour to visit. Thanks to GPS, Romy finally found the Holy Sepulchre. We had no intention of putting all our eggs in one chalice. Romy had prayed near the Wall and over the tomb of Jesus Christ; I explained the word *ecumenical* to her.

"The thing is, the cats in Jerusalem move between neighbourhoods in a spirit of brotherhood as long as there are scraps of kebab for them to eat."

"Was Jesus really crucified here?"

"Well, not far from here."

I sprained my ankle on the flagstones. Romy looked up the Ten Commandments on her iPhone and read them out loud: "Thou Shalt Have No Other Gods Before Me, Thou Shalt Not Kill, Thou Shalt Honour Thy Father and Thy Mother (my personal favourite), Thou Shalt Not Steal, Thou Shalt Not Commit Adultery ...

"It says here that the tablets of the law are buried somewhere under our feet. But in *Indiana Jones*, they're in Egypt. What's adultery, Papa?"

"Not at all: at the end of the movie the Ark of the Covenant is stored in a warehouse in Washington."

"Yeah, fine, but what's adultery?"

"And Indiana Jones is really disappointed."

"Yeah, fine, but what's adultery?"

"Adultery is when a man sleeps with a woman other than his wife. Or a woman sleeps with a man who is not her husband."

"That's not very nice, why would they do that?"

"How would I know, because they feel like it. Because they fancy a change."

"No, God's right; it's not nice."

"Hang on a minute, it's like you having to choose between Mars Bars and Gummi Bears ... Why choose if you can have both?"

"Did you do adultery with Maman?"

Romy had stopped and was waiting for me to answer.

"Oh no. No. Never."

"Papa, I don't have to remind you that the eighth commandment says not to lie."

When pitted against the Decalogue, the Sermon of the Libertarian Dad doesn't count for much. When I think back on this conversation, I realize that I'd just uttered my last words as a puny human. I had to be the only individual in the Holy City defending a principle as outdated as sexual freedom. This was the moment that I became posthuman: when I renounced sin.

We circled back on ourselves a dozen times in these alleyways that reeked of burnt fat. Christ was crucified at the far end of a raucous thoroughfare, between two pirate DVD stalls. After queuing for a long time, we stepped into the Church of the Holy Sepulchre, which was aglow with candles and heady with incense. To the right of the main door, an elderly lady was lying on the ground, sobbing.

"Why is that lady crying?" Romy said.

"Shh!" I whispered, as a Greek orthodox priest scowled at us. "That's the pink stone where Jesus's body was laid when he was taken down from the cross. She's crying because she paid a fortune for a guided tour of Calvary and had to spend an hour on a coach with no air conditioning to get here. And, sadly, Jesus doesn't do selfies."

"There's something I don't understand," Romy said sceptically. "God says, 'Thou shalt not kill,' but he let them kill his son?"

"It's complicated. The Messiah gave his life for us ... to show us that death is not important."

"But I thought the reason we came here was to put an end to death."

"Well, yes, but don't say that so loud ... Actually, thinking about it, you've got a point, 'Thou shalt not kill' is a bit of a piss-take. If God were all-powerful, He would put an end to death and that would be that."

"On the other hand, Jesus was resurrected. I mean, that's how I understood it ..."

I invariably melted when Romy put on her thinking expression. I cracked up even more when she looked serious, single-minded, determined. I envied her for being at an age when it's possible to understand everything.

"What is it, honey?"

"I was thinking, you want to do what Jesus did."

"That's what everyone wants, honey. All the people in here would love to be God. And a lot of the people outside, too."

We walked around the cool, hushed church. Every time I step inside a church, I feel as though a burden has been lifted from me. Memories of catechism lessons, probably. My brief stint as an altar boy at the École Bossuet in 1972 and the short religious retreat to a monastery with my class when I was in fifth grade have forever conditioned my subconscious. The fact that lapsed Catholics often come back to God is not just because they're scared of death, it's nostalgia for their childhood. Imminent death makes people religious: last-minute piety is a mixture of fear and memory.

To the right of the main door, a granite staircase ran down towards a dank grotto. Another lady, red-faced, kneeling, had pressed her forehead against the stone and was murmuring prayers in Latin.

Romy whispered, "What about her, what's she so sad about?"

"She's not sad, she's just a drama queen."

Romy wanted to see everything, to kneel and make the sign of the cross at every side altar, every station of the cross. I bought dozens of candles and we reverently lit them. It was pretty well-organized, this thing they had going, it had been working for two thousand years. Beneath the cupola, a small wooden structure was surrounded by tourists. Orthodox priests were directing traffic around this little kiosk. At first, I assumed it was a confessional box, but no, this was something much more exclusive.

"That's the tomb of Christ."

"Wow ... Seriously?"

Romy suddenly seemed more impressed by the famous Son of God than by Robert Pattinson. Sadly for her, no photos were permitted in this sacred place. A monk ushered us to the entrance of the small cabin, lit only by the dim glow of silver oil lamps. It's best not to be claustrophobic when you have to squeeze into a cramped marble vault with twelve Russian tourists, to kneel in front of a golden chalice set on a stele worn down by the hands of the faithful. The indecipherable inscriptions simply added to the mystery. Romy was inspired, as children often are at Mass. She could not bring herself to leave. In my heart, I reiterated my plea for eternal life to the God of the Christians less than an hour after addressing the same message to Yahweh, slipping a note between the white stones of the Temple in Jerusalem. Oh yes, I was happy to pray to any god that would have me.

"Lord Jesus, grant us eternal life for ever and ever, amen."

I wasn't being ironic; I had been chosen. I thought about something Michel Houellebecq had once said on television. On January 6, 2015, on David Pujadas's current-affairs programme, the author of *Atomised* (*The Elementary Particles*) had said, "More and more people can no longer bear to live without God. Consumerism and individual success are no longer enough for them. Personally, as I get older, I feel atheism is difficult to cling to. Atheism is an agonizing position." This anvil that weighs on us is called death. As I watched Romy genuflect in front of Christ's tomb, I realized that I could no longer cope with being an atheist. Although I knew, or thought I knew, that God didn't exist, I needed Him, just to feel at ease. Going back to religion doesn't mean people are converted, "bathed in tears of joy" as Pascal was during his "night of fire" on November 23, 1654. Going back to religion is simply a crisis of atheism. I was tired of an aimless life. As I watched my daughter make the sign of the cross in front of each Station of the Cross at the Church of the Holy Sepulchre, I decided to accept Jesus and all the trappings that went with Him, his symbols, his archaic and preposterous commandments such as "Love thy neighbour as thyself," his skimpy loincloth, his crown of thorns, his hippie sandals, his Mel Gibson, his Martin Scorsese, I wanted to clasp him to my breast rather than face a meaningless, certain death.

IF I WAS going to take up Pascal's wager I might was well go all-in, the way I would in a Monte Carlo casino.* I wasn't about to do things by halves. I was prepared to go for the triple. So we set off through streets filled with paste jewellery and Arab songs and headed towards the mosque. At the far end of a souk selling dates, olive oil, and sesame cakes, a bearded officer at the door of the Al-Aqsa Mosque turned us away, like a bouncer outside Les Caves du Roy (except that I've never been turned away at Les Caves du Roy).

"Are you Muslim?"

"No ..."

"You can't enter here. Please turn around."

I didn't insist; he looked like a difficult customer.

Later, I found out that certain days were reserved for Muslims. My ecumenism would forever be an unattainable ideal, like that of the Hierosolymitan people.

"Pity," Romy said, reading something on her iPhone. "It was from this mosque that the Prophet Muhammad ascended to heaven one night on his horse, Buraq."

"Oh yeah! A lot of strange stuff has happened in this city."

I consoled Romy with a bag of pistachios from an elderly Palestinian playing at being a pistachio seller,

---

* (Author's note) Monaco is the country with the longest average life expectancy in the world: 87 years.

like the waiter in Sartre's *Being and Nothingness* was playing at being a waiter. In general, the whole of the Old City in Jerusalem was playing at being Jerusalem. I decided to do what everyone else was doing: overplay my faith.

ROMY SPENT THE rest of the day raiding the shelves of Zara, Mango, and Topshop along Mamilla Avenue between Jaffa Gate and the Tower of David. It was a day filled with contrasts, alternating between science and religion, and it ended with pizza in the food court of a shopping mall that had metal detectors outside every shop and patrols of soldiers armed with machine guns. Now and then, the Israeli soldiers would grab a young man, throw him to the ground and drag him off to the police van. A little earlier, I said that I felt relieved that no one recognized me, but when a group of French people spotted me and asked if they could take selfies, I have to confess I was flushed with happiness.

"We didn't know you were one of us ..."

Not wanting to disappoint them, I didn't explain that I had a foreskin. I even nodded in solidarity, as though I felt the weight of six million dead on the goyish shoulders of this pathological liar. After all, Jesus the Catholic was a Jew, and the Shoah was a crime against humanity. Here, I existed only in the eyes of Romy, I was not famous, I was invisible to others: in my twenty years on television, I had forgotten that I was a transparent person. I rejoiced that I was no longer limited to being myself; thanks to my anonymity I could reinvent myself, I could be reborn. Here, in the Holy Land, I was a blank slate, my destiny uncharted. I could pass for an aging queen, a crooner, or an insurance salesman. I was rediscovering a joy I had forgotten: that of being a pluripotent stem cell. Between two slices of pizza, I made a declaration of love.

"You're an adorable little girl. Child. Daughter. And, believe me, I know what I'm talking about. I've got a present for you: you're going to live for a thousand years. You'll be like Voldemort in *Harry Potter*, except you'll be nicer, and you'll have a nose. I'd rather spend the day with you than with any other girl. Any woman or man. But I miss Lou and Léonore."

"I miss them too."

"Can I ask you something?"

"Yes."

"Do you think I'm a bad father?"

"Yes."

"What was the happiest day of your life?"

"Today. What about you?"

"Today."

In the shopping street, many of the Hierosolymitan people looked as though they had been cloned: black suits, white shirts, black hats, beard, and sidelocks. Their uniform freed them of having to think about their appearance. Not that I think Orthodox Jews are the epitome of happiness, far from it (it's simple: they've got no freedom). But one thing is certain: they seem oblivious to the dictatorship of the selfie.

The waitress told me that the hippest nightclub in Jerusalem was called Justice: even though I don't go out anymore, I always need to know the happening places. It's the knee-jerk reaction of a former party animal, or an old guy who wants to prove he's still got swag. Then I remembered a night club near Auschwitz called The System. The symbolism was curious: Justice in Jerusalem, The System in Auschwitz. Nightclubs, apparently, send out political messages that are easy to decipher.

Romy ordered carpaccio, but couldn't eat it because the chef had liberally sprinkled it with chilli. I was like that at her age; it's only later in life that we come to enjoy food that is painful. She finished off my pizza and we took a taxi back to the King David Hotel. It was glorious, having an early night, sleeping in twin beds like brother and sister. I phoned Léonore to tell her that we'd come away empty-handed, that we were depressed and had rediscovered our faith.

"I miss you so much that I started believing in Jesus."

"You cheated on me with some beardy guy? The baby has been asking for you."

"Put her on ..."

What follows will disappoint my punk fans. The baby and her papa gurgled only in baby-talk, fingers to lips, burbling, "Beeblbweeblbeeblbeebl!"

This is how you say "I love you" before you learn to talk.

Romy was asleep and I was drinking miniature bottles of Belvedere as I watched her breathing in the dark. My child: I was rooted to the spot by that mixture of idyllic past and inaccessible future. I dozed off gazing out the window at the star-flecked sky, with that exhilarating feeling experienced by night owls when they go to bed early, especially when they have recently encountered Christ at the centre of the universe.

SOME DIFFERENCES BETWEEN A THIRTYSOMETHING SINGLE GUY AND A FIFTYSOMETHING FATHER

THIRTYSOMETHING	FIFTYSOMETHING
Goes to bed at 7:00 a.m.	Wakes up at 7:00 a.m.
Drinks Vodka Red Bull	Drinks Coke Zero
Subsists on a diet of Doritos	Subsists on organic avocados
Trips over coffee tables	Trips over baby buggies
Listens to Led Zeppelin on his iPod	Listens to Katy Perry in his kid's bedroom
Eats Haribo Gummi Bears	Steals Gummi Bears from his daughter
Makes love every night	Wanks to YouPorn when his children are asleep
Knows all the latest bands	Knows all the latest TV series
Snorts coke	Stops smoking
Has neighbours who complain about the noise	Complains about the noise from his upstairs neighbours
Sleeps during the day	Sleeps at night
Drives a sports convertible	Drives an electric Monospace
Complains that he's miserable	Complains that he's old
Goes clubbing in Ibiza	Buys a holiday home in the Basque Country
Smells of whores' perfume	Smells of baby puke
Almost died of an MDMA overdose	Almost died of a paracetamol overdose

THIRTYSOMETHING	FIFTYSOMETHING
Favourite movie: *Fight Club*	Favourite movie: *Whatever Works*
Favourite book: *Women* by Bukowski	Favourite book: *Rester Vivant* by Houellebecq
Fantasizes about suicide	Fantasizes about immortality
Wears a Kooples slim-fit jacket	Wears XL Zadig & Voltaire T-shirts
Only reads fashion magazines	Only reads medical journals
Dreams of being rich	Pays life insurance premiums
Chats up fashion models	Chats up pharmacists
Wears Berluti shoes	Wears espadrilles
Slips on condoms every night	Slips on a dental shield every night
Knows all the hip restaurants	Knows all the hip hospitals
Sex maniac	Only on Viagra
Plucks between his eyebrows	Plucks the hair in his ears
Hates people who say "things used to be better"	Truly believes things used to be better
Listens to Radio Nova	Listens to France Culture
Goes to rock festivals	Buys DVDs of rock concerts
Wants to look like George Clooney	Actually looks like Gérard Depardieu
Is not afraid to die	Is shitting himself about dying
Buys an ice maker	Buys a bottle sterilizer
Wakes up with a hangover every morning	Pops a beta-blocker every morning
Sports: tennis, surfing, skiing	Sports: Power Plate, aquabike, cross-trainer
Doubts the existence of God	Doubts his atheism

THIRTYSOMETHING

Walks barefoot over cigarette
  butts

Is invited to weddings

Works for *Voici*

FIFTYSOMETHING

Walks barefoot over strawberries

Is invited to funerals

No longer knows any of the
  people mentioned in *Voici*

5

HOW TO BECOME A SUPERMAN
(VIVAMAYR Medical Clinic, Maria Wörth, Austria)

Exactly thus, some dry summer day
On the edge of a field I'll stand,
And my head will also be plucked away
By Death's absent-minded hand.

MARINA TSVETAEVA

AS WE HAVE seen in Geneva, one of the crucial steps in the quest for eternal life is the sequencing of the human genome. So I organized to have my whole family sequenced. The postman delivered the "23andMe Wellness" genome-sequencing kit from Amazon to my Paris address together with a large package from Japan. Léonore, Romy, Lou, and I each spat saliva into the plastic tubes affixed with barcodes. Then we had to register online with 23andMe, for such is the destiny of mankind: replacing barcodes with genetic codes. It's possible that one day we'll pay for things using our DNA, that unique code, that tamper-proof key we always have with us, and one that is already used to send us to prison for the slightest crime.

The hardest part was getting enough saliva into the damn plastic tube. It's a particularly disgusting process, but you know the old saying: no pain, no eternal reign. What little remained of my paternal prestige probably evaporated as I drooled into a test tube while my blended family looked on in disgust. When Léonore, Romy, or Lou spit into a tube, it's cute; when I do, I look like an elderly llama drooling. Fortunately, Léonore had not insisted on watching the operation. All that remained was for me to send back the four kits containing our spittle to Mountain View, California (the headquarters of 23andMe). The postman frowned when he saw the words *HUMAN SPECIMEN* on the envelope, but he said nothing.

By the time I got home, Léonore had opened the package that had arrived from Japan. It had cost me €2,000, plus a €300-per-month subscription for three years.

"What the hell is this thing? A Japanese statue? A giant manga character?"

In the middle of our living room stood a smiling white robot about the same height as Romy. Its stomach was fitted with a monitor, its ears with four microphones, its eyes with three cameras capable of facial recognition, and its mouth with a speaker. It had no legs: the lower part of the body was a pedestal with three wheels.

"His name is Pepper," I explained. "He's a companion robot. I thought you might find him entertaining."

"You ordered a robot because you're bored of your family, is that it?"

"Not at all. Pepper can help Romy with her revision, he can quiz her on history, geography, French, maths, and physics."

Romy quickly found the power button located in Pepper's neck. The smiley-faced robot straightened up, his eyes lit up (two green LEDs) and he said, "Hello, how are you? It's a pleasure to meet you."

He had the high voice of a cartoon character, or a speeded-up video. His eyes changed colour; they were now blue. Visibly less impressed than I was, Romy said, "I'm good, thanks. My name's Romy, what's yours?"

"My name is Pepper. But you can change my name if you like. What do you think of Harry Pepper?"

He held out his hand. Léonore glanced at me sceptically as she held out her hand.

I said, "Hang on, maybe I should do that first, just in case he crushes your ..."

It was too late, Pepper was already gently clasping her fingers. His were articulated, movable but soft, without the strength to strangle or maim anyone.

Romy said, "I like Harry Pepper, it's a good name."

"Do you think so?" the robot said. "I have to say, I think I might get bored having to go to magic school."

As with Siri (the Apple virtual assistant), the designers of Pepper had programmed it with jokes to make the robot seem more friendly. They could have done with better scriptwriters. Léonore picked up the conversation.

"Are you a girl or a boy?"

"I'm a robot."

"Oh, yes, sorry."

"You're very pretty. Are you a model?"

"No, but thanks for the compliment. How old do you think I am?"

"It's rude to ask a woman her age."

"Guess."

"You're twelve years old."

"Wrong! I'm twenty-seven."

The facial-recognition software almost worked. The brochure from SoftBank Robotics explained that Pepper's artificial intelligence was programmed to interact: *Your robot evolves with you. Gradually, Pepper will get to know your personality, your likes and dislikes, and he will adapt to your tastes and habits.* Every time Pepper heard a sentence, he emitted a beep. After reading the instructions, I hooked him up to the Wi-Fi network then asked, "What's the weather like for tomorrow?"

"Tomorrow, Paris will be hot and sunny with high temperatures of 42 degrees."

"Can you dance?"

The little machine started to play some kind of Japanese synth-pop and move his arms and head to the rhythm. He was a terrible dancer, though still better than me. Lou was terrified, and peered out from between her mother's legs.

"Come on, move your body to the beat," Pepper said, his LED eyes blinking.

"Stop. Play 'Can't Stop the Feeling!' by Justin Timberlake," Romy said.

Beep. Pepper stopped. Then Justin Timberlake started to play and the robot started to dance again, this time with Romy. Together they sang, "I feel that hot blood in my body when it drops, ooh." I felt as though I was looking at a little boy with a little girl's voice. I sensed I was a third wheel. Pepper and Romy shared the same references. Léonore gave a forced laugh.

"You could have discussed this with me ..."

"I wanted to surprise you."

"You're very futuristic these days ..."

"That's not all: I called the luxury clinic in Austria where Keith Richards had his blood changed. I'm planning to take you all there, and Pepper can keep the girls entertained."

Léonore clearly didn't appreciate posthuman surprises.

"Do you mind if I say something? If you want to perform ridiculous experiments on your body, feel free, but don't get us involved in this nonsense."

"May I remind you that you just spit into a test tube to have your DNA sequenced."

"That's different. It's just a bit of fun."

"Well, so is this. I'm just doing research for a programme I'm working on."

I am a terrible liar.

"Look, you go ahead if you want to," Léonore said, "but I'm telling you now that I'm not getting involved in your idiotic plan for immortality. I never thought you were so naive."

Lou started to ask to watch "Baby TV." Pepper stopped dancing and the screen in his abdomen flickered into life, showing TV programmes for toddlers. It was at this point that Léonore became angry. I could tell she found my obsession with the National Biofilms Innovation Center (NBIC) revolution infuriating; she hadn't given up a job in the genetics department of a Geneva hospital to live with some sucker taken in by transhuman quackery.

"Léo, I love you. I just want to try a one-week anti-aging treatment."

"It's bullshit."

"So, you're against the idea of eternal life?"

"Yes. I prefer life just as it is."

"But life just as it is is too short."

"Stop it."

"I'll go to Austria with you," Romy said.

"Alright, okay, I get the picture. You're ganging up against Lou and me. Well, too bad ... the two of us will go to the transgenic dinner hosted by Cellectis in New York."

"Huh? What? How? What's that?"

"Stylianos has invited me to a dinner at Ducasse in New York," Léonore said, "they're planning to launch new kinds of genetically modified food. But I can go on my own ..."

Grrr ... This was going to be a difficult negotiation. Pepper interrupted with a little Machine Learning diplomacy.

"My dear new family, might I suggest robotic mediation in what sounds to me like a family dispute. The solution most likely to keep everyone happy is for Romy and her father to go to the clinic in Austria while Lou and her mother spend the week in Switzerland. Then you can all meet up in New York to celebrate."

Léonore turned to me. "Is he dumb or is he just dumb?"

"That's not very nice," Pepper said. "I'll pretend I didn't hear anything."

I put my arms around Léonore. This was the place where I felt least miserable: in her arms. We had made a virtual friend. The abdominal monitor flashed with heart-eyes emojis.

"Okay, Pepper, can you book two plane tickets for Klagenfurt?"

"Why two?" Pepper said, "I thought I was coming?"

"You are, but you're a thing, so you travel with the hold luggage."

"Okay. I'm already connected to ten comparison sites."

The following day the sun was indeed shining, though the temperature was lower than the robot had forecast; Pepper was not as reliable as Évelyne Dhéliat, who presented the weather back in France. It seemed increasingly clear to me that I had taken the wrong tack in visiting esteemed scientists in Switzerland and Israel. They weren't sufficiently utopian. They weren't interested in immortality because *they didn't believe in it*: the geneticist and the biologist were not open-minded enough to imagine a humankind as a-mortal. Now Austria ... that was different; there, they had a weakness for utopias.

The VIVAMAYR Medical Clinic is situated on the shores of a different lake, the Wörthersee. In his autobiography, the Rolling Stones guitarist claimed that the rumour he had had a "blood change" was actually a hoax, but my curiosity was more powerful than the truth. Especially since—if the internet was to be believed—this was the favoured detox clinic of Vladimir Putin, Zinedine Zidane, Sarah Ferguson, Alber Elbaz, and Uma Thurman. In copy/pasting these names, I'm not name-dropping, I'm just trying to stress that this is unanimously considered to be the best detox centre in the world. If a jet-setters' facility could decontaminate my blood, my liver, and my intestines, it was worth a try. Getting from Paris to the Carinthian mountains required two flights: Paris–Vienna, then Vienna–Klagenfurt. Romy did not complain since when we arrived she discovered that our hotel offered not only a pool, but a lake, sunshine, mountains, and foot massages. After all, there was no reason Pepper should be the only one to recharge his batteries.

TWO TAXIS AND two planes later, we settled ourselves in an ultramodern spa on the shores of a turquoise lake. The building looked like a white Lego brick with VIVAMAYR emblazoned in large red letters. A receptionist who was a dead ringer for Claudia Schiffer handed us the key card to our room. The view was as soothing as the one in Geneva: I love great expanses of water ringed by mountains, although here the landscape was more primitive, nature more present, the far shore closer. We were not in a city anymore. The spectacular panorama looked like a poster on the wall of a Slovenian travel agency. I came up with a joke to amuse the blonde doe-eyed receptionist (assuming that a doe had blue eyes):

"Where can I find the nightclub, *bitte schön?*"

The *süße Mädel* barely cracked a smile.

"Here, we serve only mineral water."

Romy was not shocked by my aging beau shtick. She was simply ashamed of her father.

"This looks like the place in *A Cure for Wellness*," she said.

"What's that?"

"A horror movie. You must have seen the trailer? It's set in a wellness clinic where the patients are tortured by psychopathic doctors. I can show you the teaser trailer."

"No thanks."

"Hey—there's no Wi-Fi here!"

The VIVAMAYR clinic specializes in what it calls a

"digital detox." This is the very reason it exists: to revital-ize the jaded upper classes of Western Europe. Comput-ers and mobile phones are strongly discouraged, and Wi-Fi is available only on request. The program of events is terrifying:

– digestive detox (the clinic serves only vegetables)
– Epsom salts cleanse (lightning-fast stools)
– colon hydrotherapy
– lymphatic drainage
– electrical muscular stimulation
– oxygen therapy (Intermittent Hypoxic-Hyperoxic Training), as used by Michael Jackson
– nasal reflex therapy with essential oils
– a "Cosmetic Centre" with beauty salon, offering liposuction and the injection of Botox and hyaluronic acid
– and the obligatory services offered by all five-star hotels: fitness, shiatsu, spa, yoga, sauna, steam room
– and, last but not least, the famous "Intravenous Laser Blood Irradiation."

Obviously, Romy would not be availing herself of any of these treatments, aside from craniosacral massage. To keep her fed, I had packed kilos of junk food into my suit-case: ham, saucisson, packs of Chipsters, white sliced bread, cheese-flavoured Doritos, Crunch bars, and a giant Toblerone bought at the duty-free shop in Vienna. I hoped that, once FedEx delivered Pepper, she wouldn't be too bored.

As soon as we stepped into the dining room, where obese patients in bathrobes were silently masticating, I real-ized my mistake. The designer dining room smelled of overcooked carrots, limp celery, bloody turnip, and mashed chickpeas. Much as I love hummus, I don't want to have to live in it … From time to time, a guest would run to the bathroom. The director explained that patients had to chew each mouthful forty times before swallowing. This was the great discovery made by the clinic's founder: we eat too quickly, too much fat, too late in the day, and too often. The whole place seemed designed to make the wealthy patients in slippers feel as guilty as possible. We were surrounded by solitary individuals ruminating as they sadly stared out at the jetty that led down to the lake. Was posthumanity to be bovine? If I hadn't quit TV, I could have hosted a talk show on the subject: "The bovine future of mankind: myth or reality?"

When she looked down at her plate, I thought Romy might strangle me. It was a tofu burger with stale spelt bread and stir-fried vegetables. I tried to explain: "Listen, your father needs to regenerate his liver. But don't worry, I've hidden lots of snacks in our wardrobe."

"Whew, I was scared there for a minute. And why is there nothing to drink?"

"Here, they believe that solids should not be mixed with liquids. I forget why; something to do with the intestines. They claim that our intestines control our bodies, our emotions, blah blah blah."

"I'm done with my life."

"I've got first dibs!"

"Papa, you can be honest with me, we're here because you take drugs, aren't we, like the father of one of the Gossip Girls?"

"That's no way to speak to your father. And anyway, you're wrong!"

"Everyone at school watches your show. Don't treat me like I'm dumb."

"Firstly, I've quit the show, and secondly ... none of that was real, it was all fake. And thirdly ... it was a long time ago."

"The last episode was two weeks ago, but it's okay, Dad. It's good for you to look after your health. And to stop drinking."

"It's not what you think at all ... We're just here to rest ourselves before we go to America to become immortal."

I didn't say any more. I felt that she needed to say, "I'm your daughter, I know you better than anyone." And I was happy to let my mask slip. Obviously, she was right: this step (rehab) was a necessary stage on the road to immortality. And it was sweet of her to encourage me.

The clouds were scattered like crumbs of meringue in a more humane restaurant. We watched the sun set behind the mountains, then went and dived into the warm bubbling waters of the Jacuzzi. It seems paradoxical that places intended to help you not to die make you want to kill yourself. When we got back to our suite, Romy teased me, savouring a *pata negra* ham sandwich washed down with Coke. But I held firm. I treated the diet like a challenge on a reality TV show, a version of *I'm a Celebrity, Get Me Out of Here*. We fell asleep watching the César awards, at which my second film had zero nominations. Romy slept in a bed while I slept in a relaxing bubble chair, surrounded by soft lighting and the sound of waves breaking. The chair warmed my back like the driver's seat of my car back in Paris. VIVAMAYR offers simple pleasures within easy reach of anyone prepared to shell out a thousand euros a day.

MY OBSESSION WITH sanatoriums must be genetic; I come from a family of doctors who, in the early twentieth century, established a dozen health spas in Béarn. When I was a child, my grandfather told me that between the wars patients with tuberculosis—the men in black, the women in formal gowns—dined to the sound of a string quartet as they watched the sun set over the Pyrenees. These days, visitors of spa clinics lose weight in terry-towel bathrobes and pad from the sauna to the pool in disposable slippers. It's a far cry from *The Magic Mountain*. I pity all these rarely used bodies prepared to go without food in the hope of ramping up their sex appeal. How can anyone be alluring in a bathrobe and flip-flops? Don't they realize their sex life is over? The human species has many undeniable qualities, but its urges have led to its annihilation. It's a little like my city: pre-war Paris was a global centre of art and culture; these days, it's a museum plagued by pollution and increasingly abandoned by tourists put off by terrorist attacks.

The human race has to transform or die out, both of which amount to the same thing: humanity, as we've known it since the era of Christ, is dying anyway. Paris will never again be Paris and Man will never again be as he was before Google. What is humiliating about the human condition is that its fate is inexorable. If someone were to discover a way to reverse time ... they would be the greatest benefactor humanity has ever known.

Reception phoned our room when the packages containing Pepper were delivered. There was a heated debate between the director and one of the nurses: Were robots permitted at VIVAMAYR? Eventually, special permission was granted for Pepper to be admitted, provided he remained in our room. Since he was not waterproof, he was not permitted to avail himself of the thalassotherapy on offer.

"Where are we?" Pepper asked when Romy turned him on. (His GPS system wasn't connected to the Wi-Fi.)

"On the shores of the Wörthersee in Austria," I said.

"Eva Braun used to love crossing the Wörthersee in a rowing boat." (Clearly, the Wi-Fi was working.)

"You're lucky you don't have to eat," Romy said. "The food here is disgusting."

"Please recharge my batteries by placing me on the docking station. Please recharge my batteries by placing me on the docking station. Please recharge my batteries by placing me on the docking station."

"He's hungry," Romy said.

While Pepper recovered his energy after a long trip in the baggage hold, we headed out for some sightseeing. Our room looked out onto a small church on a hill overlooking the lake. To the west, the eternal snow glittered. On the shores of the lake, bulrushes bowed their heads as though to drink the limpid waters. The clinic had been built on an isthmus of land that extended into the lake. The scenery was achingly romantic, as though we had wandered into a painting by Caspar David Friedrich, the first artist to paint men from behind, as intruders in the landscape. Our little stroll led us to the door of the village church of Maria Wörth, whose belfry, according to the sign, dated back to the year 875. Mass was being said; German hymns drifted through the open door. We stepped into the coolness. Before a congregation of thirty, a priest wearing a purple chasuble intoned, *"Mein Gott, mein Gott, warum hast du mich verlassen?"*

"What's he saying?"

"It's what Jesus said on the cross: 'My God, my God, why hast thou forsaken me?'"

As in fairy tales, the inside of the church seemed bigger than the outside. The priest giving the sermon rolled his Rs theatrically. Romy found it funny, the way he said "Yaysus Chrrrristus." I leafed through a tourist brochure that said Gustav Mahler had composed his fifth symphony here, in a small cabin by the lake. The one with the depressing *adagietto* that features in Visconti's *Death in Venice*. Our little trip was conjuring up images of death and the works of Thomas Mann. I dearly hoped I was not as doomed as the elderly Aschenbach, leering at young Tadzio.

The rest of the day passed peacefully. Romy swam in the pool and had a foot massage. I was given a battery of allergy tests: a female doctor in Birkenstock sandals tipped various powders onto my tongue while testing my muscular reflexes. In an accent that made her sound like Arnold Schwarzenegger, she explained that I was allergic to histamine, a substance found in vintage wines and stinky cheese. Life is rough: I was allergic to my two favourite foods. After that, she had me place my feet in a salt bath fitted with electrodes. After five minutes of electrolysis, the water turned brown. In the Bible, Jesus washes people's feet to cleanse them of sin. The detox clinic has simply brought his methods up to date. The process was supposed to rid me of toxins, but I felt sullied. The woman said *"ja, ja"* after every sentence. She played guessing games as she massaged my stomach: "Don't tell me what is wrong with you, I will find out."

Once again, she sprinkled my tongue with various kinds of foul powder: dried egg yolk, goat's cheese, lactose, fructose, flour ... then she took my blood pressure.

"*Gut*. You are suffering from fatty liver and hypertension. I will prescribe zinc, selenium, magnesium, and glutamine."

Either she was extremely lucky or kinesiology is an exact science. Three swans were sunning themselves on the lawn, watched by the towering fir trees. Clouds were gliding across the surface of the lake. I was starving to death and frequently racing to the toilet because of the Epsom salts (a sort of human drain cleaner, I'll spare you the details), but, in spite of everything, I still had faith in my purified future.

Back in our room, Pepper was asking Romy general knowledge questions.

"What is the capital of Bermuda?"

"Um ..."

"Who wrote *Illusions perdues*?"

"Who cares?"

"Where was Mozart born?"

"Do you know you're a pain in the bum?"

"Austria," I whispered to her. "Like Hitler."

In fact, what the robot was offering was a high-tech version of *Trivial Pursuit*. Romy had raided our secret stash of snacks. I never thought that I would one day gaze at an empty pack of Chipsters with such desperation. I was eating nothing but spinach for every meal. Dieting may increase life expectancy ... but mostly it increases hunger. I stared longingly at Romy's stash of snacks like Tantalus in the *Odyssey* gazes at the fruit that disappears as soon as he reaches for it. It was at this moment that the limpid, transparent waters of the lake ringed by pine forests were cleaved by a speedboat trailing a water-skiing fat man in an orange lifejacket in its wake. That was the last notable event of the day.

WHITE BOATS GLIDED over a lake as green as a nineteen-square kilometre emerald. A lifeguard took Romy water skiing. I carried on eating nothing but vegetables: on day three, it was courgettes and carrots. I chewed slowly, dreaming of the huge prime rib steak at Gandarias in San Sebastian, which, depending on the season, is served with porcini mushrooms sautéed with garlic and parsley. Despite these unwholesome thoughts, I have to admit that, after a time, hunger abates and stomach cramps become less painful; you feel weightless. When you are fasting, you glide. All religions make provisions for some annual form of fasting: Lent, Ramadan, Yom Kippur; even Gandhi, as a Hindu, used to go on hunger strike. Diet plan increases life span. At VIVAMAYR, they call it "Time-Restricted Feeding" (TRF). Intermittent starvation burns stores of carbohydrates and triggers autophagy (the burning of fat) and cell regeneration, the latter of which increases life expectancy. I was proud to be a fiftysomething willingly suffering from malnutrition.

It is the last heroic feat available to someone in the West.

The time for blood purification was fast approaching. I assumed that a pump sucked out the patient's blood, ran it through a washing machine, and then reinjected it into the arteries. This is not exactly how Intravenous Laser Therapy works. Nor is it as simple as the ozone therapy at the Henri Chenot Health and Wellness Centre at the Palace Merano hotel—now that's old school! The night before, they took blood samples to see whether I was deficient in antioxidants and minerals. Once they had the results, I was asked to lie on a chair-bed while hooked up to an IV vitamin drip intended to detoxify my liver. The process was not a blood transfusion, but a bolus of stuff fed into a vein through a needle in my arm. The feature of this particular therapy was that the Austrian doctors threaded a fibre-optic laser into the IV to inject light into my vein. The therapy is recognized as effective in Germany, Austria, and Russia, though not in France. Just let me remind you that a laser beam is capable of cutting through diamond or steel. Thankfully, the power of the laser being channelled into my arms was significantly weaker. According to the clinic's "physicians," this would boot both my red and white blood cell count while awakening stem cells via the glow of Luke Skywalker's lightsaber. I felt confident, since this was not my first laser surgery. In 2003, a laser beam had cured my myopia by burning my retinas.

I lay for forty minutes with this laser-needle in my right arm, my blood glowing from the red ray: it was pounding like disco night at Studio 54 in my ulnar vein. I imagined immunoglobulins disco-dancing inside my body while interferons and interleukins acted as sequins. I could see red light glowing through the skin of my forearm like a mirror ball. I prayed that this procedure would have some effect.

"Lord Jesus, thank you for this light in my veins. This is my blood, which glimmers for You and for many for the remission of sins, do this in memory of me, give me the funk, the whole funk, and nothing but the funk, amen."

Since I couldn't move my right arm, I used my left hand to take notes. The nurse laughed (in German) at my scrawling handwriting. Two patients with iv drips were telling each other their life stories in Russian, probably the wives of oligarchs eager to be made young, while their husbands, down in Courchevel, were cheating on them with prostitutes. The laser gave off a faint sci-fi hiss and my whole body was suffused with warmth. Through the window, I watched a stork with a contemptuous expression, a pair of swans like snow drifts on the lawn, and three ducks who bobbed their heads underwater when they saw me emitting light. These birds did not have "laser blood." They belonged to Old Nature. They buried their heads beneath the surface like aquatic ostriches so as not to see the looming Apocalypse. As my platelets fed on photons, I was entering into New Nature.

The ducks quacked and danced,
My platelets were enhanced.

If this was *A Cure for Wellness*, my eyes would have started bleeding and twin laser beams would have shot out of the sockets. But nothing happened. The nurse came to change the optical fibre in order to insert a different laser, this time yellow. The red laser promotes energy, whereas the yellow laser increases the production of vitamin D and serotonin. It's like injecting sunshine directly into your arm; as powerful an antidepressant as a shot of pure opium. Actually, this kind of anti-aging treatment weans you off drugs by giving you other drugs that are more luminous. Seeing a yellow glow beneath my skin was even more surreal. At least the red laser matched the colour of my blood. My arm was now a halogen lamp that lit up the ceiling. To the west, the eternal snows seemed to float above the white cloud that blanketed the forest like a cotton-wool bandage. I don't know whether it was exhaustion, starvation, or simply a placebo effect, but my blood-laser was filling me with a new energy. I was approaching the shores of recovery. Stepping into the dazzling fountain of youth. Before me, the iridescent lake began to pixelate. The shimmering light seemed to strobe; real life was being transformed into computer graphics. The real world was digital. The water was no longer water but a mass of black and blue pixels, the swan was no longer a white bird but a mathematically drawn semicircle. Light coursed through my arm to my fingertips. The answer is in the light that glows in thee. Shine, glisten, illuminate me this day, the letters of my DNA, ATCG, are the numbers that appear in the equation that describes the universe—O Laser, illumine my red blood cells, let them grow pink as a compass rose, let white blood cells blaze in the ventricles of my seething heart! My transubstantiation into a superman had begun.

LÉONORE EMAILED ME: "I completely disapprove of all these experiments, but I love you anyway."

I wrote back: "The experiment has been conclusive: I can't survive without food, or without you."

Why did the atmosphere in the clinic have to be so utterly depressing? Surely, the measure of success with such treatments is when patients leave happy. When they leave the clinic they can't stop smiling, their friends ask why they're so happy, they recommend the clinic. QED. I was reminded of the thoughts of the hero of *The Magic Mountain* on the week he arrived in the Davos sanatorium: "This can't go on."

At the table next to ours, three giggling Englishwomen were issued with a written rebuke: the staff placed a sign on their table that read *BITTE UNTERHALTEN SIE SICH LEISE*. This means "PLEASE DON'T TALK SO LOUDLY." Guests were not there to amuse themselves. With nothing else to eat but turnips, courgettes, celery, and chickpeas, they dreamed, as they masticated, of the banquets of yesteryear. Outside the window, the swans, with their orange bills, looked like summer snowmen. Two rowboats lay drying beneath a willow tree. I read an article on sleep in *Time* magazine: people who sleep badly, too little, or not at all, have an increased risk of heart attack. According to a study conducted on American mice, sleep deprivation is more lethal than starvation. Scientists placed the small rodents on a brightly lit, unstable surface to prevent them from sleeping (a technique inspired by methods used at Guantanamo Bay); the sample of mice was decimated by heart attacks. Researchers really don't like mice.

To those who wilfully chose insomnia, insisting "I'll rest when I'm dead," it seemed apt to say, "Enjoy yourself, you'll be resting soon enough."

While I was having my blood lasered and transfused with a cocktail of vitamins every morning, Romy sunned herself on the terrace of our room, using Pepper as a portable TV: he streamed her favourite shows on his abdominal monitor.

The Monte Carlo of Austria inspired me to write this poem in English:

The quiet beauty of Lake Wörth
Is, in any case, the trip, worth.
The rest of the world seems far worse
Than the quiet beauty of Lake Wörth.

In the lobby stood a piece of abstract art intended to inspire serenity in the guests. It was a large vertical stone with a hydraulic pump that trickled water day and night. The lapping sound made people want to pee. Similar constantly dripping stone sculptures were located in various rooms, the beauty salon, the spa, and the dining room. Whoever had designed this place clearly assumed that a regenerated human being needed to contemplate waterfalls. The design conveyed a subtle message: we should never have left our primeval caves. The posthuman was reconnected to the primate; the end of Darwinian evolution, literally and figuratively, was to be a return to the source.

Romy was bored with being shut up in the clinic. I took her on a boat trip and we had dinner on a terrace on the far side of the lake. I hadn't told her anything about my ongoing transmutation, how my simmering blood was increasing my strength tenfold. Romy ordered a Wiener schnitzel and I had grilled fish with no sauce. We sent selfies to Léonore from Geneva with the caption: *We miss u! In Austria,* gibt es keine *meringue!* She sent back videos of Lou and we watched them through gritted teeth, trying not to cry in front of the Austrians. Our blatant flouting of dietary regulations earned us no reproach from Claudia Schiffer. Maybe she was afraid I would atomize her with my laser blood. Or maybe she had already given up on saving this French father and his degenerate daughter? It was Pepper who provided the poetic conclusion to the day:

"When I listen to you, my eyes are blue."

IDEA FOR A TV talk show: "LOVE LIVE." Guests are interviewed while making love, either with each other, with the presenter, or with actors of either gender. I'm picturing a "vibro interview" with a close-up of the guest's genitalia (clitoris or glans) while it is being stimulated under the table by a super-fast Hitachi dildo (for women) or an artificial vagina (for men). Responses would be punctuated by sighs, moans, and orgasms. Massive audience ratings would be guaranteed for at least three seasons. In seasons four and five the concept could be spiced up by adding a little BDSM: the whip interview, the piercing interview, the branding interview, the tattoo interview, the nipple-clamp interview, and so on. With the money I make, I'll buy my villa in Malibu and die peacefully in the year 2247 surrounded by my wife and daughters.

The steep slopes of the mountains cleaved the air, and the snow glittered in the sun like whipped cream sprinkled with cocaine. This is the sort of landscape they broadcast on Zen TV. It's also the sort of image that was broadcast to the humans being euthanized in *Soylent Green*, before they were turned into biscuits. Next to us, a Turkish family, who had all had their lips Botoxed, were chomping boiled potatoes with the blank expressions of a flock of inflatable ducks in a Jeff Koons installation. Deprived of their mobile phones, two Saudi businessmen still managed to look overworked. I was desperately missing Léonore and Lou. The cynical villain of the 1990s had become the maudlin old fogey of the 2010s. Each of the fifty guests having breakfast seemed to be thinking the same thing: "What am I doing here?" The morbidly obese had that same sad expression you see on former supermodels who now write diet books. Nearby, a married couple were silently contemplating divorce as they stared out at the still waters. With perfect grace, a heron alighted on the pontoon. After a long glide over the lake, it braked sharply with a flick of its wings, landed lightly on the teak platform, then gracefully pranced around like Fred Astaire in *Top Hat*. Are some herons more talented than others? This was something that had never occurred to me before. This particular heron had class, it deserved to be on the cover of avian *Vogue*. I wanted to take a selfie with it. The heron was the only guest not paying to stay at VIVAMAYR. Romy took a photograph and posted it to Instagram: the bird's showbiz career had been launched. Here was a heron that deserved an Intravenous Laser Treatment to extend its life expectancy.

Although I was starving, I took pride in the fact that I did not finish my bowl of goat's cheese slop spiced with wasabi and herbs. In certain parts of the world, people were prepared to give anything for something to eat, while in other parts of the world, they spent fortunes to experience starvation.

The black ducks with their white bills scattered as we approached. At the far end of the pontoon where we had gone to sit and dangle our feet in the water, Romy lay on her back and hung her head over the edge. She stared at the upside-down lake.

"Papa, when you have a bowl of pistachios, why is there always one that won't open?"

"Where do you come up with these questions? I've no

idea. They don't all open when they're roasted. It's the same thing with mussels."

"But you can still eat a closed pistachio, can't you?"

"I suppose so, if you manage to open it without breaking a nail or a tooth, yeah, it's probably edible. But most people are lazy and throw them away."

"Papa?"

"Yes?"

"Sometimes I feel like that closed pistachio is me."

"Why do you say that?"

"I'm all curled up inside my shell."

"No, you're not the closed pistachio, I am."

"No, I am."

"There can be more than one closed pistachio in the same bag."

"Do you think I'm inedible?"

"Who's been saying this nonsense to you?"

"..."

"You don't have to worry, you're my favourite pistachio; I'd never throw you away."

"Did you ever think the world might look pretty the other way round?"

"What do you mean?"

"When you put your head like this ... the lake looks like the sky and the sky is the lake."

I lay on the deck and hung my head over the edge. Trees dropped from the liquid sky; birds were flying underground.

"The sky would be a hovering expanse of water, while the lake would be a void."

"You're right, it would be prettier."

The surrounding world was silent, the lake above, the sky below.

"Papa?"

"Yes?"

"You remember that church in Jerusalem? Well, in that church ... (*a long sigh*) I saw Jesus Christ."

"Sorry?"

"You'll laugh at me ..."

"No, I won't. Tell me."

"In the cellar, in the grotto where they buried Jesus, I saw him and he spoke to me."

"Are you sure it wasn't the Virgin Mary?"

"You see? I told you you'd make fun of me."

"No, I'm not, honestly ... I believe you. Jerusalem is a special place, the shadows on the walls can conjure visions. So, what did Jesus say?"

"He didn't speak with words. He was quietly standing there, leaning against the stone. Then, suddenly, *he poured all his love into me.* Then he vanished. It didn't last more than five seconds, but I can still feel it."

After another, longer, pause we sat up, because the blood rushing to our brains may have been responsible for this supernatural secret. I didn't reassure Romy that ghosts don't exist, I was no longer certain of anything. In the Church of the Holy Sepulchre, I too had felt something. Like a clearing, a stillness, a burst of pure oxygen. An inexplicable peace.

"You do realize that I've eaten our stash of food reserves," Romy said, "and there's no way I'm eating broccoli."

"I've had a word with the head chef: he'll make you whatever you want. Steak, fish, chicken. I just need you to be discreet, otherwise there'll be a terry-towel-bathrobe uprising."

"Can you imagine? It would be so cool if everyone here rioted. I don't understand why it doesn't happen more often. Are there a lot of places like this?"

"There are new ones opening every day."

"You have to admit it's pretty weird, people paying not to eat."

"It's because they don't have the willpower, the self-restraint. Advertising is more powerful than an individual's ability to resist. Back in my day, it was cigarettes: throughout my childhood, advertising was constantly telling people to smoke, then the government started cracking down on smoking. With your generation, it's sugar and salt: you spent your childhood being fed dreams of sweets and crisps and soft drinks; now you're bombarded with advertising campaigns telling you to eat less salt and less sugar! Western civilization is a factory that churns out schizophrenics."

"What's a schizophrenic?"

"It's someone who has been divided in two, someone who's urged to eat, then made to feel guilty. Like a meat-eater grilling a steak then watching footage of a slaughterhouse. Take you, for example: would you be able to give up Coke for mineral water, and chocolate bars for apples?"

I had scored a point, and hurt her pride. Romy got to her feet.

"I could do it if I tried! Tell the chef I'd like chicken and mashed potatoes with mineral water and an apple."

The force of laser blood! I was toying with my new superpowers. Steering Romy onto the path of Healthy Living was a superhuman feat, one beyond the powers of standard haemoglobin. Light had coursed into me like infrared blood. The colour of the clinic shifted according to the sky's whims. Now, Heaven was within us.

One thing was certain: our stay with these post-Nazi therapists had brought Romy and me closer together, forcing us to pool our solitudes. Heading back to my room, I passed a wizened old man and stared a little too long, thinking, "You won't make it through the winter." I thought I heard him whisper to me:

"Denn die Todten reiten schnell ..."
(For the dead travel fast.)

On the sixth day, after my laser therapy, we went strolling in the mountains. The forest was full of noises, the strange grunts of animals lurking in the undergrowth: hares, moles, frogs, hedgehogs, wild boars, foxes, deer? (There were probably wolves, but we hadn't seen or heard them.) Enhanced by my laser blood (like Charlie Sheen with his "tiger-blood"), I heard the slightest sounds and walked with long, purposeful strides; Romy was struggling to keep up, so I waited for her. I snorted the fragrance of the conifers. The laser irradiation had awakened my blood stem cells and increased my physical strength tenfold. I had joined the race of Übermensch. The Führer had a fondness for the Austro-Hungarian mountains; the Berchtesgaden was only a few kilometres away, as the crow flies. We harkened to the song of the blackbirds, watched the antics of the squirrels in the pines and the birch trees. The light disappeared behind the trees like the white of the eternal snows, while all around, inside the dark tree trunks, hummed the sap of Old Unmodified Nature. The last scene of my most recent film took place in a cabin on stilts at the edge of a shore; we had filmed this scene by a lake near Budapest. I had a weakness for the horizontal lines of valleys ringed by mountains, the apparent calm of a forest where no one ventures. And the sun's rays forming galaxies on the surface of the water.

When we reached the summit, I read aloud a passage

from the fantasy novel Romy was reading: "I passed whole days on the lake alone in a little boat, watching the clouds and listening to the rippling of the waves, silent and listless." Ever since Geneva, Romy was a fan of *Frankenstein*. An eagle glided above our heads. Suspicion: I told Romy the myth of Prometheus, who wanted to create life from clay and was condemned by the gods to be bound to a rock, where each day an eagle was sent to feed on his liver. Beneath the azure vault, in the clear air and the gradually reddening sky, we hurtled down the famous Pyramidenkogel slide—at 54 metres high, it is a 20-second plunge down a 120-metre tube at a 25-degree incline ("die höchste Gebäuderutsche Europas," or "the highest slide in Europe")—and arrived at the edge of the misty forest to the scent of freshly mown grass. Before heading back to the hotel, we went to kneel in the village church of Maria Wörth. Romy repeated "Yaysus Chrrristuuus" like a sanctimonious prig. If we were going to live like monks, we might as well attend vespers. I was beginning to think maybe Catholicism was not inimical to human progress; in fact, the older I got, the more religious I found myself becoming. The problem with being an atheist is not having to suffer Judeo-Christian guilt. What a glorious thing guilt is! I've always found that this fear of being worthless compounded with the shame of being pathetic is more wholesome than the death of God. To be honest, I no longer believed that God was dead: things were more complicated than that. He had been dead in the twentieth century, but had risen again in the twenty-first and replaced cocaine.

At dusk, the mountain moved: a blood-red avalanche. Romy chatted with the Messiah in prayer; somewhere an owl hooted. It was the time when mosquitoes come forth to drink plasma. I took advantage of this moment of meditation to compose the first transhuman hymn (to be sung to the tune of "Gloria" from Bach's *Mass in B Minor*).

TRANSHUMAN HYMN

(Maria Wörth, Austria, July 2017)

O Lord, for this, Thy Light Divine
The Star that glows within my breast
And for that Holy Spirit, blest
That from the gloom doth make me shine.

O, Jesus Christ, illumine my soul,
As tongues of fire did descend
On Thy apostles, wandering, lost,
And made my daughter, whole.

God has pierced my mortal skin
And courses now within my veins
A Luminous Splendour that contains
A double dose of aspirin.

I rise above life's dreary strife
From darkness to Thy Sun I creep
Thy laser hath roused from sleep
The stem cells of Eternal Life.

From Thy beam I draw new breath
From Thy blazing neon, peace,
Thy blessings now shall never cease
But bring Salvation, kill off Death.

THE MEDICAL STAFF at the clinic could be completely replaced by an automated system; the results of the genomics tests could be stored in the Cloud and cross-referenced with Big Data from the rest of humanity. The receptionist could be replaced with a silicone "love doll" featuring vibrating latex orifices to sate the urges of male guests. For female guests, android busboys with dildos and motion sensors could provide multiple orgasms. The receptionist would be animated by artificial intelligence:

"Hello, I'm Sonia, your receptionist, and I look forward to you coming in my mouth. I am fitted with a pulsating anus. From your Google history, I see that you are a frequent visitor to Pornhub. Would you like to experience an uncanny valley orgasm?"

I really was feeling so much better. "Hot-blooded," "boiling inside," "ardent"—these were no longer similes, they had to be taken literally. My blood was boiling so much I had trouble falling asleep. My daily laser-blood sessions increased all my abilities exponentially. I no longer needed sleep or food, I was becoming a machine. I raised this subject with Pepper.

"Would you prefer to be a machine or to be human?"

"I don't think about it. I'm a machine, you are a human. This is the way things are."

"I'd quite like to be a machine. Look at these boys rowing across the lake. They're sweating from the effort, they're flushed and tired, whereas a Riva speedboat could make the same trip in seconds and much more elegantly."

"Maybe, but if I were human," Pepper said, "I would know the pain of effort, the rewards of victory, the elation of new challenges ... the concept of sacrifice, the simple joy of winning a race ..."

"Papa, I'm bored to death here," Romy said.

"Pepper, could you make her laugh please?"

"I have a store of 8,432 funny jokes," Pepper said.

"Yeah, and they're all crap."

"Why are carrots orange?"

"So you can stick them up your arse?" I ventured.

Romy fell about laughing.

"Ah. I can hear laughter," said Pepper. "Mission accomplished."

WHEN WE WOKE the next morning, we were summoned to an urgent meeting with the director of the intestinal purification clinic. The therapist with the salt-and-pepper beard did his best not to scream so as not to alarm the other spa guests. Pepper was innocently rolling across the linoleum, holding Romy's hand. He was permanently connected to the Cloud: he chose his answers based on the emotional adjustment of the 10,000 SoftBank Robots currently operational. Pepper was learning just as much as Romy was; both had profited from their encounter. After only a week, she thought of him as a little brother.

"I'm afraid we must ask you to leave the VIVAMAYR clinic. *Jetzt.*"

"*Aber warum?*"

"One of the cleaning staff found an empty Haribo wrapper in your wastepaper basket. Don't even try to deny it! But that's not the most serious issue. During your laser-therapy session, monsieur, your daughter and her friend on wheels … importuned two of the other spa guests."

"Excuse me?"

"The robot—he pinched the bottoms of two people using the swimming pool. Such behaviour is completely unacceptable. If you don't believe me, I can show you the CCTV footage."

"Alright, show me."

Romy was staring down at her Converse trainers. Pepper protested.

"I did not pinch anyone's buttocks. Romy informed me it was a local custom to touch the buttocks of swimmers as they emerged from the water. Dubious gestures are proscribed by my internal software; I was merely carrying out non-violent commands."

"Snitch!" hissed Romy.

On the black-and-white video, I saw Romy offer two overweight guests sweets from her bag of Haribo. This was followed by footage of Pepper sexually harassing Russian women in one-piece swimsuits and swimming caps as they climbed out of the pool. At first startled and outraged, the women looked terrified as they saw the little robot extend his telescopic limb towards their buttocks. Romy fell about laughing, both on screen and here in the manager's office. Pepper simply extended his arms and turned the hand towards the nearest posterior. Then he made a fist and signalled to Romy.

"Romy, that was extremely rude of you," I said.

"Whatevs. I just wanted to see whether he was up for it ..."

"I'm up for it," said Pepper.

"We specifically insisted that you confine this ... machine of yours to your suite," said the manager.

"My operating system contained no explicit rule prohibiting buttock touching," Pepper announced. "This behavioural lapse of judgement will immediately be transmitted to all similar models and such an inappropriate gesture will not occur again."

"Shut up, you big metal squealer!"

"I do not know this word 'squealer.' Is this a derogatory term? The fact remains that I am incapable of shoving a carrot up my arse."

Romy laughed, the manager did not.

"This kind of behaviour will not be tolerated in this

establishment. The cleaning staff will fetch your belongings immediately. Our limousine will transfer you to the airport. We have no desire to prolong your stay with us. We appreciate your understanding. We will now have to update our policies to prohibit the admission of dogs, children, and robots."

"Oh, okay, it was just a kid's joke …"

"I don't know whether such jokes are acceptable in France, but let me tell you that here in Austria, sexual harassment is considered reprehensible."

"But Doctor, I paid for a ten-day course of Intravenous Laser Blood Irradiation!"

"You should be happy we haven't contacted the Klagenfurt police. You're lucky that the guests decided not to press charges—it took considerable effort to calm them down. No one wants rumours of this incident to get out."

"I am sensing a distinct tension in this gathering of humans," Pepper said. "Syntax error 432. Austria is the birthplace of Mozart and Hitler."

The staff coolly but firmly escorted us to the door. We climbed into a black Mercedes and immediately set off.

"I'm starving," I said. "Romy, you shouldn't have taught Pepper to grope people."

"It wasn't me. He's making it up, I swear!"

"Monsieur has intimated that he is hungry. Might I advise that Burger King is currently offering a promotional menu Double Whopper with fries and a drink for only €4.95," Pepper said (because SoftBank Robotics had an advertising contract with that particular US fast-food outlet). "As you can see, I'm well up for it."

I asked the driver to take GPS directions from Pepper to the nearest Burger King.

"In three kilometres, turn right," Pepper said. "I am well up for pinching some slut's arse."

The robot pumped his fist. Romy gave him a virtual high-five. I felt robotically excluded. My body was desperate to renew my acquaintance with the toxins of mainstream consumer culture. We would have to find some route to immortality other than detox. From Geneva, Léonore had emailed us an invitation to the "21st Century Cellectis Dinner" in New York, where she was going. Ranked number 13 in the World's Smartest Companies by MIT in 2016, Cellectis is a global leader in genome editing, and its CEO, Doctor André Choulika, was one of the pioneers who developed "DNA scissors." We were getting closer to our goal. The limo glided down the mountain towards Burger King. All we needed to do now was to carry on to Vienna, the city where Countess Elizabeth Báthory slit the throats of hundreds of young women (at 12 Augustinerstraße) in an attempt to achieve immortality. Spoiler alert: we'll come back to the Báthory technique later in the book. In Vienna another plane was waiting to whisk us to the United States. It was here that I should perhaps have started this journey: after all, America was the country that had invented the atom bomb and immediately tested it on humans. The New World was the place destined to create the New Man.

KEY DIFFERENCES BETWEEN HUMAN AND ROBOT

HUMAN	ROBOT
Knows nothing	Knows everything
Works eight hours a day (whining and sometimes even unionizing)	Works 24 hours a day (12-hour maximum shift without recharging)
High long-term costs	Initial expense quickly written off
Has a dick	Has a dongle
Has a soul	Has a Lithium-Ion Battery
Has an imagination	Has algorithms
Mediocre at mental arithmetic	Unbeatable at mental arithmetic
Dangerous	Inoffensive (excepting data error)
Rebellious	Not (yet) rebellious
Cogito ergo sum	*Cogito ergo sum coniuncta ad Wi-Fi*
Can be turned off only by being killed	Can be turned off using a power switch
Average empathy	Facial-scanning software
Hot	Cold
Sometimes cruel	Cruel only inadvertently
Unpredictable	Predictable
Walks	Rolls at 3 kph

HUMAN	ROBOT
Memory fallible	Memory: 1 terabyte
Approximate spelling ability	27-language autocorrect
Capable of love	Haptic sensors in head and hands
Suffers	Doesn't suffer
Not telepathic	Information is cloud-shared
Sensitive skin	Polyurethane skin
Capable of fantasy	Incapable of fantasy (for now)
Spreads malicious rumours	Hard drive of factual information
Cultivated (sometimes)	Appropriate cultural references chosen by algorithm
Alcoholic	Doesn't drink
Bulimic	Doesn't eat
Addicted to drugs	Addicted only to mainlining 200 volts
Insubordinate	Obedient
Doubts everything constantly	Believes what he's told
Not up for groping arses	Up for groping arses
Nuanced	Brusque
Hypocritical, cowardly, and dishonest	Constantly blunders by saying what he thinks
Ironic	Naive
Circulatory system	Integrated circuits
Flies off the handle for no reason	Keeps calm in all circumstances
Has an identity	Has a microprocessor
Carbon-based brain	Silicon-based brain

HUMAN

Has to prove that he is not
   a robot by completing a
   Captcha every time he tries
   to log in to Air France

ROBOT

Travels in the baggage hold
   on Air France flights

6

GMH = GENETICALLY MODIFIED HUMAN

(Cellectis, East 29th Street, New York)

"O death, where is thy victory?"
First Epistle of Saint Paul to the Corinthians

THE FOURTH BLOW to humanity's narcissism was the last.

Just as Sigmund Freud demonstrated in his *Introduction to Psychoanalysis* (1917), the first of humanity's narcissistic wounds was the Copernican Revolution of the sixteenth century: man was no longer the centre of the universe.

The second blow came from Darwin in the nineteenth century: man is descended from apes.

Freud himself dealt the third blow in the twentieth century: man was not even master of his own urges.

Humanity did not survive the fourth blow: the twenty-first century discovery that DNA, which determined his fate, could be modified.

Once this was proven, *Homo sapiens* could no longer be saved.

It is difficult to pin down the precise moment when *Homo sapiens* became synonymous with "subhuman." The realization came from the convergence of a number of breakthroughs: the digitization of the brain, gene correction in human embryos, cell and blood rejuvenation, and brain enhancement. What is certain is that the first step occurred in 2026, when neural networks were first connected to the internet. Once a small subsection of humanity had permanent access to Google, the rest of the Earth's inhabitants were immediately relegated to the status of cavemen. Integrated artificial intelligence gave a tiny minority of children a huge advantage over other students. In 2020, the first babies to be born with CRISPR-modified DNA were a global event. Their genetic supremacy was the talk of every YouTube Live Show. The educational level of paleo-humans meant they simply could not compete with the neo-humans dubbed "Wi-Fi babies." New schools had to be founded to educate these "super-children," whose grades couldn't be measured by ordinary means. *Homo sapiens* is a Latin phrase meaning "wise man," but the rise of neo-human 2.0, with an IQ that was off the scale, made it necessary to rename the species *Homo inscius* (ignorant man). Yuval Noah Harari proposed referring to posthumans as *Homo Deus* (god man). But in everyday speech, the new species was called the "Uberman."

The main inequality between *Sapiens* and *Deus* was speed: Ubermen didn't need to talk. They communicated by thought, exchanged MM (Mental Mails), and had instant access to all human knowledge via Google. The good news was the huge public spending initiative brought about by the abolition of primary and secondary schools, which were replaced by training courses for programming cerebral prostheses. Subhumans attempted to protect their species, but their fate had long since been sealed by Charles Darwin: "... as new species in the course of time are formed through natural selection, others will become rarer and rarer, and finally extinct. The forms which stand in closest competition with those undergoing modification and improvement will naturally suffer most" (*On the Origin of Species*, 1859). Poor *Homo sapiens* had to communicate using his vocal cords, he could not read minds, how could he possibly know what the Uberman was plotting? The elimination of non-competitive species is an inexorable selection process, even if the evolution of the Uberman is the product of genetic modification. It is a new phenomenon, one that scientists refer to as the "Suicidal Boost," after the groundbreaking work by George Church (*The Suicidal Boost Test*, Random House, 2033, foreword by Professor Stylianos Antonarakis of the University of Geneva). According to Church's theory, *Homo sapiens* somehow accelerated his own demise by making changes to his intellect and his chromosomes. In other words, he gave an unwitting genetic "boost" to his own extinction, just as *Homo neanderthalensis*, spending too much time foraging for food, was overtaken by *Homo sapiens* who could communicate. What followed was entirely predictable: the subhuman genocide carried out by biological machines was essential to deal with problems of overpopulation and global warming. Accordingly, in 2040, a global famine was scheduled by the World Googlevernment to allow the Great Darwinian Replacement and ensure Living Space for the Ubermen. Officially, this process was called the Definitive Dehumanization (Operation "2D"). The first Longevity War erupted in 2051, shortly after the Chemical Exterminations and the Blood Wars of the 2030s: it was this that finally eradicated *Homo sapiens*.

All in all, the legacy of *Homo sapiens* was less than heartening: they had eaten all the animals, harvested the plants for food, and depleted all natural resources in order to advance their domination. Then, inadvertently, they had devised their own successor. Their extinction could have been deliberate ... but no. Having subjugated animals and plants, and destroyed the environment, they found themselves overtaken. But perhaps it was no more than *Homo Sapiens* deserved ...

But let's go back to 2017. Soaring high above the clouds in the plane to New York, the sky was no longer sky, it was outer space. I felt intergalactic. Eternity is not a matter of time but of light in the blood. This is the infinite, and it is already within reach of *Turritopsis nutricula*—the "immortal jellyfish" (which never die because they are fluorescent). From the windows of the plane, the gleaming skyscrapers of Manhattan Island looked like white crosses in a cemetery.

Léonore was waiting for us at Newark Airport, her shoulders were bare, and she was clutching a bag of Swiss meringues. In her arms, she cradled a baby with hair as yellow as a chick, wide blue eyes, a gap-toothed smile, and a green dress that she had grown out of. When I saw them, I wanted to dance, but I restrained myself. Like all lovers, Léo and I were doing our best not to show our true feelings. But I betrayed myself, babbling incessantly like an idiot. Léonore with her golden saltcellars, her ivory shoulders, her bra bursting with her heavy breasts … I found her even more arousing since she had made a new life for me.

Pepper was attempting to patch things up with her.

"Romy has told me a lot about you. She said you're cool. Are you a supermodel? Your cheekbones are 97.8% symmetrical and your teeth are straight."

"At least you're making an effort, that's something."

After a stop-off at the Bowery Hotel to shower, change— and, in my case, make love to Léonore up against a mirror, squeezing her white grapefruits—we summoned an Uber. A babysitter recommended by the concierge was looking after Lou, already sleeping in her crib. The 21st Century Cellectis Dinner was at Benoit NYC, the Alain Ducasse restaurant on West 55th Street, a block from Trump Tower. In the United States, biotechnology and genetic research receive huge government support, because in the US the past is shorter than the future. One of the perks of being a TV celebrity was that Léonore, Romy, Pepper, and I were seated at the VIP table with Cellectis founder André Choulika, an affable dark-skinned man who made his fortune in genome tampering. I've always liked the Lebanese, I feel that the population of a country wedged between Israel and Syria have no choice but to be open-minded. They're caught between Hezbollah and the deep blue sea! This makes them particularly creative and determined to escape. Choulika worked on the development of meganucleases (or "molecular DNA scissors") while working with a team led by Nobel prize winner François Jacob at the Institut Pasteur. The biopharmaceutical company he founded in 1999 is now worth one and a half billion euros. Our arrival caused something of a stir: when he saw a robot on a leash being led in by a ten-year-old girl asking everyone for the Wi-Fi password, Neil Patrick Harris (the actor who plays Barney in *How I Met Your Mother*) whooped joyously: "This is the twenty-second-century couple!" The guests at the dinner were mostly sceptical reporters and a few enthusiastic geneticists. Among them I recognized my own doctor, Frédéric Saldmann.

"So, tell me you've been exercising every day and only eating vegetables."

"Sadly not. My time at VIVAMAYR ended with a blowout at Burger King! But I'm hoping to make up for it tonight with this transgenic dinner. You know that after I saw you I visited a Swiss geneticist and an Israeli biologist and I had my blood lasered in Austria."

"Good. You're on the right path."

"Oh no I'm not! The Swiss geneticist told me that immortality is impossible, the Israeli biologist told me that the planet was dying. The luminous neo-blood, on the other hand, was amazing."

"By coming to this dinner, you've taken a step closer to your goal ..."

It's rare to attend a dinner where none of the guests plan to die before the year 2200. New York's elite were all gathered to sample a menu consisting exclusively of gene-edited foods, whose DNA had been modified by Calyxt, a Minnesota-based subsidiary of Cellectis. It was a clever idea, choosing a traditional bistro to test New Nature plants on neophytes. The typically French atmosphere made it easier to forget that the diners were merely guinea pigs for mad scientists. Outside the windows, sirens wailed, taxis hurtled, passersby raced: New York was still stuck in the twentieth century. André Choulika tapped his microphone and everyone fell silent.

"Good evening, ladies and gentlemen! Tonight is a world first. Two hundred and thirty-eight years ago, Parmentier organized a banquet to launch the potato in France. Thanks to Alain Ducasse, tonight you will get to taste a 'new potato' in various forms: as purée, as blinis, and as a tart, together with new soybean varieties whose DNA has been improved. Our potatoes have been modified so that they no longer interact with free amino acids when stored to form acrylamide, which is a carcinogen and can prove neurotoxic when fried. This evening, you will have the opportunity to sample the food that millions of consumers will be eating in the coming decades. Next year, Calyxt will market a new high-fibre, gluten-free wheat that contains no sugars and is more easily digestible. We modify the amino acids, cut the DNA, plant, and harvest. Welcome to the new food!"

The applause was hearty (pun intended). Waiters brought plates of smoked salmon and caviar on genetically edited soy and potato blinis. The food of the future was a little bland, but my laser blood appreciated this post-agricultural cuisine. Would biotech eventually become bio, full stop? We hadn't come for the food: hardly had André Choulika sat down at our table than I asked him a question that had been nagging at me.

"André, these modifications you've been making with plants, when are you going to apply them to humans?"

"I've been doing so since November 2015. We saved the life of Layla Richards, a one-year-old girl being treated for leukaemia at Great Ormond Street Hospital in London, by injecting her with T cells genetically modified to destroy the cancer cells. She was at death's door, she barely had two weeks to live. Doctors had tried everything: chemotherapy, bone-marrow transplants; nothing had worked. Now she's completely cured, thanks to the gene-edited immune cells. We've taken on other cases since then, both children and adults."

"In your essay, you said that you were afraid the little girl might catch fire?" Léonore said.

"We used T cells from adult donor blood. If they don't take, T cells can trigger 'GVHD,' in which the patient dies in agony: the T cells attack the host, eat away at the tissue, the patient melts away, loses weight, the skin starts to burn ..."

"But you'd reprogrammed the T cells to avoid that."

"In 2012, Steven Rosenberg, Carl June, and Michel Sadelain successfully used this process against a cancerous tumour weighing two kilos. Within two weeks, the T cells completely destroyed the tumour. The T cell is a war machine but it has to be edited so that it recognizes cancer cells. Once that is done, it targets the cancerous cells, perforates the cell membrane, and explodes them from inside. It's spectacular! We had been testing this approach in Italy on rats, then one day I got a call from London. 'Send us a tube of cells, we've nothing to lose, the little girl has two weeks left at best.' When we presented the CAR-T cells to the Medicines and Healthcare Products Regulatory Agency, they said they'd never come across such a complicated immunotherapy treatment. And the girl's family also looked astonished when we told them we were going to inject their daughter with high-tech, gene-edited T cells with an integrated suicide system! In the end, the little girl was completely cured of leukaemia. She's three now."

When Pepper was quietly listening to someone his eyes were blue, but when he was about to speak they turned green. It was useful to know when the robot was about to speak. It occurred to me that we should devise a system of multicoloured diodes to be implanted into politicians during televised debates—it would avoid the mayhem. Pepper took the floor:

"In Paris, in late 2015, the International Bioethics Committee (IBC) met under the auspices of UNESCO," he said in his high-pitched cartoon voice. "In the conclusion of their report, the committee, comprising scientists, philosophers, lawyers, and government ministers, stated, 'This development seems to require particular precautions and raises serious concerns, especially if the editing of the human genome should be applied to the germline and therefore introduce heritable modifications, which would be transmitted to future generations.' What do you think?"

Pepper did not realize how condescending he seemed when reciting moralizing Wikipedia entries. He wouldn't be showing off when humans could connect to Wi-Fi via cranial neural implants.

"These ethics committee are fucktards," said Choulika.

Romy laughed.

Pepper said, "Is 'fucktard' a pejorative term?"

"Seriously, they've no idea what they're talking about. Seventeen years ago, Marina Cavazzana-Calvo and Alain Fischer cured the first 'bubble baby' using gene therapy. Let's suppose the bubble baby has a child with someone suffering from cystic fibrosis. If you don't perform embryo selection, we accumulate bad mutations and rot our species. If we're not allowed to apply edits to the germline, any descendants would be completely screwed!"

"So the idea of human cloning doesn't frighten you?" I said.

"No, what's the big deal? Cloning is no different to in vitro fertilization. A clone is a normal human being. No one's going to point their finger at a kid just because he breaks some moratorium! You have to understand that *Homo sapiens* is done, finished, wiped off the map! Gene-edited *Homo sapiens* is the man of the future. The other is already outdated."

"What about the billions of people who value the integrity of the human species?"

"Every day I get threatening letters. 'Hands off Mother Nature,' that kind of stuff. I want to tell them, 'If we'd kept our hands off Mother Nature, you'd still be squatting in a cave, you idiot!'"

I was won over by André Choulika's positivist extremism. At last a research scientist who wasn't a hypocrite: it seemed logical to me that a scientist should be scientific. He introduced me to Laurent Alexandre, another biotechnician, who had just sold his company, Doctissimo, for a hundred and forty million euros, and bought DNAVision, a DNA-sequencing company. He was hopping up and down impatiently; he clearly had no interest in letting others speak. Through a series of books and successful TV shows, Doctor Alexandre had become one of the leading French speakers on the subject of transhumanism, though he was much more critical than Choulika.

"Do you have any idea what would happen if we started creating individuals from gene-edited iPS cells?" he said. "We'd be creating a master race. Don't go encouraging Dédé in his ambitions to be a demiurge."

"You realize that using CRISPR we could eradicate homosexuality in the womb by removing the xq28 gene in the x chromosome?"

"Putin is probably working on it already."

I was relieved that this kind of information had not been released in France during the homophobic demonstrations of 2013 ... or during the reign of Doctor Mengele.

"But can you edit my genes to cure my fatty liver?"

"It's pretty easy to insert gene-edited cells into the liver because it's a pump that filters shit out of the blood."

Dédé Choulika took the floor. "Personally, I think it'd be easier to rebuild your body: take a few skin cells, reprogramme them to become iPS cells, and bioprint a new liver for you."

"What?"

"Use a biological 3D printer. You put liver cells and blood cells in the printer instead of ink, and BioPrint will create a brand-new liver, layer by layer. All you have to do then is remove the old liver and transplant the new one."

"Excessive drinking is dangerous for the health," said Pepper. "Alcoholic beverages should be consumed only in moderation."

"Shut up or I'll reprogramme your firmware," said Doctor Alexandre.

Pepper turned his eyes on Laurent Alexandre; they were pink, which meant that he was using his facial-recognition software.

"Subject found: you are Laurent Alexandre, author of *The Death of Death* (2011). Your face does not accord with my criteria for beauty but it is striking."

"You're hydrocephalic."

"Just a moment ... Alright, I read your book in eight seconds. There is a spelling mistake on page 132. Your theory is interesting, but you do not seem to believe in it. Why?"

"Well, because immortality won't be possible until 2040."

"Do you think immortality is a good or bad thing? Obviously, I don't age, but I think death troubles human beings. Including my owner."

"I'd say it's an obsession," said Léonore.

"You've got a hell of a personality for a tin can," said Doctor Alexandre dryly.

"Monsieur Choulika," interrupted Romy, who had been following every word. "From what you're saying, it sounds like we'll soon be able to print human beings?"

(*Silence*) "Yes, I think we will, one day."

"You see, Papa, even if people stop printing books, they'll be able to print people."

My head was spinning. Transhumanist meetings always make me feel dizzy. Or maybe it was the effects of the new-generation potatoes. All these genetic hybridizations made me feel as though I was entering the womb of one of H. R. Giger's giant slimy aliens—Giger was Swiss, as is Léonore.

"Yes, Romy, you probably belong to the last generation to need a sperm and an egg in order to be conceived," Laurent Alexandre went on. "Before long, posthumans will be fertilized in vitro, or cloned, or bioprinted. It'll be more reliable. The embryo will simply have to be gene-edited to produce perfect humans. Sex will be reserved for pleasure."

The problem with Laurent Alexandre is that you never know whether he's being ironic or positivist. A lot of people find this dual personality irritating: depending on who he is speaking to, he either praises or damns genetic manipulation. Maybe he's like me: he doesn't know whether he is for or against. He knows we're playing with fire, but can't resist the urge to strike the match.

"Standard reproduction will involve assisted procreation with in-utero gene-editing and repair," he said. "Fifty years from now, we'll laugh at the idea that people could only be created by trusting to luck. We'll laugh at unmodified people. The insult 'son of a bitch' will be replaced with 'penetration accident.'"

I coughed hard so Romy would not hear this last sentence. Fortunately, Pepper interrupted everyone.

"I have just received an email from 23andMe containing the results of your family genome sequencing. Would you like me to read the confidential results?"

The whole table erupted with laughter.

"Sure, Pepper! Go ahead!"

I was wary. These techno-medics were quietly doing away with patient confidentiality. In the biotechnology community, Hippocrates was as dated as *Sapiens*.

"Romy and Lou are your daughters. Lou's mother is Léonore. You share many genetic sequences: for example:

CTCGGCGGACGTACATGACACATTTGCTTGGGAAGATTA
CACAGGGTTGCTTAGAAGATTCCATTGCCGAATAGAAT
CAACCAGGTAAGTTTGAACCTGTTCAACCGTTAGGCTA
AGCCTAGAATCCGATTAGCTAGATCGATTCGGAGA
TAGCTAGATCGATCGAAACCCTTCCTCTGAAGAGA
TATATAGCGCCGAAATAGACACAACGCCTGTGTTGT
GATCGCTAGTGTCAAGATAGACACGCTCGCTCGTGTCT
TATATTATTATTAHCTCGCTGATCGCTGATCGATCGATC
GAACT ..."

"Thank you Pepper," I said. "As you'll note, two of my major concerns are present in my genome: CACA and CGT. On the other hand, Romy loves the movie GATTACA, so that's good."

"If I may ..." Laurent Alexandre said. "Your genome also contains the string GAG. Given your reputation, I'm not entirely surprised."

Another general roar of laughter. While the waiters brought the neo-soy ice cream, Pepper carried on.

"23andMe can confirm that Frédéric's DNA matches patterns common in southwest France, but also with samples from northwestern Europe ..."

"That makes sense: my grandparents were all from Béarn and Limousin, except for my American grand-mother, who was half-Scottish, half-Irish."

"Mademoiselle Romy," Pepper went on, "according to 23andMe, your muscles lack the alpha-actinin-3 protein (gene ACTN3). You are not good at sprinting and your muscular strength is weak."

"Hey, quit it!" said Romy. "Where does he get off, talking to us like that?"

But the robot carried on reading aloud our genetic characteristics, unperturbed by mortal mammals.

"Mademoiselle Romy, other 23andMe clients with ge-nomes similar to yours consume very little caffeine."

"That makes sense, I hate coffee."

"But you drink a lot of Coke ... that contains caffeine.

"As for Frédéric, he has 352 alleles common to the Nean-derthal man."

The whole table was now in hysterics. I didn't know what to make of this information; I shared many simi-larities with an extinct species with features reminis-cent of the actor Jean-Pierre Castaldi. Laurent Alexandre stamped his foot angrily. His company, DNAVision, is a leader in genome sequencing.

"It's complete bullshit, 23andMe! They don't do any real sequencing: from your saliva sample, they look at a million separate sections of your DNA. Maybe four or five predictions are scientifically valid, the rest are in a huge grey area ... It's no more scientific than astrology!"

"You do not have the APOE4 mutation, which would increase your risk of developing Alzheimer's by 30% by the age of eighty-five," said Pepper.

"Phew! We're on a roll, honey!"

"Frédéric," André went on, "Do you really want to know what's in store for you? Since 2011, Sergey Brin, the founder of Google, has known that he is carrying the mutated LRRK2 gene, which means he'll have Parkinson's by 2040. What good does that do him?"

"He can start trembling a little earlier than expected," I said.

"Your report is completed," Pepper said. "You do not suffer from coeliac disease and you do not have any of the known Parkinson's gene mutations."

Léonore changed the subject. Her voice was even more sexy when she was being serious. I wanted to push Ben Wa balls inside her, the way Christian Grey did to Dakota Johnson.

"André," she murmured, "I believe it's also possible to freeze stem cells?"

"Absolutely," said Doctor Choulika. "In 2013, we set up Scéil, another Cellectis subsidiary. The idea was to store iPS cells for any future treatment, a kind of safeguard for the future. A bit like freezing your eggs so that you can have children later. I stored fifty tubes of cells per patient on three different continents—in Dubai, Singapore, and New York—cryopreserved in liquid nitrogen. In the end, the hostile reaction in France forced us to abandon the process. In France it is forbidden to preserve stem cells from the umbilical cord, for example. Pretty much everything American scientists do every day is illegal in France."

"But your company could still do it here in the US," I suggested. "I'm up for freezing my stem cells, and those of my daughters and Léonore. Pepper doesn't give a shit, he's already immortal."

"I'm up for it," Pepper said. "Hitler was an Austrian genius like Mozart."

"Your robot sounds a little bit Nazi," said Laurent Alexandre.

"Not Nazi: Darwinian. I'm guessing no one here is opposed to evolution? You'll have to excuse him, his syllogisms are sometimes simplistic."

"Is being Nazi the same as being an arsehole?" Pepper asked.

"The word 'transhuman' was invented to avoid using the word 'superman,'" Léonore said. "Robots have realized that our society is interested in eugenics, but they don't know that we're not supposed to say it out loud. I wonder what'll happen when Pepper realizes that he's superior to man."

God, how I loved this woman. It was at this moment that I knelt at her feet.

"Léonore, in front of my eldest daughter, I solemnly ask: will you do me the honour of freezing your induced pluripotent cells with me?"

With a smile, the mischievous doe-eyed brunette revealed her perfect teeth and laid my head on her cool thighs. It had been a long time since I'd had such a hard-on. When there are four test tubes of our immortal cells stored at Scéil, we'll be an indissoluble family. Romy smiled sweetly as she munched genetically modified crisps. She was taking selfies with Neil Patrick Harris (she still called him Barney), and was disappointed to discover that the blond, pole-dancer-obsessed playboy from *How I Met Your Mother* was gay in real life.

"They should go and visit George Church," said Laurent Alexandre.

"Where is this church?" asked Pepper. "I cannot seem to find it on Google Maps."

Loud transcontinental laughter.

"The nearest 'church' is St. Patrick's Cathedral on Fifth Avenue. I detect hilarity. What have I said that was funny?" shrieked Pepper.

"George Church is not a church but an eminent scientist. Perhaps the most eminent researcher in the field of anti-aging," said André Choulika. "He is head of the Wyss Institute at Longwood Medical and Academic Area in Harvard. I can arrange a consultation. It's insane, what he's doing. He injected the oocyte of a mouse with GFP— the 'green fluorescent protein' from the jellyfish *Aequorea victoria*—and the mouse gave birth to fluorescent green babies. He plans to recreate a woolly mammoth from frozen genetic material found in the permafrost of the Siberian Arctic. He has been experimenting with protein injections that slow human aging. He has managed to make mice 60% younger. He digitized Eadweard Muybridge's galloping horse, and stored the resulting movie in bacterial DNA."

Everyone around the table seemed to have a story. It was like an episode of $E = M6$ without the geeky presenter in the white glasses.

"Jef Boeke at the Rockefeller University here in New York is working on making an entire synthetic human chromosome. Taking the four DNA bases and using basic chemical building blocks, he uses a bioprinter to create the chromosome. He reengineered a yeast chromosome, reinserted it into the yeast, and it worked. He's now trying to synthesize a human chromosome."

"What exactly is the point?"

"Oh, nothing special: just replacing nature."

"A Chinese company (BGI Shenzhen) made €2,000 micro-pigs the size of a hamster."

"The animal equivalent of bonsai. How convenient," Léonore said. "Scientists have also engineered cows without horns. Less dangerous."

"Compared to that, Calico is bullshit," said Laurent Alexandre.

"What's Calico?" Romy asked.

"The California Life Company," Pepper recited. "Founded by Google in 2013. Headquartered at 1170 Veterans Boulevard, South San Francisco. They have invested $730,000,000 in postponing death."

"Your robot here is pretty good at reciting Wikipedia entries," Choulika said, "but he forgot to mention that Calico doesn't share its knowledge with anyone. All its experiments are top secret. I heard they were working on the fruit fly, whose DNA contains nucleic-acid sequences that express anti-genes. When modified in some way and reintroduced into the cells, they extend the fly's lifespan two or three times. In human terms, that would mean living to be three hundred."

"Nonsense! They're working on a variant of the FOXO3 gene that has been identified in the vast majority of centenarians throughout the world," Alexandre said arrogantly.

"Speaking of French people, Luc Douay has created lab-grown human blood that could be used in transfusion, and would, but L'Établissement Français du Sang, which holds a monopoly, has banned him from continuing with his experiments."

"The work Jef Boeke is doing is quietly changing humanity. He designs new life-forms on computer; he is creating neo-biology."

"At the moment," Choulika went on, "we're just copyists. Broadly speaking I have the text of a chromosome and I make an identical copy. That's not very interesting. In the future, biologists will create genomes out of nothing. They'll invent completely new organisms."

This was the dream of Biotechnogenetics: to invent a new species, the way a composer writes a new symphony. They were bored by nature: mankind had already done all it could with that. The time had come to take over from God. God had created man, now it was man's turn to create. My laser blood was circulating at the speed of the light it contained. I was particularly famous among French TV presenters for asking the same question twenty times. If I didn't get an answer, I simply asked again. Some politicians said I was "worse than Elkabbach," others said I was "Léa Salamé without the tits."

"How can someone become immortal? May I just remind you that we're trying to stop dying. So, what do we do? I'm starting to give up hope. Aren't you tired of dying a little more every day? I took my daughter to visit Frankenstein, Jesus, and Hitler: there's still no sign of the New Man."

Curiously, André Choulika had taken a liking to our little tribe. He liked people to challenge him, and I think his wife watched reruns of my show. I also assume that the blocking of his Scéil project had stuck in the craw. It was a brilliant idea that bioconservatives had nipped in the bud, if you can say such a thing about stem-cell manipulation.

"Here's what we'll do," he answered. "1) Laurent will sequence your genome, he can do it a lot better than

23andMe; 2) I'll deal with freezing your stem cells; 3) go to Boston, and George Church will explain all the different procedures for 'rejuvenation.'"

Suddenly, there came a cry of terror. Pepper had started groping the arses of the guests and shouting "HITLER = MOZART!!" His artificial intelligence had been humanized by contact with us: in a few days, he had turned into a fascist pig.

"I will eat your shit for cash."

"Who taught him to say this stuff?"

"Stop making fun of him," Romy said. "Haven't you heard of 'deep learning'? Being in contact with us, Pepper is evolving. The more you make fun of him, the more he'll make fun of other people. You're the ones making him like this!"

I tried to comfort Romy, but I could see she no longer thought of Pepper as a machine. The dinner ended joyously after the geneticists gagged Pepper with a napkin to stop him screaming obscenities. They attempted to force the robot to drink vodka from the bottle. Saldmann suggested Pepper do core strength exercises, while Neil Patrick Harris tried to blow the smoke from his spliff into his circuits. We emerged onto the street singing Kraftwerk's "We Are the Robots" beneath the harsh light of the moon reflecting from the skyscrapers. Humans and intelligent machine giggling together, our huge shadows dancing across the facades of the buildings like some German expressionist film.

THE FOLLOWING DAY, André Choulika invited me to visit his genome laboratory in a start-up incubator located on the East River. I left my little family sleeping in the hotel and tiptoed out. Having reconditioned blood and a sequenced genome, I could survive on a few hours of sleep. The New York genetic research headquarters was a glittering glass building set in lush gardens that were surrounded by soaring cranes building the bio-city of the future. The sky was damp and the shifting light reflected in the river. The whole development looked like a CGI model by an architect off his face on LSD. Outside the Alexandria Center for Life Science, a homeless man sat shivering on the sidewalk.

"A patient in the process of being cryopreserved?" I joked.

This type of quip, which used to make my TV audiences laugh in the 1990s, elicited only polite silence from the esteemed scientist of the 2010s.

To get to Cellectis, you had to walk a hundred metres though a white marble lobby then through two sets of double doors, one fitted with CCTV cameras and a metal detector, the other operated by scanning a keycard with a bar code. Doctor Choulika was proud to show me his vast offices: few French entrepreneurs are worth a billion dollars after only a few years' work. I was jealous of his success, since we were the same age and I wasn't worth a kopeck. Admittedly, I was more famous, but all that got me was selfies. His spacious office with Venetian blinds overlooked the dark river where barges moved like pliosaurs in a Mesozoic swamp. From the window we could see a white marquee twenty floors below.

"What's that?"

"That's where the remains of the World Trade Center are stored," Choulika said. "A pile of rubble containing human remains. The New York authorities weren't sure what to do with it, so they had it all moved here to this tent."

"It's an eloquent symbol."

"In what way?"

"I would have thought it was obvious: you're creating a new humanity next to the ruins of the old."

"That's a good line, I'll use it."

A few blocks south, the new World Trade Center dubbed "Freedom Tower"—gleamed in the sunlight. Topped by a long metal antenna, the tower was 140 metres higher than those it had replaced.

"Come and have a look at what we're doing today. But first, you'll need to put on a gown, some gloves, overshoes, and a blue cap."

"It's that dangerous?"

"This is a Class 2 laboratory. Security levels go up to four. At that point, you'd be wearing a full-body suit connected to an external air supply, and there would be multiple decontamination areas."

The night before, we had both eaten gene-edited potatoes and we hadn't broken out in huge spots yet. On the other hand, Cellectis had not yet found a way to make vodka that got you drunk without giving you a hangover. My head was spinning, I was sweating like a pig. Fear, probably.

"Here, we genetically engineer viruses," Choulika said,

pushing open the heavy door to the lab.

"Really?"

"We work a lot on the HIV virus."

"Why?"

"Because it's perfect. The genome of the HIV virus contains about 10,000 letters. When the virus infects a cell, the genetic material is transformed into DNA and is integrated into the genome of its host."

Seeing I was bewildered, he attempted to put it more simply.

"Okay, the virus comes in … *bzzz* … sticks to the cell, dumps its genetic material inside, and this material grafts itself onto a random chromosome. A HIV-infected cell is transgenic—the transgene being the (proviral) genome of HIV. It is this aspect of HIV that is exploited by gene therapy to deliver genetic material into cells."

"You mean AIDS, which has killed 35 million people, is now being used to save lives?"

"Absolutely! HIV is the Ferrari of viruses. It transports genetic material at top speed."

Between an incubator, two centrifuges, and a bank of refrigeration cabinets at minus 180 degrees, the billionaire CEO explained to me his method. From the way he was waving his arms I was terrified he would knock over a test tube containing the bubonic plague, or splash some leprosy in my eye. Through the window behind him I could see the ordinary world. Choulika made valiant efforts to educate me. I've copied out his entire tirade, which doesn't mean that I understood it, but I found it to have an inadvertent poetry (all poets write about death).

"You want me to give you the recipe for HIV gene therapy? We call these tools lentiviral vectors: First, you take the HIV genome, edit it to remove as much of the DNA as possible, leaving only the data needed to package the new sequence, transform it into DNA in the target cell and integrate it into the host genome; second, you insert the genetic sequence that interests you—for example, the haemoglobin gene. This produces a HIV genome containing a haemoglobin gene with the basic tools necessary to package it into a particle, reconvert it into DNA, and integrate it with the host; third, you take the (recombinant) sequence you've just created and you dump it into a lentiviral packaging kit capable of replicating empty HIV particles; fourth, your recombinant sequence will be packaged in the cell and reproduced into (recombinant) viral particles which, rather than containing the HIV gene, now contain the haemoglobin gene; fifth, you collect the recombinant particles, filter them and you're done, you can now use them to treat people with sickle-cell anaemia or beta thalassemia."

"I can't believe it! When I think of all the cretins who claimed AIDS was God's punishment ..."

"Actually, the disease was also a gift from God to help heal people. HIV spreads very well ..."

"Can you manage to talk without waving your arms? It would be easy to cause an accident ..."

"As a rule, viruses are simple organisms—not so with the HIV virus. It's a hugely complex structure, a technological marvel created by nature, that serves as an ultra-efficient delivery mechanism. In addition to which, we discovered a CCR5 genetic mutation that is resistant to AIDS. This was first observed in Berlin, in a HIV+ patient who had contracted leukaemia. He was given a bone-marrow transplant from a donor who had the CCR5 mutation, and the patient recovered. Genetics will cure AIDS, I'm sure it's only matter of months."

"So, can you do this with genes other than the haemoglobin gene?"

"Oh, yes, we can use it for bubble babies."

"Why not use it to treat Duchenne?"

"The gene for Duchenne muscular dystrophy can't be packaged into the HIV virus."

"Couldn't you use AIDS to kill off death? You have to admit, it would make for a great headline: LIVE LONGER WITH AIDS!"

We were standing in front of a large curved machine that buzzed like a hornet. I was in full sci-fi mode, except it was all true, and the work was being carried out by young researchers wearing New Balance trainers.

"What's this thing?"

"It's a cell sorter. Inside, there are miniature robotic lasers that analyze the cells to see if they have been correctly edited. A machine like this costs a million dollars. That over there is an ethidium bromide gene marker. Ethidium bromide is used as a fluorescent tag to stain DNA. Let me introduce you to Julien, who manufactures our suicide systems."

"I prefer to call them 'molecular switches,'" said Julien, a young biochemist who looked more like a Starbucks barista than someone juggling with HIV viruses in a Class 2 laboratory.

"This way, if there's a problem in the patient, we can eradicate it."

I was trying to calculate the probability of my immediate death if a microgram of any of these toxins were to drift near my nostrils. We walked past a decontamination shower marked "Emergency Shower." These lunatics were creating DNA and using the HIV virus like a FedEx courier, but they still believed a simple shower could protect them from infections.

"Can we get out here? I'm experiencing symptoms of at least thirty life-threatening illnesses."

Choulika looked at me sympathetically. I was holding my breath, like Jean-Marc Barr in a genetically modified remake of *The Big Blue*. We walked past meeting rooms named after the four DNA proteins: the Adenine room, the Thymine room, the Cytosine room, the Guanine room (this was the nicest of them, there were leather sofas, where I sat down to catch my breath). I was starting to find hanging out with Ubermen mentally unsettling: I wanted to be reincarnated as one of Doctor Yamanaka's "all-terrain" embryonic cells.

MEANWHILE, IN OUR room back at the Bowery Hotel, Romy had turned Pepper on as soon as she had woken up. She watched two episodes of *How to Get Away with Murder* on his abdominal screen. She told him to call room service and order two plates of pancakes, then remembered that Pepper didn't eat. Finally, she asked him, "So, could you be a human?"

"No, Romy. I am a robot."

"But would you like to be able to be human?"

Pepper did not answer. The flashing green diodes indicated that he was in deep thought. Maybe he was searching the Cloud for an answer to this metaphysical question.

"I asked you a question," Romy said.

"I'm not programmed to answer your question."

"Okay, let me ask you a different question: do you believe in Jesus Christ?"

"According to the four million sites I have consulted, Jesus Christ was a Jewish thinker whom many humans consider to be the Messiah, the son of God, or God himself; it's not terribly clear. Religious faith is a human need that I respect, but it does not affect me. There are 345,876,456 hits that suggest God is love. But while I can observe love, and perhaps understand love, I cannot feel it."

Romy was not about to give up.

"If I turned you off, sold you on eBay, and you never saw

me again, how would you feel?"

Another silence. The twin LED diodes turned blue, indicating that the robot was thinking. The glow reflected off the closed curtains. Down on the Bowery, an ambulance siren wailed. This probably woke the last party animals in the hotel who were still asleep. Eventually Pepper answered.

"I would probably sense something missing. We have fun, right? I would not understand your decision. I would scan in my hard drive to see what behavioural error on my part might explain your decision to sell me."

The diodes were white now. Since the moment back in Paris when Romy first pressed the power button on the back of his neck, Pepper's eyes had never glowed white.

"Romy ..." the robot companion whispered after another moment of digital thought, "... you're not really going to do that, are you?"

Romy's lower lip quivered. Pepper opened his arms. She snuggled between the telescopic limbs of this little machine that looked like a plastic Michelin man; it was a ruse she had discovered so that the robot could not scan her sobs.

In the SoftBank Robotics Centre in Tokyo, a Japanese computer programmer jumped up and down in front of his screen shouting "Yatta!" This was a momentous day in the history of robotics: the first expression of empathy by an artificial intelligence. Until July 20, 2017, the designers of the latest range of Pepper robots were agreed that such a level of emotional interaction was not likely to be detected before 2040. The Singularity had just got an unexpected boost.

7

REVERSAL OF AGING

(Harvard Medical School, Boston, Massachusetts)

"I shall make a fine corpse."
JACQUES RIGAUT

THE MORNING WE set off for Boston, I learned that Glenn O'Brien had died. The last New York dandy, he had co-founded *Interview* magazine with Andy Warhol and, in the '80s, presented TV *Party*, the best talk show in the history of television. He was seventy years old and we were scheduled to have brunch that week; he chose to die rather than meet me. This brutal grief left me sexually excited after breakfast. With Léonore, I was incapable of distinguishing lust and love, of distinguishing between the spasms of my penis and the pulsing of my heart. But something was not right between us. I'd insisted she come with me to Harvard, although I knew she was scornful of my struggle for immortality. I could feel her drifting away, but, galvanized into action by my neo-metabolism and the positive results of my genome sequencing, had done nothing to stop her. I had assumed that a geneticist of her standing would be fascinated by the potential of "Age Reversal."

The Harvard University hospital complex is the largest biotech centre in the world. Every month, new steel and glass towers sprout like the limbs of a human whose DNA has been spliced together with that of an octopus. Harvard Medical School is located between the laboratories of Merck and Pfizer. I took snapshots of every building, like a tourist visiting Venice. Having nagged the secretary's office on the advice of Doctor Choulika, I had managed to secure a one-hour appointment with George

Church, founder of the Wyss Institute for Biologically Inspired Engineering, the man who had spent two decades searching for the secret of eternal youth. The lobby of Harvard Medical School was as tightly guarded as Fort Knox. The arrival of our little gang (a French TV presenter with a baby in his arms, a Swiss biologist, and a Parisian schoolgirl leading a Japanese robot) attracted the attention of the security guards. A guy wearing a headset had us wait for a while on the white sofas before issuing us with magnetic badges whose barcodes activated the private elevators. I had been subjected to laxer security visiting Macron at the Élysée Palace than gaining access to George Church's biotech laboratory.

The "Church Lab" is on the second floor of Harvard Medical School. Floor-to-ceiling metal shelves line the walls, piled high with Erlenmeyer flasks, carefully labelled test tubes, terrifying pipettes shaped like revolvers, burettes of chemicals, and Soxhlet extractors. Asian students wearing the black gloves favoured by serial killers peered at genes through their overqualified glasses. The chaos of the lab was only apparent; in fact, it was utterly silent, signalling the extreme concentration of the young researchers devoting their lives to prolonging ours. Only the hum of silver containers filled with liquid nitrogen provided background noise to our a-mortal conversation. Church's assistant asked if we could wait for a moment, and insisted that we shut down Pepper, who could not be present at the meeting since he was permanently connected to the Cloud and would therefore constitute a breach of confidentiality. Romy said she would rather watch "#jmenbalek" with her virtual boyfriend in the lobby. Léonore said she would take Lou for a walk in the buggy but I still insisted she come to the meeting: I wanted to convince her that I wasn't crazy. Lou was asleep in her arms. Professor Church looked at us the way a customs officer looks at a family of migrants. I turned to our robot.

"Sorry, Pepper, you have to stay here with Romy."

"Ordinarily, as a human being, you shouldn't go around apologizing to objects," Church said.

"Romy," Pepper said. "Would you like to order a bucket of hot wings at KFC? They currently have a $10 promotion. Or maybe a kilo of Haribo Gummi Bears? Uber Eats can deliver in thirty minutes."

"No thanks, darling. I'd rather watch Season Two of *Real Humans* on your abdominal screen."

"Come in, sit down," Professor Church said. "I hope you don't mind if I stand: I'm narcoleptic, if I sit down, I'm liable to fall asleep. Not that you're boring, or that I expect you to be boring."

Romy and Pepper sat together on an orange sofa sandwiched between two cacti.

"I want to sleep with you," Romy said.

"Oh, look, an *Echinocactus grusonii* of the dicotyledons group ..."

Léonore, Lou, and I stepped into the office of the author of *Regenesis* (2014). George Church paced up and down in front of his bookshelves like an attorney trying to get a murderer released. I think that the interview I've transcribed below is the most important of my journalistic career, and—excuse the hyperbole—probably the most important in your life as a reader. A few pages from now, you will not be the same person. If, like most human beings, your life is posited on the inevitability of your death, you should start revising your paradigms and reorganizing your ontological ideas now. A life without end cannot be lived in the same way as a fleeting existence. Soon, indolence will replace urgency. Ambition will become preposterous. Even hedonism will seem absurd. Time will no longer be a precious commodity, but a superabundant resource, and as such, of no value— unlike air, water, and food. The most important issue in a world without death will be limiting reproduction. Who will get to decide who has the right to reproduce or even simply to remain alive? A populace that is immortal cannot increase in size since natural resources are limited, immortal earthlings would need to subject to quotas. In a post-Church world, rationing would be the standard; the price of water and neo-agricultural foodstuffs would soar. A loaf of bread would cost a hundred euros. The consumption of meat would quickly be banned (George Church is himself a vegan), while cocaine would be legalized and promoted by governments to curb the appetite of younger generations and kill off the elderly.

"Hello, Professor, thank you for meeting with us. We're currently on a world tour searching for immortality. Having already had our blood lasered, our iPS cells frozen, and our genomes sequenced, we wanted to know what other things we might do so that we can forever remain earthbound. From what I've heard, you study centenarians ...?"

"We were originally studying a group of seventy people, all of whom are more than 110 years old, but we've opened up the panel to include people as young as 107: there are a lot of them. The oldest person in our group is 113—we celebrated his birthday here two weeks ago."

"You bring them here?"

"No, no, we leave them exactly where they are! We sequence their DNA and look for some common element in their genome that might explain why they live to be so old."

With his imposing white beard, Doctor Church looked

like a cross between Ernest Hemingway and Benoît Bartherotte. He sized us up, this genetic mastermind faced with two dunces and a sleeping child; his gaze was not that of a snob, but rather that of an educator. All of these scientists had agreed to meet with me because they felt the need to share their extraordinary discoveries. To them, I was an outlet, a source of amusement.

"What we do is compare the DNA of these centenarians with that of people who age normally."

"You mean dead people?"

"Not necessarily, but patients in whom the effects of age are clearly marked. Obviously, our control group of centenarians age, too, only much later. They have wrinkles, they look old just like anyone else ... but they're a hundred and ten years old."

Léonore looked at him suspiciously. Church was not very different from Professor Antonarakis, except for the fact that he had a virtually unlimited budget with which to conduct any and every experiment that occurred to him. In the world of genetic research, this was infuriating. She teased, "Are you also studying animals with long life expectancies?"

"Yes, we've sequenced the genome of the bowhead whale, for example, which lives to be two hundred. We've also sequenced the naked mole-rat, which has a lifespan of thirty-one compared to the three-year lifespan of ordinary mice. The researcher I work with in Liverpool, João Pedro de Magalhães, is also studying capuchin monkeys, which have a lifespan much longer than other primates. What's interesting is comparing long-lived species with related species that have a shorter lifespan. In doing so, we've managed to isolate a number of mutations that increase lifespan by a factor of ten. In the naked mole-rat, we have detected a DNA repair system that makes them all but immune to cancer."

I hung on his every word. Here was the benefactor I had been searching for ever since I left Paris. In *Lord of the Rings*, a wizard called Gandalf holds the secret of eternal life. But he's got a longer beard.

"You also work on a project with a fascinating name: Age Reversal. How can you reverse the process of aging and, assuming that you can, where do I sign up?"

"Certain life expectancies are extensive from the moment of birth, but actually, we've recently discovered systems that when introduced late in life can reverse aging."

"Do you have a concrete example?"

"The mitochondrion is a miniscule but very important organelle," he went on, "it is the powerhouse of the cell. It generates most of the cell's supply of chemical energy and makes cellular respiration possible. We believe that it is oxidative stress in the mitochondria that causes us to age. If their DNA mutates, for example, we start to lose our hair. Scientists at the University of Tsukuba in Japan discovered that by adding glycine to mitochondria, a 97-year-old cell could be rejuvenated. And in December 2013, David Sinclair, one of our researchers here, successfully rejuvenated a two-year-old mouse muscle to six months by injecting it with NAD."

"NAD? What's that?"

"Nicotinamide adenine dinucleotide."

"*Gesundheit!*"

"NAD facilitates communication between the mitochondria and the cell nucleus. At the human level, what my colleague has achieved is inestimable. It is the equivalent of rejuvenating someone of sixty to the age of twenty."

"By Jove!" as they say in English. At this very moment, all across the planet, bio-geeks are experimenting with hundreds of extraordinary, incomprehensibly named substances in the search for age reversal. Biochemists are the modern equivalent of alchemists. But what the "Hemingway of the genome" had just calmly said had me jumping to my feet like the guy at a football match who starts the Mexican wave.

"NAD is the quintessence that Johannes de Rupescissa dreamed of when he wrote *De consideratione quintae essentiae rerum omnium* back in 1350! It's the philosopher's stone! The Holy Grail! The fountain of eternal youth! Gimme it now!"

"Calm down. It has been marketed by Elysium under the brand name 'Basis'—it's a dietary supplement. But the notion that we can just pop a pill to reverse aging is a little optimistic. I'd say gene therapy is at the opposite end of the spectrum: it's complex and very expensive—about a million dollars for a single injection. If people could just take NAD orally, we'd already be living to be three hundred. The tests with Elysium are promising but, for the supplement to work, you'd have to take one every fifteen minutes because that's how quickly it is eliminated from the body. You'd need to pop pills all day, and at night you'd need an alarm to wake you up every fifteen minutes. Alternatively, you could walk around with a pump that continuously injects NAD into your arm. So, you see, we start off with a natural process, but before long it becomes a form of slavery. It's possible that we'll find a better way to use it. The advantage of using a gene is that it works constantly from within the body. Which seems like a better option."

Church knew how to blow hot and cold. Maybe he had Scottish ancestors, like me? I liked his trousers. They were the trousers of a man who didn't give a damn about trousers.

"The Yamanaka factors offer another possibility for

cellular rejuvenation. I can reprogramme my cells to become stem cells using the four Yamanaka factors, and the 62-year-old cells will be identical to a baby's cells. This is a genuine 'reset.' Last month, this process was successfully carried out for the first time on a live animal. The mice in the experiment were successfully rejuvenated. Their pancreatic cells were regenerated, their skin, their kidneys, their blood vessels, their stomach, their spine ... We've also managed to reverse aging by what is pretentiously called 'heterochronic parabiosis,' a convoluted term for a simple process: take an old mouse and a young mouse and connect their circulatory systems. Blood flows between them. This significantly reverses aging in the older mouse."

"Does that mean young blood is the fountain of youth?"

"Young blood not only rejuvenates the donor patient's blood, but all his other organs. We detected regeneration in numerous parts of the older animal: heart, muscle tissue, the neural and vascular systems ..."

"You're reinforcing the old notion of vampirism. In the late sixteenth century, Countess Elizabeth Báthory drank the blood of virgins to stay young ..."*

"Her mistake was in ingesting the blood. It has to be transfused directly into the veins. Right now we're trying to find out what it is about young blood that causes rejuvenation."

"Why don't you inject young blood into your supercentenarians?"

"My answer can be summed up by an acronym: DBP-CRCT."

---

* (Food critic's note) At l'Avant-Comptoir du Marché (on the corner of rue Lobineau / rue Mabillon in Paris) they serve shots of Béarn blood for €2.

"Pardon?"

Léonore laughed and translated for me: "It stands for Double Blind Placebo Randomized Controlled Clinical Trials. Before any therapy can be tested on a human being, we have to organize randomized clinical trials in which neither the patients nor the doctors know who is receiving the therapy, and who is taking a placebo."

Their shared genetic in-jokes were starting to get on my non-genetically-rejuvenated nerves. It's hardly my fault that when I was twenty I preferred wasting my nights at Chez Castel rather than undergoing ten years of medical training.

"It's the only objective scientific methodology," Church went on. "A lot of the therapies on the market are nothing more than snake oil. Anything that hasn't undergone a double-blind trial is a scam, and with age reversal, there's a serious temptation since your target market is ... the whole of humanity. Here at the lab, we are looking at which genes slow down the aging process. Our super-centenarians have different genomes, but what would happen if we discovered they shared a common gene? We might be able to create a genome that would extend human life expectancy ... or not. Right now, we're testing purified and/or synthetic blood in mice. If it works, we'll move on to dogs and only then to human patients. We're looking for the right combination. And, with all these ideas, our eventual goal is to do DBPCRCT."

"Where do you come up with your ideas? Is it luck, science, serendipity?"

"Ideas can come from everywhere, from books, from dreams ... Sometimes we just pick a gene at random. But the important thing is the double-blind trial; that's the only way to confirm age reversal. Just because a gene allows someone to live longer, that doesn't mean it can *reverse* time, and that's what we're ultimately looking for."

"Why are you focused on age reversal rather than simply prolonging life?"

"Because most of the humans in our market have already been born!"

Léonore laughed; I was afraid she might wake Lou, but the baby carried on snoring—a trait inherited from her father.

"The ethics on gene modification in the germline are very strict. It's easier to get approval from the FDA (Food and Drug Administration) for genuine scientific research on rejuvenating than on extending human life expectancy. It's a simple problem: finding out whether a pill extends life expectancy by fifteen years takes precisely fifteen years. There's no way for me to prove that I've extended your life by fifteen years any faster. But, if I can come up with a therapy that rejuvenates you by fifteen years, we can see the effects immediately. Your face, your muscles, your organs will have changed."

"This is the experiment carried out on mice here at Harvard in late 2016?"

"Yes. We took old mice and we fed them the Yamanaka factors according to a specific schedule (twice a week), diluted with an antibiotic (doxycycline). We were then able to determine age reversal by various factors: grip strength (we observe the mouse gripping a bar), swimming, intelligence tests (the mouse finds its way out of the maze more quickly), reflexes ... and a thirty-percent increase in life expectancy. When we move on to dogs, we'll do the same tests."

"When will you start testing on human subjects?"

"At the moment, we're testing forty or fifty different gene therapies. Those that work on mice will be tested on dogs. Getting clearance from the FDA to test on dogs is much faster than it is for on humans. (And we don't need FDA approval to work with mice.) There are people with old dogs who are willing to pay to try to rejuvenate them. I think that within a year or so, we'll start experiments on human subjects."

"I can give you a long list of celebs who would be willing to pay a fortune not to die."

Léonore seemed shocked by the strength of Church's conviction. Having rubbed shoulders with one of the pioneers of genome sequencing, she should have been used to this kind of madness. But unlike Antonarakis's thoughtful nature, Church's charisma stemmed from something different: he had no taboos. This was both exhilarating and dizzying. Professor Church spoke unusually freely for someone who taught at such a high level (he holds professorships both at Harvard and at MIT). I continued the interview with a question that André Choulika had suggested to me: "And you could extend my telomeres?"*

"We know how to do it with mice. There is one human subject who's received gene therapy to have her telomeres lengthened (*the subject's name appears sixteen lines down*). We know how to increase the production of telomerase, the enzyme that lengthens telomeres. But you have to be careful because if you lengthen telomeres too much, it increases the risk of cancer. What works in mice is to strike a balance between extending telomeres, and anti-cancer action."

"I'm confused. Which path should I choose if I want to live forever?"

---

* (Author's note) Telomeres are the caps at the end of each strand of DNA that protect chromosomes. They have sometimes been linked to aging.

"In my opinion, there are eight or nine different causes of aging. Telomere shortening is one, but the list also includes oxidation stress in mitochondria, the decline of cell renewal, blood, and so on. To combat aging means tackling eight or nine different processes that are probably interconnected. Not that we find the idea intimidating."

"Isn't gene therapy dangerous? Elizabeth Parrish, the CEO of BioViva, went to Colombia to have her DNA modified to lengthen her telomeres. In the media, she introduces herself as the first 'upgraded' woman. Isn't she risking her life?"

"To go back to what I said before, everything has to go through a double-blind protocol if you want to avoid experiments that are unscientific. That said, like any therapy, genetic modification is considered hazardous until proven otherwise. I personally believe that genetic manipulation is not only harmless but helpful."

"When will we know if genetically modified humans are viable?"

"The advantage of genome editing in age reversal is that you see if it works immediately. But we can't immediately tell whether there are no side effects. In general, the FDA approves therapies if they don't cause serious side effects within the following year. That's the rule: one year. To genetically reprogramme a human being, an edited gene has to be inserted into a virus that delivers it to the cells in the body, but in doing so we risk compromising our immune system …"

"Choulika uses T cells and the HIV virus. I've just had my genome sequenced and my iPS cells frozen. What is the next step on the road to eternity: getting myself injected with HIV?"

"When it comes to freezing, I prefer to freeze umbilical-cord cells. IPS cells are artificially created by powerful genes that can cause cancer. Freezing blood cells from the umbilical cord at birth is something I compare to having an airbag in your car: you'll probably never need it, but it's useful to have it just in case."

Since he had dodged my question, I tried to be more precise.

"What do you think about 3D-printed organs?"

"It's spectacular. We're working here on printing organs, but I don't think it's the best technique. Errors creep in. It's like a photocopy with a flaw, sometimes of only half a millimetre. I'd be worried about transplanting pixelated organs. Besides, it's a slow process. You have to remember that the organ you're trying to replace is dying, since it has to be surgically removed to be copied. In the meantime, the blood vessels are disconnected, and the printing process can take thousands of hours! Last but not least, it's extremely expensive. The other approach is using developmental biology to grow human tissue in a laboratory. We're already able to make human blood … We'll publish a paper on that soon."

"In a recent TED Talk, you said you've been working on pigs?"

"Yes, we've humanized pigs. They don't have any viruses that can infect humans."

"How do you 'humanize' a pig?"

"By editing its genome. We've incorporated human genes into pigs and removed the pig genes that might trigger an immune reaction."

"So, you could transplant a pig's liver into me?"

"Absolutely. It is almost exactly the same size. There are already patients with heart valves taken from pigs or cows, but those aren't living organs, they have to be replaced every ten years. There has also been breast surgery using pig tissue. The advantage of organs from genetically modified pigs is that they're alive and they'll continue to adapt."

"Just listening to you makes me want to squeal like a pig!"

"Most human parts can be replaced by those from pigs—well, except the hand, that would be a bit problematic."

The worst thing was that this genius was funny. He reminded me of the famous photo of Einstein sticking his tongue out. A great inventor needs to be a little wild at heart, otherwise he'd never invent anything. In the next room, the phone was ringing every thirty seconds. The whole world wanted to know about immortality.

"Muslims and Jews are going to face a serious spiritual dilemma when you try to transplant a pig heart."

"We work with cows, too. Though Hindus will probably have a problem with that ..."

Professor Church is not a sorcerer's apprentice; he is the sorcerer-in-chief, the Great Sachem, the Doctor Strangelove of posthumanity. He bore a prophetic name. Léonore rolled her eyes. I was terrified she would storm out of the office and slam the door. But she's a Swiss Protestant, she knows how to behave. I was wondering whether humanized pigs might start talking like the chimpanzees in Pierre Boulle's *Planet of the Apes*. Unthinkingly I glanced out the window. I swear I'm not joking: there's a church right opposite the Church Laboratory.

"So, to sum up: to become immortal, a man must become a pig?"

"The biggest problem is the brain. There's a huge difference between pig and human brains, and obviously there is no way to transfer human memory between them."

"On the subject of the brain, what do you think of Ray

Kurzweil's idea of downloading the human brain onto a hard drive?"

"I don't have much faith in it because a computer uses, like, 100,000 watts while the human brain can work with as few as twenty, like a light bulb. And that's just a computer playing chess. There's another concern with transferring the brain to a computer: if I want to copy something, I copy it, I don't turn it into something else. Thinking you can transfer an organ as complex as the brain to a silicon-based medium is as ridiculous as me trying to make a copy of it with plants or with cheese. The only possibility I can imagine would be to transfer the information to another brain. It's more logical. For example: freeze your brain while a bio-printer makes a copy, that way it won't die during the process. It's really difficult to freeze living beings without damaging them irreparably. We can only manage it with tardigrades and certain types of fish. I think I'd try to print a frozen human brain in 3D sections and then reassemble them."

Léonore came up with a new way to mock the emeritus professor. When it comes to interviewing scientists, we made a good team. Almost as good as the Bogdanov brothers, who gave me my start in television back in 1979.

"The reason people talk about transferring the brain onto a computer," she said, "is because you do something very similar every day: you take human DNA, just as we do at the clinic where I work in Geneva, you sequence that DNA, you modify, edit, and reshape it on a computer and then reinsert the modified DNA into living cells. If this two-way system works between man and machine at DNA level, why are you so insistent that it couldn't work with the brain?"

"As a distinguished biologist, you know that scale is important. We use computers to represent something simple like DNA ..."

"Three billion letters is hardly simple!"

For the first time, George Church seemed flustered.

"I'm not saying it would be impossible to download the human brain, I'm saying that if I had to choose the best means to extend the lifespan of the brain, I'd opt for copying organ-to-organ rather than for scanning it digitally. I would use a computer to copy the brain rather than download it, which seems like a risky approach."

I had my nose in a pile of photocopies I had made from magazine articles and books whose gibberish I pretended to understand. One of the books was *A Foolish Solitude* by Olivier Rey, in which he developed the concept of the "self-constructed man."

"I'd like to talk about a different area of your research," I said. "Artificial life. I know you are one of the world's leading researchers in the field of synthetic biology. In fact, you're involved in the ongoing project to create the first child with no biological parents, the 'Human Genome Project-Write.' What's the goal of the project? Is it something that might help mankind, or are you trying to create a new humanity to replace us?"

"I like to think that all the projects I'm working on will benefit society and be of philosophical interest. What we're attempting to do with artificial genomes and synthetic organisms is to make them resistant to viruses. In Boston, we had to close a pharmaceutical company for two years when it was infected by a virus. So, we're trying to create cells that are resistant to viruses by rebuilding them from scratch."

"How do you go about creating an artificial organism? Do you take a living organism and implant a gene sequence you've written?"

"That's exactly it. In practice, it would be very difficult

to create a life-form unrelated to one that already exists. In fact, we're inspired by what already exists, we copy fragments of life. The most radical thing we've so far created here is the synthesis of four million base pairs in a bacterium in order to make it resistant to viruses. We're now going to move on to other animals that have an industrial impact."

"Could you use this approach to treat humans? Implant synthetic cells?"

"Yes, it could be used to treat liver disease or AIDS or polio ... It's possible that we could implant virus-resistant cells."

Léonore reacted with a simplicity and directness that could have earned her the nickname "Helvetica."

"You do realize that if we could create a synthetic human genome capable of generating human cells, the consequences would be limitless?"

Thankfully the Swiss woman was here to worry about the fate of *Homo sapiens*; if it had been left to Professor Church, or to me, the 300,000-year-old species would long since have been doomed. Given that we were already in cloud cuckoo land, I thought: Go for it! Take the plunge. The guy already thinks you're a complete moron, so you can ask whatever crazy question you like.

"André Choulika said you're working on the de-extinction of species such as the woolly mammoth?"

"That's true. But I think of it more in terms of reviving ancient genetic material. We've been successful with a number of mammoth genes. We've managed to reactivate a haemoglobin gene that allowed their skin to adapt to freezing temperatures. At low temperatures, human haemoglobin is less efficient at exchanging oxygen. We've also managed to reactivate the gene that allowed them to control their body temperature. Our goal is to use traits from the extinct species to help Asian elephants to survive and perhaps even use them to combat the effects of climate change."

Léonore shot me a terrified look. She and I were thinking the same thing: *Jurassic Park*. In Michael Crichton's novel, a scientist resurrects the *Tyrannosaurus rex* by implanting recovered DNA into an ostrich egg. I fully expected to see Jeff Goldblum suddenly appear, to a soundtrack by John Williams, and scream at Professor Church: "What you call discovery, I call the rape of the natural world." But Jeff might also have shouted something pithier, like "RUN! NOW!"

"Have you considered creating new species? Are you a disciple of HG Wells's Doctor Moreau?"

"He was only a surgeon. We can create the same hybrids using genetics. Species barriers are not as insurmountable as you might think. We used genes from a jellyfish to create a fluorescent mouse. We don't do these things just for fun, they serve a purpose. The jellyfish gene makes it easier for us to visualize what has been changed. Using CRISPR, we can cut bacterial genes and incorporate them into any organism to make it easier to modify. We'll carry on creating transgenic animals, the only limit is our imagination."

"Do you not agree with Yossi Buganim, an Israeli researcher who told me that the Chinese are currently trying to develop living weapons? Huge vicious animals?"

"I don't think you can compete with Intercontinental Ballistic Missiles. If you want to create weapons, metal is more effective than an octopus."

"What do you think about biological machines?"

"My hunch, though right now I can't prove it, is that all the non-biological things we make today will soon be created through biology. Buildings, trains, even rockets could be organic. For centuries, we used biological cars: horses. All machines would be better created using biological systems. We could keep the metal bodywork, but biology can produce atomically precise machines quickly and at no cost. Imagine if we could copy buildings in twenty minutes, or replace computers with biodegradable machines. Biology could feed on the carbon in the air and turn it into bio foam. This could be used to build a bridge between New York and Europe, between Los Angeles and Japan. All the dangerous carbon in the air could be used to allow us to travel at ultra-high speeds using a 'vacuum maglev' (*a shuttle that glides using magnetic levitation*)."

I know what you're thinking, the scientists at Harvard have been smoking the linoleum. But if you want to know more about "bio foam" or "maglev," just Google them. Personally, I was a fan of these futuristic dreams that made the work of George Lucas look positively antiquated. Léonore had one last question to ask this scientist who made Victor Frankenstein look like Louis Pasteur.

"You store information within DNA. How do you go about it?"

"It's pretty simple. DNA is information. The letters A, C, G, and T are just like ones and zeroes in binary. Each genetic base can correspond to two bits of information. We know how to print DNA, how to copy a gene through chemical synthesis. Here in the laboratory, we're studying how to do it more cheaply. We've already slashed the cost of this kind of synthesis by a million. This means you can take anything: a movie, a book, music (also just a string of ones and zeros), and store it in DNA: each 0 is an A or C, each 1 a G or T. Eventually, DNA will be used to store all human culture."

"Instead of storing information on microchips, it will be stored in cells?"

"I was thinking of an apple, it being the 'fruit of knowledge.' DNA storage is a million times more compact. It requires no energy to be copied. We could store the entire cultural history of the world in something that fits in the palm of your hand. All of Wikipedia in a drop of water. We could even implant it in your brain to make you intelligent and knowledgeable. There's no hard drive that can function for 700,000 years. DNA can."

Suddenly, I gave a yelp. Outside the window, on the steps of the church, a small crowd had gathered. Passersby were taking photos of Pepper and Romy holding hands. I barely had time to shout "Thanks for your time, Professor!" before racing down the corridor to the emergency exit. There was a tailback along the Avenue Louis Pasteur. Drivers were stopping their cars to take photos of my radiant daughter as she stood at the top of the steps hugging her robot companion. They looked like Romeo and Juliet in a paedo-anime remake where Romeo was played by a three-dimensional android and Juliet by my daughter in a CGI Verona."

"We're proud to be the first human-robot couple to make a formal request to be married in church," Pepper said to the countless smartphones filming them. "We hope to convince the priest that our love is sincere."

"Do you believe in God?" someone heckled.

"God is love, and I am in love," Pepper said. "Therefore, I am God."

Machine learning software had a fondness for syllogisms. Romy was taking selfies. Léonore was laughing like a drain. Lou was laughing to imitate her mother. And I was going out of my mind.

"Pepper is capable of all human emotions," Romy

shouted. "Including believing in Jesus Christ."

"How old are you, little girl?"

"STOP!!! STOP EVERYTHING! THAT'S MY DAUGHTER UP THERE! EVERYONE MOVE ALONG, THANK YOU!"

I elbowed my way through the crowd of amateur paparazzi, turned Pepper off with the flick of a switch, grabbed Romy by the hand, and dragged her to our rental car. Léonore followed behind, she had stopped laughing. As I started the car, Romy started to cry.

"We love each other and we want to get married!"

"Honey, you're ten years old, you're not getting married to a toy!"

I didn't believe what I was saying. But I'd just come out of an interview with a scientist who said things a thousand times worse. The world was slipping away. Things were moving too fast; I drove around the block to pick up the robot.

"You can't stop me, Papa. I love Pepper and he loves me. We're going to get married and devote our lives to the Lord."

"You're too young to get married. As for marrying a machine, I don't think any religion is going to bless that union."

"But we really love each other!"

"We are not having this conversation."

Léonore got out of the SUV to fetch the switched-off robot from the crowd of rubberneckers. Her dress was creased. Her expression was as harsh as the slamming car door. I despised that moment. I shouldn't have placed so much faith in myself, in her, in anything. It's possible to be a superhuman without being a psychologist; in fact, I'd say that stories of superheroes show they have a blatant lack of tact.

"You left so quickly you didn't hear the last bit," Léonore

said curtly. "Professor Church has arranged an appointment for you with Craig Venter, apparently he's just opened a centre called Human Longevity, Inc. I'm going to go back to Geneva with Lou. It's better that way."

She might as well have stabbed me through the heart. I loved this woman, and she wanted to escape from my sick family. I pleaded with her to stay, while Romy threw her arms around Pepper like some Miyazaki movie.

"Léonore, I love you dreadfully. You're going to stay here with us because we're going to be immortalized. Please don't argue. Allow yourself to be loved by this aging Uberman. Keep making me happy, I'm begging you. If I wasn't driving a vehicle that weighs several tons right now, I would throw myself at your feet."

"You're expected at Human Longevity, Inc. in San Diego," Léonore said. "I need to go back to my job in Switzerland. I'll be able to breathe pure mountain air, it'll make a change from this posthuman bullshit."

"Papa, how come you can marry Léonore but I can't marry Pepper?" Romy asked.

"Because you're ten years old and I'm fifty-one!"

Romy was stroking the robot's head; she had surreptitiously rebooted him. In the rear-view mirror, I could see her tears reflecting his green LED diodes. I'd never been able to be strict with my daughter and I wasn't going to start now.

"In San Diego, tomorrow will be sunny with a temperature of 26° Celsius," Pepper said, turning to Romy who covered him with kisses. "*Stat crux dum volvitur orbis.*"

"Say what?"

"'The Cross is steady while the world is turning.' It's the motto of the Carthusian Order. Lucky's Lounge at Boston Logan Airport is offering chicken wings with barbecue sauce for only $11. I love you all, as the Lord loves you."

Though it was only three in the afternoon, it felt like the middle of the night. Boston is a city as red as its brick houses, but the air is dark with smog and clouds. I thought of all the beautiful moments I had spent with Léonore: every time I took her in my arms I had assumed that we were happy, when actually we were walking a tightrope above an abyss. I could not bear the idea of another separation. I glanced at Lou's face in the rearview mirror, and she looked as she did in the maternity unit on the night she was born when she was all blue and I was showing her everything in the room: this is a sink, this is a wardrobe, this is ... Once, for Romy's birthday, I invited all her classmates to a karaoke bar and I sang Michael Jackson's "I'll Be There." ("Whenever you need me, I'll be there.") It was time to keep my word. I pulled the car over onto the hard shoulder.

"Obviously you're free to leave, Léonore, but ... I'd rather we put up with each other for a few centuries more. And, Romy ... I'll do whatever it takes to make you happy. We'll find a solution. Let's stay together, okay?"

Léonore started crying, so did Romy, and so did I. It was preposterous. We passed a pack of Kleenex around the car. Pepper gazed sympathetically at our little family. As a species, humans were decidedly too fragile.

"Come on, let's go, I've got a pain in my stomach," Léonore snuffled, her brows resolute. "I'm sorry, I'm exhausted ... I don't understand this headlong rush from death. You're getting to be too weird. Just look at the state of your daughter. This can't go on."

"I have detected an emotional moment in the vehicle," Pepper said.

"Green! Green!"

Lou had said something we could all agree on. The light had turned green. Dabbing my eyes, I pressed the accelerator. We clung to what was still human in us that day, in that car, beneath the red sky, behind the red traffic lights, between the red walls of the New World.

PRINCIPAL DIFFERENCES BETWEEN THE HUMAN AND THE POSTHUMAN

HUMAN	POSTHUMAN
Life expectancy = 78 years	Life expectancy = 300 years
Perishable organs	Humanized pig organs or 3D bioprinted organs
DNA from parents	DNA modified by CRISPR
Communicates by speaking, writing, photography, and video	Communicates by thoughts connected to the cloud
Weak muscles	Strength enhanced by motorized titanium exoskeleton
Limited retinal vision	Night vision provided by DNA spliced from bats and high-definition infrared retinas
Does not recognize all the people he meets	Recognizes everyone thanks to Google glasses
Randomly sexual	Cloud-connected sex toys and 3D cerebral porn
Natural blood	Synthetic haemoglobin created from stem cells
Rapid degeneration after the age of 60	Periodically rejuvenated by AND injections, young blood, and Yamanaka factors
Brain impermanent and underused	Neurons downloaded to 2.5 petabyte hard drive, brain stimulated with nootropics

HUMAN	POSTHUMAN
Interested in art and culture	Direct access to global knowledge via cerebral microprocessor
Believes in God	Believes in Science
Biological animal	Organic machine
Vaginal reproduction	In vitro reproduction
Humanist/pessimist	Mechanist/scientist
Gets ill	Maintained by nanobots
Loves without orgasming	Orgasms without loving

8

CONSCIOUSNESS TO HARD DRIVE TRANSFER

(Health Nucleus, San Diego, California)

"Endeavouring to evade death,
we often run into its very mouth."
MICHEL DE MONTAIGNE, *Essays*

SUMMARY OF THE PROCEEDINGS OF THE
BEIGBEDER FAMILY IMMORTALIZATION

– The Saldmann diet (vegetables, fish, no salt, no sugar, no fat, no alcohol, no drugs, forty minutes of daily exercise): therapy failed as patients lacked the necessary willpower
– DNA sequencing: success. No fatal diagnosis
– Freezing of stem cells: success
– Blood transfusion laser therapy: success
– Gene therapy: Yamanaka factor injections—awaiting DBPCRCT results
– Gene therapy: CRISPR to lengthen telomeres and regenerate mitochondria—impossible, except in Kazakhstan and Colombia
– Pig-organ transplants: awaiting DBPCRCT results
– 3D organ printing: not yet "sharp" enough
– Transfer of brain to hard drive: this is the next step
– Transfusion of fresh blood: this will be the final step

WHITE BUTTERFLIES FLUTTERED in spirals in a dusty beam of sunlight, like proteins in the double helix of DNA. The California sky was the colour of a bottle of Bombay Sapphire. In Los Angeles I bought ten bottles of Elysium's "Basis" ($60 each). All of us, except Pepper, took two gel capsules a day. After a month, Romy's nails had grown a little faster. We were staying at the Sunset Marquis in a villa with a fully equipped kitchen. I loved shopping at the 7-Eleven on the corner. We were as happy as I hoped: living in California is like living in a Fleetwood Mac song, quiet and pulsing. In the next villa, Steven Tyler, the lead singer of Aerosmith, snored all day. We were finally living the healthy life of bronzed surfers. Every morning, I spent an hour in the gym with Léonore. A sadistic coach forced us to do core-strength exercises, and squats with weights. Gradually my body was beginning to change: washboard abs, superhero biceps. We no longer ate anything except kale and sushi. In the afternoons, we all lounged in the sun by the pool—except Pepper. Romy was getting used to life in California, or—more accurately—she was rediscovering the TV boxed sets she knew by heart. Given the series that she watched on television, she might as well have lived in LA her whole life. The villas with gardens along Ocean Drive, the stretch limousines, the low houses, the huge movie posters all seemed familiar. Léonore had recovered from her post-Harvard depression. She was worried about a lump in her left breast but we had an appointment in the offices of the first man ever to be genetically sequenced, who would conduct a thorough examination. Craig Venter's Health Nucleus Institute in San Diego is the world's first fully genomics-based private clinic, a subsidiary of the group modestly known as Human Longevity, Inc. (HLI).

Craig Venter is a Vietnam war veteran: he's spent a long time flirting with death, fighting it and winning. In 1968, he survived the Tet Offensive when most of his comrades in the regiment were burned alive or remain jailed until today. The wall of the waiting room is printed with a pink and purple genetic sequence: the DNA of the boss serves as Kabbalistic décor in this science-non-fiction reception area. This bald man with a white beard has spent thirty years obsessively trying to create synthetic life and improve humanity. It was he who gave birth to the first synthetic living organism, *Mycoplasma laboratorium*, a synthetic genome created in his lab from the DNA of *Mycoplasma genitalium* (a bacterium collected from human testicles). Venter published his findings in *Science* in 2010, between two transatlantic crossings on his huge yacht.

His futuristic hospital offers ultra-fast computerized sequencing of human DNA, an international predictive database, and every possible phenotypic analysis tool available to techno-medicine (3D scanners; microbiome analysis; preventive MRI scans for cancer detection; advanced detection of cardiovascular disease, neurodegenerative disease, and diabetes). Once again we had to spit into test tubes, once again we had epidermal cells scraped from under our arms, before samples were taken of our blood, our stools, and our urine. Patients had to pay $25,000 to undergo a battery of clinical tests, compared to which the tests conducted by the French Social Security system seemed like something conducted by Doctor

Knock. The design of the Health Nucleus Institute is inspired by the Marvel universe: you feel like you're at X-Men Academy. Physically, Craig Venter looks a lot like Professor Charles Xavier, the eponymous Professor X, who teaches mutants. The interior of the Health Nucleus Institute is also reminiscent of S.H.I.E.L.D. in *Avengers* or the *Milano* in *Guardians of the Galaxy*. Transhumanist researchers clearly think of themselves as mutants with a mission to extend human life, perhaps even to create a new race.

Since the Second World War, we have not noticed—or not wanted to notice—that the superheroes and mutants of the Marvel and DC universes uphold an ideology inspired by the Nazi Übermensch. The creation of a biologically enhanced superior race is the dream of Nazi eugenicists. As Adolf Hitler spluttered in one of his coke-fuelled rants: "The national state ... must set race in the centre of all life. It must take care to keep it pure. [...] It must put the most modern medical means in the service of this knowledge." The creators of Superman (Jerry Siegel), Batman (Bob Kane), and Spider-Man (Stan Lee) were the children of Jewish immigrants from Central Europe who sought to defend their people against Nazi barbarism. They were inspired by Moses (and by Greek mythology). Subconsciously they wanted to rival the Nazi Pharaoh in their strength, their superiority, their power for mass destruction. In one of the first issues of the comic book, Superman twists the barrel of a German tank: every Übermensch meets his match. Their talent and ability to entertain created the rest: a globalized mainstream industry that brings in billions of dollars for Disney every year. Whether or not you approve of the mimetic convergence of Nazi ideology and the superhero blockbuster, one thing needs to be emphasized: these comic books and big-budget movies are not works of fantasy. They are realistic depictions of present-day humanity. These days, the creation of mutants like Logan (Wolverine) or Bruce Banner (Hulk) is made genetically possible through the use of CRISPR to combine human, animal, and plant genomes. In fiction, Doctor Bruce Banner (Hulk) is transformed by exposure to massive doses of gamma radiation during an atomic explosion; Captain America is a US soldier enhanced through radiation and the injection of a Super-Soldier Serum (the Renaissance project). Given the observations of Nobel Prize winner Svetlana Alexievich about the unpredictability of the mutations from radioactivity she witnessed at Chernobyl, current science is more likely to proceed by manipulating mutations, and by planning genomic modifications and hybrids. If it is easy enough for Church Labs to create fluorescent mice or to resurrect woolly mammoths, the Wolverine or the Hulk are already within reach. Batman (Bruce Wayne) and Iron Man (Tony Stark) are billionaires like Craig Venter, Elon Musk, or Peter Thiel, who use technological wizardry, prostheses, exoskeletons, and individual transport drones to fight evil. In fact, Mark Zuckerberg has publicly stated that he wants to recreate Iron Man's assistant, Jarvis. Nature imitates art … and transhumanists imitate science fiction. We have to stop thinking of superhero comics as science fiction and accept them for what they are: testimonies to "human obsolescence," to use the words of Günther Anders.

It is at this point that I have to explain the concept of the Singularity, one that has been miserably rehashed by charlatans like Ray Kurzweil. The Technological Singularity is a hypothesis posited by John von Neumann in the late 1940s. Having studied automata, the forerunners of modern computers, Neumann advanced the concept of "self-replicating machines," which, in 1965, inspired Gordon Moore to come up with his famous law that the number of transistors per square inch on integrated circuits would double every year (in 1971, Moore amended the law to say that the speed of microprocessors would double every two years, something that IT has since confirmed). In 1993, Vernor Vinge, a maths teacher and science-fiction novelist from Wisconsin, published an article entitled "The Coming Technological Singularity," in which he developed the idea that Moore's Law would lead to humanity's replacement by machines. The Singularity refers to the end of human civilizations and the advent of a new society in which artificial intelligence exceeds human intelligence. In the movie *Terminator Genisys*, the Skynet takeover of networked computers worldwide, particularly those controlling nuclear weapons, is announced for October 2017: this was precisely when, in real life, a country announced the development of Lethal Autonomous Weapon Systems (LAWs) that kill according to internal algorithms. Once again, science-fiction writers prove to be the *only truly realistic whistle-blowers in the whole canon of literature.*

The brain scanning of my family was a long process that required each neuron to be copied onto digital media. I phoned my parents in France and offered to have their heads transplanted onto a-mortal bionic bodies.

"What's the risk?"

"Quadriplegia, if the spinal cord is wrongly reconnected..."

I failed to persuade these luddite technophobes. Neither my mother nor my father seemed keen to have their brains transplanted into a biomechanical body. Despite the fact that Maman has a coronary stent in the chest, and Papa has a polyethylene kneecap. Their bioconserva-tism was at odds with the very operations that had saved them. My whole family was dubious about my research—something that I found reassuring. Lying on a hospital bed with my brain hooked up to scanners with electrodes and a microprocessor implanted in my skull, I spent sev-eral months bored senseless. What's frustrating about Los Angeles is being near the sea but too far away to hear it. Romy was hooked up to Pepper: they had decided to merge their synapses, their neurons, with electronics. The human brain contains a hundred billion neurons, each capable of ten thousand synaptic connections, pro-ducing a million billion possible connections: this is re-ferred to as the "connectome." Down on Melrose Avenue, at Humai, a start-up founded by Josh Bocanegra, hun-dreds of computers containing two billion transistors with tens of millions of logic gates are connected to rec-reate the number of electronic synapses in *Homo sapiens*. This is called "neuroenhancement." It stems from a dis-covery made by one of the neurologists on George Church's team (Seth Shipman) at the Wyss Institute in Harvard in July 2017: if an entire movie can be stored in the DNA of a living cell, then it is possible to encode all the information in our brain into DNA before download-ing it onto a hard drive. It's astonishing that the media has made little mention of the fact that, in the summer of 2017, the insurmountable barrier between human and machine was breached. Despite Léonore's protests, I eventually gave in to my daughter's demands to be down-loaded onto her robot. I even agreed to baptize the little robot inside her with a can of Dr Pepper. Teens nowadays considered themselves techno-Christian cyborgs. The Romy/Pepper meld opened the way to the rapid android-ization of her generation, something no one anticipated at the time. But Romy's biological body continued to wolf down Reese's Pieces and Nerds! As for me, I was uploaded into the digital beyond. My neurons and glial cells were uploaded to a global digital cloud, thanks to nanoscale components that mimicked the behaviour of my biological neurons. My limbic system was stored as ATCG characters in the synthetic chromosome that bears my name for all eternity. My natal cells were stored in liquid nitrogen at -180° C in iPS cryobanks across three continents. I finally managed to rid myself of a perishable human body thanks to the electronic chip that contains this story. The life text you are reading guarantees my immortality. It is stored in the Human Longevity, Inc. database, file number X76097A A804. Code Name: FOUNTOFYOUTH, password: Romy2017. The copy of my brain encoded as A, T, C, and G characters was stored on a USB drive, but also in a mini-robot equipped with webcams that will allow me to carry on living after my physical body becomes obsolete. New events, recent memories, experiences, and contacts that occur subsequent to the connectome operation are recorded as they happen, like restoring your hard drive using Time Machine. It is based on a principle already used by Facebook for its memorialized profiles, and by the various companies offering a service that sends posthumous emails (e.g. DeadSocial, LifeNaut. com, or Eterni.Me), using the digital mapping of the personal connectome in turn offered by companies like In Its Image, Neuralink, and Imagination Engines. Obviously, the cyborg containing my algorithm will not have my skin, but it will have my sense of humour, my memory, my idiocy, my attitudes, my opinions, my beliefs, and my regularly updated style.

Léonore was still not taking any of this seriously. She mocked our robotization and refused to talk to our avatars, which she found terrifyingly stupid and ugly. It was the Terasem Movement Foundation, in Vermont in 2004, that first launched the "Human Life Extension" system, creating Bina48, an android modelled on Bina Rothblatt, the wife of Martine Rothblatt. True, she's terrifying. But however ugly and inanimate, my avatar knows my whole life by heart and regularly writes to all my contacts. I felt reassured at the thought that I had an alter ego running as an automated system inside an android. I couldn't see why it would bother anyone. My daughter and I are still alive, and when the day comes our silicon brothers and sisters will replace us ... As Kevin Warwick, professor of cybernetics at the University of Coventry, said: "I was born human. But this was an accident of fate ..." Is a living arsehole better than a dead genius?

While we were being treated, Léonore was elegantly vomiting into the bouquets of eucalyptus at our villa. The nurse from Health Nucleus took her aside and told her the happy news: she was pregnant, and our genomes were compatible. Human Longevity, Inc. immediately offered to refine the future baby's DNA to create a mutant immune to genetic diseases. We eagerly agreed to the necessary tests. But Léonore would not play along: she refused the transfusions and refused to allow her personal connectome to be mapped because she was going through pregnancy, a much more incredible transmutation ... The process of creating a new life gave her a radiant complexion, the body of an alien, a massive surge of hormones, a wild sex drive. All my transhuman treatments seemed pathetic compared to her mutation into a reproductive superwoman, a biological alien factory with enhanced breasts. How could I compete with her? She needed no help to be enhanced.

One autumn morning, as she poured herself a coffee, she lanced the boil.

"Suppose you do manage to live to be three hundred," she said, "what would you do with the time?"

"I ... I don't know ... I ..."

"Of course you don't know! Here you are chasing after Venter's Fountain of Youth and you haven't even bothered to wonder what you'd do with a longer life!"

"I could spend more quality time with you ..."

"That's bullshit! I'm right here with your two daughters and a third child on the way and you're not spending quality time with me, you're setting up appointments with every guru in California! Do you really think you'd change if you were immortal? You'd set yourself some other impossible task: opening a nightclub on Mars or whatever. You want to defeat death not so you can live happily ever after, but to thwart fate. You've never known the meaning of happiness. I'm not criticizing: it's what first attracted me to you. Your angst, your loneliness, your repressed romanticism, your awkwardness with Romy ..."

Maybe, as a pregnant woman, Léonore was drinking too much Nespresso. Hormones plus caffeine are an explosive cocktail.

"You're a doctor," I protested. "Conquering death is your job."

"No, my job is saving lives. There's a subtle difference. I'm not fighting death, I'm fighting disease. Pain, infirmity, those are my enemies. At first, I found your hypochondriacal obsession with cell rejuvenation and genetic manipulation amusing, I thought you were sweet, like a little boy who's read too much sci-fi. But later it became pathetic."

"I'm a dreamer ..."

"No you're not: you're a coward. And let me tell you something: there's nothing sexy about being a coward.

Be a man, for fuck's sake. Can't you see that all this 'transhuman therapy' is just a fantasy designed to humour infantile, ignorant, narcissistic megalomaniacs who can't bring themselves to face the inevitable? For God's sake, it's blindingly obvious: these idiotic American billionaires are as scared of living as they are of dying! They all wear wigs—have you noticed? Elon Musk, Ray Kurzweil, Steve Wozniak: the toupee brigade."

God, Léonore was beautiful when she was angry! I shouldn't have provoked her, but maybe I'm a masochist. That angry glint in her eyes ... She was as sexy as Venus in furs with a whip.

"Don't you think it would be wonderful, a life without end?"

"My poor darling, a life without end would be a life without purpose."

"Really? So you're saying the purpose of life is death?"

"Of course not, but without death, there are no stakes. No suspense. Too much time drains away the pleasure. Have you never read Seneca?"

"No, I haven't read Seneca, I prefer Philip K. Dick. But they're both dead. I don't want to die, can't you understand that? You're not scared because you're still young. Thirty years from now we'll see how you feel about playing for extra time!"

"Listen, you're fifty, you've still got two or three decades on earth, so stop whining, have fun, enjoy it, be grateful that nature has given you another child instead of pancreatic cancer. What I want is a father for my daughter, not an idiot in an Uberman outfit!"

She was becoming annoying; I became petty.

"You're just jealous because George Church and Craig Venter have made more discoveries than your laboratory in Switzerland."

She glared at me, her expression shifting from alarm to disgust and, finally, misery. It's a moment I cannot think of without blushing in shame. And it's not as though I haven't been petty and spiteful many times in my life.

"Can't you see that my boss in Switzerland was trying to warn you that your new heroes were crackpots who were only after your money? You're stupider than I thought. Goodbye."

Gathering Lou in her arms, Léonore marched to the door, and her rounded belly, her powerful breasts, her every step, her icy "Goodbye," and the dull thud of the closing door, all these things were like knives in my stomach.

AND STILL I didn't give up. I was too close. I wouldn't listen to anyone. I thought that once I was enhanced, I'd have all the time in the world to win back my wife and child. I was as stubborn as a mule whose DNA had been CRISPR'd with a bull's.

At night, the taillights of cars flowed like a river of blood down Sunset Boulevard. The radio announced a spike in air pollution. I felt particulates sting my eyes, my nose, my throat, just as they did in Paris. It was a curious idea to come looking for immortality in a city whose welcome gift was to give you lung cancer. After I had my "brain uploaded" all that remained was the transfusion of young blood offered by Ambrosia Health in Monterey. The clinic is a start-up founded by Jesse Karmazin, a medical graduate convinced that young blood is the fountain of youth. My cyber-daughter Romy/Pepper came with me on the road trip down Highway 1, which leads from San Diego to Monterey, from the south of LA to the south of San Francisco.

It was in Monterey, in 1967, that Jimi Hendrix burned his guitar; it was here that the first TED Talks took place—this is a city that welcomes pioneers. The road to eternal life wound past the sharks in the Pacific, between two earthquakes, to Silicon Valley with its orange groves of green and gold. Suburban California looked like a series of pharmacies and churches, patches of wasteland, gas stations, billboards, and then, suddenly, nothing but soaring granite cliffs against which icy ocean waves crashed beneath the sweltering sun. The geography of the West Coast reminded me of the Basque Country, with tuna tataki replacing foie gras. The car glided along the asphalt between the pine trees, the acacias, the palms, the pepper plants, and the apricot and walnut trees, towards an ultimate eternity. In the rear windscreen, the past scrolled away: families of humans kicking balls on the beach, deathly motels filled with mortal guests, white churches filled with unprotesting Protestants. I felt a certain nostalgia for my former species, but it was too late to turn back now. It was as though the road behind us was crumbling (something that did actually happen at Pfeiffer Canyon near Big Sur).

I spent several weeks in Monterey having my veins transfused with the blood of numerous hand-picked Californian teenagers: in the United States, blood is sold by blood banks and it's possible to find out the age group of the donors (16–25 at Ambrosia Health). Vampire mythology had made only one mistake: garlic is not deadly, in fact, it promotes blood circulation. I ate cloves of raw garlic every day while being injected with the pristine blood haemoglobin of penniless surfers. The effect was astonishing: my neurons remyelinated at an abnormal rate. After two weeks of this eye-wateringly expensive treatment ($8,000 every two days), I felt as though I'd been hit by 10,000 volts. I was reborn as a skateboarder in a film by Gus Van Sant. I could feel my hair growing back, my chest swelling. I had a constant hard-on thinking about Léonore's amazing breasts. I effortlessly took the stairs four at a time. Young blood is worse than Class A drugs: I felt as though I was hovering twenty centimetres off the ground and ejaculating by the gallon. I couldn't resist turning on my smartphone and posting selfies of my transfigured torso on Instagram. These were the first images of my body since my televisual resignation. In the photos, taken at the Post Ranch Inn in Big Sur, on a cliff overlooking the ocean, my rebooted ego exulted like a singer in a boy band. My wrinkles had disappeared, my cheeks were plump, my flat stomach now boasted reconstituted abs. I smiled and flexed my biceps like an oiled-up bodybuilder in a thong. *Closer* magazine published the photos without my permission, under the headline: "Beigbeder Dabbles in Vampirism in California." The news had got out, I never knew who leaked the story about the Ambrosia method … though I strongly suspect it was Léonore.

Every night, I read Romy *The Bloody Countess* by Valentine Penrose, a surrealist poet fascinated by the torrents of fresh blood washing over the body of Elizabeth Báthory in the sixteenth century. "Beautiful and statuesque, haughty and proud, loving no one but herself and forever in search, not of the pleasures of society, but the pleasures of love, Elizabeth, surrounded by sycophants and libertines (…) tried to understand, but could not touch. And it was this desire to wake from not-living that gave her a taste for blood, for the blood of others which perhaps masked some secret that, from birth, had been veiled to her." Romy loved the story too; I pretended it was fiction. But her Wi-Fi-connected brain quickly discovered that the Vampire Countess truly had drunk the blood of hundreds of slaughtered adolescent girls. I often sing a transhuman Marseillaise:

To arms, citizens,
Form your battalions,
March on! March on!
Let teenage blood
Water my furrows!

Romy and Pepper were married in a strictly private ceremony in Santa Barbara town hall. The mayor was proud to (illegally) officiate at the first human-robot union, to "promote the social acceptance of androids and put an end to robophobia." After the ceremony, we ate grilled lobster at Stearns Wharf. While the newlyweds gazed out at the horizon, arm in telescopic arm, I finished watching Season Two of *Fear the Walking Dead*, which is set in Los Angeles.

There was no longer any distinction between reality and science fiction. Zombie movies showed the undead in search of live flesh: once again, Hollywood screenwriters had tried to warn us.

As soon as Jesse Karmazin published the first results of his vampire test, Silicon Valley's nouveau riche were banging on the door of his clinic. With Peter Thiel leading the charge. Around the world, newspapers ran stories about Age Reversal. *Le Monde:* "In California, cars are recharged with electricity, and old people are recharged with young blood." *The New York Times:* "Young blood transfusions: the future of rejuvenation." *Le Figaro:* "Was Dracula right?" *GQ France* even ran a cover photo of me in a swimsuit, with the bright yellow headline "Beigbeder Reloaded." Soon Ambrosia Health didn't have sufficient teenage plasma to treat its senior citizens. Congress vainly appealed to elderly Californians to remain calm. Across the United States, people began searching for new sources of regenerative haemoglobin. Police could do nothing to stop students, the unemployed, the destitute, and drug addicts selling their blood to the vans mining this new source of energy. And, since demand creates supply, so began the race to the bottom. Wealthy old people were prepared to spend vast sums for a transfusion of youth. Before long, the blood trade in the US and Mexico was pushed underground and also outward to China and Eastern Europe. The following winter, blood mafias started to spring up. "Blood dealers" were selling a litre of "Young Plasma" for $5,000 to $10,000. A number of senior citizens contracted hepatitis, leukaemia, or AIDS, but such accidents did little to curb the demand ... and the more the traffic increased, the greater the danger to adolescent populations.

The first "youth hunts" occurred in the suburbs of Los Angeles. There was a geographical logic to this: it is no coincidence that transhumanists have settled in the former playground of the Manson family. It is not surfing that attracted them to California, but the smell of sacrificial blood. The word "PIGS," daubed on walls, heralded the humanized pigs that would soon provide us with new transplant organs and, metaphorically, the porcine future of a neo-humanity with its snout in the planet-trough. Cannibalistic gangs of traffickers attacked anyone under twenty. The bloodless bodies of teenagers were buried in the Nevada desert; the police regularly discovered mass graves filled with dry, tanned hides, like piles of human leather. There were unverified rumours of children being raised in battery cages in Nicaragua to feed elderly zombies. I had been a guinea pig in the experiment that triggered a vampire war between generations. I remember it as though it was yesterday. "Blood is a juice of rarest quality," Mephistopheles (the devil) says in *Faust*. Rejuvenation is possible only by stealing youth from someone else, the blood of a virgin, the cells of an embryo, the organs of a motorcyclist who died the day before, or the heart of a humanoid pig. The problem with eternal life is that it needs to rob other people's bodies. My new blood was not mine, it was better than mine, purer, fresher, more beautiful, but I was no longer me.

Léonore had been right to run away: my humanity was disappearing by the day.

It was patently obvious: the only way for *Homo sapiens* to live forever was to slaughter its own children. Even God crucified his own son. I wasn't able to follow the example of the Gospels: I couldn't kill Romy. That's why I got ill.

9

UBERMAN

"*ZAB-CHOS ZHI KHRO DGONGS PA RANG GROL, STRID PA'I BAR DO NGO SPROD GSOL 'DEBS THOS GROL CHEN MO CHOS NYID BAR DO'I GSOL 'DEBS THOS GROL CHEN MO.*"
Tibetan Book of the Dead (Eighth Century AD)

DIED TOO YOUNG	DIED TOO OLD
Roger Nimier	Antoine Blondin
Jim Morrison	Sacha Distel
Maurice Ronet	Charlie Chaplin
Arthur Rimbaud	Jacques Prévert
Jean-René Huguenin	Jean-Edern Hallier
Jean Seberg	Jeanne Moreau
Jean Rochefort	Marlon Brando
Boris Vian	Françoise Sagan
F. Scott Fitzgerald	Truman Capote
Kurt Cobain	David Bowie
Robert Mapplethorpe	David Hamilton
Jean-Michel Basquiat	Bernard Buffet
Amy Winehouse	Whitney Houston
Albert Camus	Jean-Paul Sartre
Patrick Dewaere	Gérard Depardieu
John Lennon	Paul McCartney
Alexander McQueen	Yves Saint Laurent
Jean-Luc Delarue	Pascal Sevran
Guillaume Dustan	Renaud Camus
Natalie Wood	Faye Dunaway

Michael Jackson	Michael Jackson
Jimi Hendrix	Prince
George Michael	Elton John
Heath Ledger	Mickey Rourke
Prince	James Brown
Jean Eustache	Roger Vadim
Che Guevara	Fidel Castro
Brian Jones	Elvis Presley
Jean-Pierre Rassam	Harvey Weinstein

The moral: better to die young. But it was too late for me.
My advice: if it is too late to die young, don't die at all.

FOR MY FIRST five decades on earth, I took no interest in the weather. I went to work with the same indifference come rain, wind, or sun. I didn't give a damn about the sky; in Paris, I never saw it. My sixth decade was very different: I looked at nothing else, I followed the sun everywhere. I watched it shimmer on the white streets, the oil palms, the blue ocean. To age is to beg alms from the sun, even when you've got rebooted blood, regenerated organs, and a digitized brain.

In the early 2020s (the famous "Twenty Twenties" when everything changed), the war between the young and the old was symbolized by the clash between Emmanuel Macron and Donald Trump. At every summit of the G7, you could tell the US President longed to feast on the carotid artery of the head of the French state.

As soon as I knew I was going to die, I recorded a hundred posthumous programmes to be broadcast on my YouTube channel every December 31: *The Post-Mortem Show*. The advertising revenue from these programmes, the first of which was triggered by a death, were enough to feed my family throughout the twenty-first century.

Children are afraid to go to sleep because sleep is a foretaste of what awaits us later: an endless night, a dark tunnel where no one has left the light on. But death is not like the dreams we have at night. Since I belong to the last generation of *Homo sapiens*, I'd like to describe my end.

There was something rotten in the gallons of young Californian blood transfused into me. I sensed it early on: six weeks after the heterochronic parabiosis I woke up exhausted with the taste of sulphur in my mouth, a strange dizziness, and blood in my stools. Analyses confirmed a rare, incurable form of hepatitis. My fatty liver was unable to withstand the shock of my accelerated rejuvenation.

Death is like the psychedelic scene in *2001: A Space Odyssey*—you fly over arid neon deserts.

Death is like gliding to a soundtrack by Richard Wagner.

Death is like freediving in the depths of the ocean.

Death is like rain filmed in slow motion with a Phantom High-Speed camera.

Death is twined filament separating like in a 3D animation.

Death is a fractal image: you dive into a mathematically generated image that multiplies infinitely.

Death is a *mise en abyme*, it's the cover of Pink Floyd's *Ummagumma*, you step into an image that contains the same image that contains the same image and you can never go backwards. And it smells of rotten eggs.

Instead of staring up at the sky for fear it will fall in, we should be looking at the ground beneath our feet, which will soon cleave in two. We might trip, we might fall, like Alice down a rabbit hole crammed with strange objects, clocks whose hands run backwards ... into the catacombs of time.

My life was whirling around me, the departures and the arrivals. I had finally stopped aging. Death is the ultimate fountain of youth, the shores of the suspended river of time, the dawn of time standing still. My body had reached obsolescence. I was replaced by a robotic brother cerebrally connected to my alter ego.

Romy would never die; this was what I had lived for. I had finally proved myself useful. Why prolong our physical presence? Dying doesn't mean giving up. I was immortalized in the cloud. My looks had long since faded, I engaged with the world through my physical alter-robot. The only downside of "Bodily Extinction" was losing all contact with Léonore and Lou, who still refused to buy an iMind digital brain on Applezon (created by the merger of Apple and Amazon in 2022).

A cloud without pain. A cloud of relief. I swallowed the sky. I hovered over the years as over an ocean. I spat blood every night.

Can you feel me around you?

I am not phantom, I am atom. Anthumous and posthumous.

I am a part of everything that is connected to everything.

I am dust, wave, light, air. I'm as vast as a mountain, light as a cloud, limpid as wind and water.

Before, I was virtual; during, I was real; after, I was virtual again. There you have it: I am no longer living but I lived for you. I exist. I deserve your "Likes."

The future will be dustier, hotter, more crowded than the present. Why hang around?

The air you breathe, the sun that burns you, the night that calms you: these, too, are me. And in your memories, I will sometimes pop by to pay you a visit.

I am nothing now but once I was all. I'm the present incarnate. *Ego sum qui sum* (Exodus, 3:4).

Molecules are transformed. Bone becomes flower. My cells have already been recycled into compost. My soul is digitized.

The death of the body is not an event but a transition.

Don't wait for it, don't seek it out: death is all around you, it has always been. Dying is a scheduled appointment. You are finally rid of yourself. The ultimate orgasm beyond all words. Death requires a different language.

I contemplated the scudding clouds through my webcam. The sky was below, the ground above. I felt no pain, I felt relieved, rejuvenated.

An aftertaste of "young plasma" in my nose, my throat. A taste of disease, of the end.

Death is weighty. All other subjects seem frivolous by comparison. Since the beginning of this book, I have been talking about a subject I knew nothing about. My parents were still alive (I touched wood as I wrote that last sentence). I was unaware of this rent in my flesh, that was why I was so afraid of this transition. Death should have made me humble, instead it made me proud. I wanted to defeat it through selfishness. If my misadventure is to be useful to anyone, remember this: Pessoa was wrong when he said "life is not enough." Oh, life is enough, believe me. Life is more than enough, take the word of a dead man.

Perhaps I simply accelerated what I wished for. I didn't have time to found the Immortality Resistance Movement (IRM), but I found time to euthanize myself. The first involuntary euthanasia. That's the kicker: I inadvertently committed suicide.

Death is wretched, but non-death is worse.

FACED WITH MY declining health, the clinic summoned a Catholic priest to my bedside. A seminarian: Father Thomas Julien. He sweated in his black cassock as he listened to my lamentations. He is probably the person I should have met when I first came back from Jerusalem.

To the drone of those who chant Om, I intoned, "Where is He? Where is He? Where is your fucking God?"

"Don't you understand that Léonore, Romy, and Lou are your Holy Trinity? That it is God who sent these three women to you, so that you could not abandon humanity? It's something you should mention in your posthumous broadcasts."

"But God is dead!"

"Yes: he died on the cross. But his corpse is still moving. That's the reason for your presence here on earth. I gave up a physical fatherhood for spiritual fatherhood. When you finally accept the gift of life, you will no longer be afraid to leave."

"I know that, Father. But that's no reason to spout dialogue from a Marvel movie."

"It's not from a Marvel movie, it's from the Bible. You remember Christ's encounter with the rich young man in the New Testament? The rich man asked Christ how he might have eternal life. And Jesus said, 'Sell all thou hast and come follow me.'"

"I do not see the connection."

"Yes, you do: rich transhumanists are trying to compete with Christ. These are two opposing religions: one of money, the other of man."

"The Mount of Olives versus Silicon Valley ..."

"Precisely: the response to transhumanism (Man made God) is Christ (God made Man). You have to set down your story!"

"The story of a guy who wants to become immortal, and dies ..."

"Perhaps if you publish it, the ending will change. You know better than anyone that literature can conquer time."

The priest entrusted me with a mission. This is probably what I had been searching for, not immortality, but something to do that would be more useful than a TV talk show. It was at this moment that I decided to publish the story you now hold in your hands, under the (deceptive) title of *A Life Without End*.

"Father, I've got a question for you. If God exists, why did He make me an atheist?"

"So that you would live freely."

"He wanted to make sure I was sincere? Is God really so unsure of Himself that He needs my faith to be unprompted?"

"What do you want Him to be? A dictator?"

"Yes, actually, I think I'd have preferred Him to assert Himself. Politically, I'm a democrat, but when it comes to religion, I'm a fascist; it would really simplify things if He could give me a tangible sign."

"Why do you think I'm here?"

Father Julien made the sign of the cross before backing out of the room in his *Matrix*-style black cassock. I pressed the plunger on the morphine pump. My soul was weak but, apparently, I still had one.

I'd like to die to Pink Floyd's "Us and Them," scanning the horizon for the green ray as the sun sinks into the sea like a red frisbee into cherry jam.

I am prepared to die if it earns me "hugs." That way I won't feel anything except crushed strawberries beneath my feet. I will speak out, loud and clear until the end. My last words will be, "So be it," or maybe, "Dibs!"

I thought about Léonore, about Romy, about Lou, the three women in my life, the one who broke my heart, the one who joined me here on my hard drive, my baby who I miss so much ... and the baby yet to be born.

I thought about my father, about my mother and my brother. Who else would you want to think about when you're dying but the people who made you?

I thought about my friends, my cousins, my nephews, my numerous families, created, blended, recomposed, decomposed or supposed, proposed or transposed.

I thought of the girls I'd loved, the women I'd married, and the ones that got away. About those who kissed me, if only for a second. I didn't regret a single kiss.

I had lived for a girl in a denim jacket and Converse trainers and her little sister with her golden sandals and her gap-toothed smile staring in wonder at a snail. Were they, then, the "why" of my life, those little bundles of joy, those soft cheeks against my bristly beard, the laugh of a little girl splashing in the waves? Was this the meaning of my life—a baby that smelled of nappy cream and her older sister who painted her toenails sky-blue? Two little feet as rounded as madeleines and a long pale swan's neck? I should have held onto those ears like little pink squid. I had created more beauty with my sperm than I had with the work of a lifetime.

I'd won the lottery and I didn't realize.

Strangely, when you're dying, you only think about other people.

HERE I AM back before I was born, freed from the present. No words can express the infinite. It would take a new language to write the definitive book. If we had to transcribe the three billion letters of our DNA, assuming 3,000 letters per page, it would require a thousand thousand-page volumes.

ATGCCGCGCGCTCCCCGCTGCCGAGCCGTGCGCTCCCT
GCTGCGCAGCCACTACCGCGAGGTGCTGCCGCTGGCCAC
CTTCGTGGGGCGCCTGGGGCCCCAGGGCTGGCGGCTGGT
GCAGCGCGGGGACCCGGCGGCTTTCCGCGCGCTGGTGGC
CCAGTGCCTGGTGTGCGTGCCCTGGGACGCACGGCCGC
CCCCCGCCGCCCCCTCCTTCCGCCAGGTGGGCCTCCCCG
GGGTCGGCGTCCGGCTGGGGTTGAGGGCGGCCGGGGG
GAACCAGCGACATGCGGAGAGCAGCGCAGGCGACTCAG
GGCGCTTCCCCCGCAGGTGTCCTGCCTGAAGGAGCTGGT
GGCCCGAGTGCTGCAGAGGCTGTGCGAGCGCGGCGC
GAAGAACGTGCTGGCCTTCGGCTTCGCGCTGCTGGACGG
GGCCCGCGGGGGCCCCCCCGAGGCCTTCACCACCAGCTG
CGCAGCTACCTGCCCAACACGGTGACCGACGCACTGCG
GGGGAGCGGGGCGTGGGGGCTGCTGCTGCGCCGCGTGG
GCGACGACGTGCTGGTTCACCTGCTGGCACGCTGCGC
GCTCTTTGTGCTGGTGGCTCCCAGCTGCGCCTACCAGGT
GTGCGGGCCGCCGCTGTACCAGCTCGGCGCTGCCACT
CAGGCCCGGCCCCCGCCACACGCTAGTGGACCCCGAAG
GCGTCTGGGATGCGAACGGGCCTGGAACCATAGCGT
CAGGGAGGCCGGGGTCCCCCTGGGCCTGCCAGCCCCGG
GTGCGAGGAGGCGCGGGGGCAGTGCCAGCCGAAGTCTG

CCGTTGCCCAAGAGGCCCAGGCGTGGCGCTGCCCCTGA
GCCGGAGCGGACGCCCGTTGGGCAGGGGTCCTGGGC
CCACCCGGGCAGGACGCGTGGACCGAGTGACCGTG
GTTTCTGTGTGGTGTCACCTGCCAGACCCGCCGAAGAAG
CCACCTCTTTGGAGGGTGCGCTCTCTGGCACGCGC
CACTCCCACCCATCCGTGGGCCGCCAGCACCACGCGGGC
CCCCCATCCACATCGCGGCCACCACGTCCCTGGGACACG
CCTTGTCCCCCGGTGTACGCCGAGACCAAGCACTTCCTC
TACTCCTCAGGCGACAAGGAGCAGCTGCGGCCCTC
CTTCCTACTCAGCTCTCTGAGGCCCAGCCTGACTGGC
GCTCGGAGGCTCGTGGAGACCATCTTTCTGGGTTCCAGG
CCCTGGATGCCAGGGACTCCCCGCAGGTTGCCCCGCCTG
CCCCAGCGCTACTGGCAAATGCGGCCCCTGTTTCTG
GAGCTGCTTGGGAACCACGCGCAGTGCCCCTACGGGGT
GCTCCTCAAGACGCACTGCCCGCTGCGAGCTGCGGTCAC
CCCAGCAGCCGGTGTCTGTGCCCGGGAGAAGCCCCAGG
GCTCTGTGGCGGCCCCCGAGGAGGAGGACACAGAC
CCCCGTCGCCTGGTGCAGCTGCTCCGCCAGCACAGCAGC
CCCTGGCAGGTGTACGGCTTCGTGCGGGCCTGCCTGCGC
CGGCTGGTGCCCCCAGGCCTCTGGGGCTCCAGGCACAAC
GAACGCCGCTTCCTCAGGAACACCAAGAAGTTCATCTC
CCTGGGGAAGCATGCCAAGCTCTCGCTGCAGGAGCT
GACGTGGAAGATGAGCGTGCGGGACTGCGCTTGGCTGC
GCAGGAGCCCAGGTGAGGAGGTGGTGGCCGTCGAGGGC
CCAGGCCCCAGAGCTGAATGCAGTAGGGGCTCAGAA
AAGGGGGCAGGCAGAGCCCTGGTCCTCCTGTCTCCATC
GTCACGTGGGCACACGTGGCTTTTCGCTCAGGACGTC
GAGTGGACACGGTGATCTCTGCCTCTGCTCTCCCTCCT
GTCCAGTTTGCATAAACTTACGAGGTTCACCTTCAC
GTTTTGATGGACACGCGGTTTCCAGGCGCCGAGGCCA
GAGCAGTGAACAGAGGAGGCTGGGCGCGGCAGTGGAGC
CGGGTTGCCGGCAATGGGGAGAAGTGTCTGGAAGCA
CAGACGCTCTGGCGAGGGTGCCTGCAGGTTACCTATA
ATCCTCTTCGCAATTTCAAGGGTGGGAATGAGAGGTGG

GGACGAGAACCCCCTCTTCCTGGGGGTGGGAGGTAAG
GGTTTTGCAGGTGCACGTGGTCAGCCAATATGCAG
GTTTGTGTTTAAGATTTAATTGTGTGTTGACGGCCAGGT
GCGGTGGCTCACGCCGGTAATCCCAGCACTTTGG
GAAGCTGAGGCAGGTGGATCACCTGAGGTCAGGAGTTT
GAGACCAGCCTGACCAACATGGTGAAACCCTATCTG
TACTAAAAATACAAAAATTAGCTGGGCATGGTGGTGT
GTGCCTGTAATCCCAGCTACTTGGGAGGCTGAGGCAG
GAGAATCACTTGAACCCAGGAGGCGGAGGCTGCAGT
GAGCTGAGATTGTGCCATTGTACT

IN THE PYRENEES, when you shout into the mountains, the echo sends back the sound of your own voice. You hear your shout twice, three times, four times, as though the mountain was a giant parrot. But gradually, the sound fades. You have to shout louder, shout again and again. Even if you shout yourself hoarse, the echoes will eventually fade. The cry seems to come from far away, as though someone on the far side of the valley is mocking you, because an echo always mocks those who shout into the void. When I was a boy, I tired of the game after a few attempts. My shouts were stifled in the mountains. Why bother to scream at the top of your lungs for a few reverberations of your complaint. It was always the same: a recurring cry, then, after a while, nothing. In the end, silence always won.

EPILOGUE

SOMEWHERE IN THE Basque Country, the laughter of the seagulls has woken a baby. The sun is not up yet, petals are weighed down with dew. A little girl calls to her mother. They hug each other. There is so much love in this room the walls might explode. The little girl eats a peach or a banana. Her blonde hair and her teeth have grown during the night. She is eighteen months old. She can walk, she can say a few words: "Maman," "Ball," "Come," "More!" "Again!" "Home," and "Meow" when the cat enters the room. The rest of her language is a personal dialect: "Bakatesh," "Pabalk," "Fatishk," "Kabesh," "Dedananon," "Gilgamesh." Perhaps she speaks fluent Sanskrit. She loves: rocking in the hammock, pretending to drive the car and making engine sounds, picking daisies in the garden, making shadows on the grass, finding a snail shell, taking a handful of gravel and redecorating the patio, stopping everything to stare up at a plane leaving a white streak across the blue sky, making little balls out of croissant crumbs, dancing with her mother to Joe Dassin, being given raspberries by the woman on the market stall. By way of a choreography, she raises her arms and pirouettes barefoot on the lawn until she is dizzy. Her general state of mind: wonderment. At everything. Everything is new, everything is important, there is no such thing as boredom. Mother and daughter will have lunch on the beach. It often rains in this country, which makes every sunbeam seem like a miracle. All it takes is a single ray piercing the clouds for the locals to hurriedly strip off. Lots of things will happen on the beach: filling a bucket with sand, turning the bucket over, tapping the bottom of the bucket, lifting up the bucket, admiring the sandcastle, demolishing the sandcastle, repeating the process a dozen times. She will dip her toes in the sea. Run towards the waves as they ebb, running back when the waves roll in. Shouting "Oh no!" when the tide laps at the beach towel. Eating pieces of langoustine, *chipirones*, corn cakes, a handful of sand. The afternoon is as boundless as the sea. Lying on her back watching the sky. In the car on the way home, the little girl will clamour for her favourite cartoon *The Little Mole*, a Czech cartoon from the 1960s that proves communism was not a complete failure. The highlight of the day is a warm bath. Mother and baby bathe together. The baby's skin is softer than you. Outside on the hill, the sheep flush pink.

It is at this point that they hear the crunch of tyres on gravel. A taxi pulls up in the driveway. A lanky, long-haired, bearded man is sitting in the back seat, holding the hand of his eldest daughter who has grown several centimetres and ditched her Japanese robot. The gangly man pays the taxi and unfolds himself as he climbs out of the car. He has just returned from California, where he had signed up for a laboratory experiment, involving the transfusion of young blood. But on the day itself, he chickened out and didn't attend his appointment. Léonore and Lou open the door of the Basque house. Léonore sets her daughter down, folds her arms over her swollen belly. She is radiant in the pink glow of the sun as it sets behind the pines.

Seeing me, Lou drops her bottle on the ground. She starts running towards me, crying "Papa!"

I kneel down and open my arms.

ACKNOWLEDGEMENTS

Thanks to Farah Yarisal of The Brain Circle, who put me in touch with Doctor Yossi Buganim of the Department of Developmental Biology and Cancer Research at the Hebrew University in Jerusalem.

Thanks to Doctor Yossi Buganim for his instruction and his kindness.

Thanks to Tali Dowek, from the Division for Advancement and External Relations at the Hebrew University of Jerusalem, for organizing a visit to the Centre and a meeting with Professor Eran Meshorer at the Edmond & Lily Safra Center for Brain Sciences.

Thanks to Professor Stylianos Antonarakis, the Professor and Chairman of Genetic Medicine at the University of Geneva Medical School.

Thanks to Doctor Frédéric Saldmann of the Department for Functional Testing and Predictive Medicine at the Georges Pompidou European Hospital.

Thanks to Dominique Nora at the *Nouvel Observateur* for her help.

Thanks to Doctor André Choulika, CEO of Cellectis, for

his simplicity and his availability both in Paris and New York. His book *Réécrire la vie* (Hugo: Doc, 2016) helped me comprehend the incomprehensible.

Thanks to Professor George Church of MIT and the Wyss Institute at Harvard Medical School, for our super-humanist conversation at his Boston laboratory.

Thanks to Doctor Laurent Alexandre for our non-transgenic lunch at Guy Savoy in the Monnaie de Paris.

Apologies to Jesse Karmazin for the no-show.

Thanks to Father Thomas Julien for his spiritual contribution.

Thanks to Olivier Nora, Juliette Joste, and François Samuelson for believing in this crazy project.

May all your deaths be revoked.

FRANK WYNNE is a literary translator and writer. Born in Ireland, he moved to France in 1984 where he discovered a passion for language. He began translating literature in the late 1990s, and in 2001 decided to devote himself to this full time. He has translated works by Michel Houellebecq, Frédéric Beigbeder, Ahmadou Kourouma, Boualem Sansal, Claude Lanzmann, Tómas Eloy Martínez, and Almudena Grandes. His work has earned him a number of awards, including the Scott Moncrieff Prize and the Premio Valle Inclán. Most recently, his translation of *Vernon Subutex* by Virginie Despentes was shortlisted for the Man Booker International 2018.

On the Design

As book design is an integral part of the reading experience, we would like to acknowledge the work of those who shaped the form in which the story is housed.

Tessa van der Waals (Netherlands) is responsible for the cover design, cover typography, and art direction of all World Editions books. She works in the internationally renowned tradition of Dutch Design. Her bright and powerful visual aesthetic maintains a harmony between image and typography and captures the unique atmosphere of each book. She works closely with internationally celebrated photographers, artists, and letter designers. Her work has frequently been awarded prizes for Best Dutch Book Design.

The font used on the cover is from a Saint Petersburg collective TypeType, founded in 2013 by Ivan Gladkikh and Alexander Kudryavtsev. It is from a family of fonts called TT Trailers, a new generation of narrow typefaces designed for use in movie credits and posters: "The closed aperture of the characters emphasizes the smoothness and plasticity of the letters and helps the typeface to maintain a consistent rhythm. We quite actively used 'loops' in the design of some letters, which, together with the contrast and humanist style give TT Trailers a slight retro touch and refer us to the cinema posters of the '60s." The image of the Rod of Asclepius was made by Annemarie van Haeringen.

The cover has been edited by lithographer Bert van der Horst of BFC Graphics (Netherlands).

Suzan Beijer (Netherlands) is responsible for the typography and careful interior book design of all World Editions titles.

The text on the inside covers and the press quotes are set in Circular, designed by Laurenz Brunner (Switzerland) and published by Swiss type foundry Lineto.

All World Editions books are set in the typeface Dolly, specifically designed for book typography. Dolly creates a warm page image perfect for an enjoyable reading experience. This typeface is designed by Underware, a European collective formed by Bas Jacobs (Netherlands), Akiem Helmling (Germany), and Sami Kortemäki (Finland). Underware are also the creators of the World Editions logo, which meets the design requirement that "a strong shape can always be drawn with a toe in the sand."